Spice

Spice

Lilah Suzanne

interlude press

BOOK DESIGN by Lex Huffman
COVER DESIGN by Buckeyegrrl Designs
COVER AND INTERIOR ILLUSTRATIONS by Gladys Garcia

Love is friendship that has caught fire.
It takes root and grows,
one day at a time.

ANN LANDERS

◥◤ Chapter One

Ask Eros: Dangling on the Hook

Q: *I've been with this guy for almost a year and we have a lot of fun together. The sex is great, and we hang out at my apartment all the time. He's met my friends and family. The problem is, I know almost nothing about his life. He won't let me meet his friends, claiming they won't like me. He says he's not close to his family, but he goes home all the time. We don't go out on dates. We aren't even Facebook official. Not even "it's complicated." Should I push the issue and ask him to commit? I think a year has been long enough for him to figure out what he wants.*

A: *Instead of trying to suss out what he wants and thinks and needs, why not spend more time on what you want? Which is not, I'm guessing, a guy who thinks so little of you that he won't take you out and show you off to his friends and family and the greater world at large. Because the thing is, that's is exactly what you should get. And nothing less. Spending a year with a guy who wants to keep you hidden away and confused is 364 days too long. Time to get off that hook and swim away to bigger and better things, little fish.*

Simon pats his face with a damp paper towel, the automatic sink clunking on and off as he repeatedly leans close to the mirror. A toilet

1

flushes, and a man in a crisp suit comes out, adjusts his tie, checks his teeth and leaves without washing his hands. Simon watches him go with a shudder.

He tosses the paper towel into the gleaming silver trashcan—who knew trash cans could be so elegant?—and takes a deep breath. His hair stands up in the back, that whorl that seems determined to defy gravity no matter how much he spends on hair product. He'd just swoop it all up instead of fighting nature, but Andrew prefers his hair tamed. His pants need tailoring, but, in a bit of a rush, he'd bought the outfit at the only department store still open on his way to this hotel.

The bathroom attendant watches Simon fret with a distinct air of boredom; arms crossed and slumped against the marble sink. Another man comes out, washes his hands and takes a paper towel, but doesn't leave a tip. The attendant sighs and uncrosses and re-crosses his arms, resumes his position against the lip of the counter. Simon digs in his pocket, flips open his wallet and takes out some bills.

He's not sure what is the appropriate amount to tip someone who stands in the men's room of a swanky five-star hotel all day passing out paper towels and mints. Simon is curious about what leads to such a career choice. Is the guy upwardly mobile? Does he someday want to own a bathroom attendant empire across Manhattan and the outer boroughs?

Simon stuffs the money in the jar to a grunted *thanks bruh* and then checks the time on his phone. Okay, he's officially stalling now.

"Do I look like a man who's ready for a serious, committed relationship to you?"

The attendant, *Toph* according to his name tag, has thick black-rimmed glasses that he probably doesn't need, a piercing through the middle of his nose and an eighties-era Flock Of Seagulls-style haircut that Simon desperately hopes is meant to be ironic.

He never uncrosses his arms or stirs from his position, but obliges Simon with a quick once over. "Nope."

Simon frowns down at his outfit; too big slacks and a dress shirt still stiff and starchy, all topped off with a Ralph Lauren tie. The overall effect is a little less epic love story and more Episcopalian heading to Sunday services, now that he looks closer at it. "It's the tie, right? I knew the tie was too much."

"Nah man," Toph says, still unmoving. "It's like... You look miserable. Love should lift you up where you belong, you know what I'm saying?"

Simon opens his mouth to argue, but Toph looks well past done with the conversation, so Simon shakes the comment off and opens the bathroom door with an elbow. He's just nervous. That's all. Andrew finally invites him out to a beautiful fancy hotel when it's just been quick lunch dates so far, but Simon knows Andrew has feelings for him. Or—Simon thinks he has. It's hard to tell what Andrew really feels.

On the elevator up to the top floor, Simon yanks the tie loose enough to pull over his head, can feel the cowlick getting even worse, stuffs the tie in his pocket and bounces on the balls of his feet.

His palms are clammy, and his pulse races too hard against his throat. The ride up seems endless with people getting off and on, barely sparing him a glance before moving to the far opposite side of the elevator. He's out of place and uncomfortable. He's sure everyone can tell: Andrew calls when Simon is already tucked into bed, says he needs him—aren't those the words he's been waiting to hear? So if this is what it takes to show Andrew that he's serious—that they should be serious—then that's what he has to do.

Simon stares at the heavy door of the hotel room for slightly too long, then knocks just once before Andrew pulls the door open. The sleeves of his dress shirt are rolled up; his blazer has been discarded on the king-size bed that's still pristinely made up. He's on the phone, so he beckons Simon in with a nod, then moves to the side of the room with two chairs and a handsome oak table strewn with papers. Above it is a wide window covered with heavy red velvet curtains pulled tight.

Simon sits on the very edge of the bed, hands folded and tucked between his knees, trying to politely ignore whatever Andrew is saying on the phone in a hushed, placating tone.

"Yeah. I've got it covered," Andrew says at normal volume, tapping his phone to end the call and then turning to Simon. "Advertising. So needy. Anyway, thanks for coming."

"I, uh—Sure. I mean I was just hanging out at home anyway—"

"Great. Great. Listen, sorry we couldn't meet at my place. I'm repainting."

It sounds like a flimsy excuse, not that Simon minds the hotel. Though he was maybe hoping for a little wining and dining room service style, or maybe— "Do you want to go down to the bar? I could use a drink," Simon says with a small laugh.

Andrew sits next to him, the bed dipping so they're close enough that Simon can feel the heat of Andrew's body and smell the scent of cedar and pepper from Andrew's cologne. Their knees brush, Andrew smiles and then—his phone chimes with a text.

Andrew pats his knee once, then stands to retrieve his phone. Simon releases a shaky breath.

"Fuck," Andrew mutters under his breath.

"Everything okay?" Simon croaks. He really could use a drink. Or two. Or several.

"Yes, I'm sorry. I've got a meeting with someone who's on the way, and they're arriving early, so we'll have to do this quickly."

Simon blinks, frozen on his perch at the edge of the bed. Andrew peels the suspenders from his shoulders, heads to a drawer in the nightstand and digs around in it for a moment as Simon watches with anxiety spiking through his body. Andrew is the epitome of Simon's ideal partner: blond and average height, classically handsome and put together, muscled but not overly so. A guy just like he imagined he'd find when he moved to New York and found his place. Simon has wanted this relationship since his first day at *Ravish*, has wanted him. He just wishes it seemed a little less as if he was forcing himself to just go for it already. Nervous. He's just nervous.

Andrew returns to the bed and Simon stands. He's ready, ready to be whatever Andrew needs him to be and—

"Here."

Simon frowns at Andrew's outstretched hand, at the small blue flash drive in his open palm. Simon takes it. "What's this?"

"It's a flash drive. Oh fuck, you do know how to use one, don't you?" Andrew runs a hand over his face. Simon notices his jaw is shadowed with stubble, and he has dark circles under his eyes, something Simon's never seen in the years he's worked with him at the magazine. He's never looked anything less than perfect.

"Yeah, of course. But why?"

"I need you to organize all of those spending reports and see if anything unusual crops up. Don't do anything or tell anyone. Just make a note of it, then call me immediately so we can discuss it." Andrew folds his fingers over Simon's, pressing the flash drive hard into his skin. "This is really important, and I'm asking you because I trust you."

"Okay... But don't you have accountants for that sort of thing? I thought we—I thought this was—"

Andrew's phone chimes again. He drops Simon's hand, grips him by the arms. "I need you for this, Simon. I know you have the time—"

"I'm a writer. I have time for *writing*," Simon interrupts. "I have the weekly column for the website, plus monthly special features for the print magazine that require a lot research and planning."

Andrew steps back and scrubs his hands through his hair, making a mess of its perfect part. "You give women advice about what dildos to buy. I'm sure you can find room in your schedule." He picks up his phone and fires off a text. Simon's jaw clenches, and he fights off the defensiveness churning sick in his gut. It is true, after all.

"I'm sort of working on an exposé about a school superintendent accepting bribes..." Simon tries weakly. He isn't, not lately anyway. Because it's boring and he only started it because he thought he should do something more meaningful. But he likes the stuff he does write, even if it is pointless fluff. He slips the flash drive in his pocket.

Andrew is staring down at his phone, doesn't even glance up in acknowledgment. "Hey that's great." He finishes texting, drops his phone on the high thread-count duvet. "So you can do that for me, then?"

He moves close to catch Simon's eyes with his own intense gaze, icy blue and searching. Andrew brushes two fingers along Simon's hip, just enough to stir the familiar heat in Simon's veins that he can never quite help when Andrew touches him or looks at him.

Simon swallows. "Sure."

He's hustled out as quickly as he was hustled in and the door closes behind him before Simon can get his head around what just happened. He shuffles down the long hallway to the elevator just as it dings.

A cute, sandy-haired kid gets off—all of eighteen or so, in pants so tight he must have spray painted them on—looking at his phone and heading in the direction that Simon just came from. The doors slide shut before Simon can be sure, but he swears the kid stops in front of Andrew's room.

He's out in the cool, busy night before he realizes he lost his tie somewhere. It was his only one. By the time he makes it back to his apartment, not only is he too tired and out of sorts to look at the info Andrew gave him, he's completely missed a *Friends* marathon and realizes he'd forgotten to set his DVR to record. Simon kicks his shoes off into his tiny closet, bangs it closed, throws his keys, wallet and phone on the Formica countertop and sheds his uncomfortable slacks and dress shirt.

Walt looks up from the couch with a sleepy glance, whaps his skinny tail against the cushions twice, then goes back to sleep.

"Don't get too excited, Walt. It's just me." He flops down next to the dog, turns the TV on to Gordon Ramsay yelling at a chef for undercooking the chicken marsala. At least the night isn't a total wash.

"I didn't even get laid," Simon groans. Walt sighs. He gets it. Simon will get to those spending reports later, or maybe call and try talk to Andrew about them. Because Simon still doesn't really understand why he should be doing it. Not his department. Not his expertise. But for now he snuggles up to the only thing in his life he knows will always be there for him—even if he does smell as if he rolled in something that's been dead for a month—and watches other people's screwups for a little while.

ᴼᴼ chapter Two

Ask Eros: No Scrubs

Q: *Lately, my boyfriend hasn't really been in the mood for sex, but I guess he's still in the mood for porn because I can hear him watching it. To make matters worse, he's leaving stains from when he, you know. Finishes. It's ruining my couch. Any tips for getting rid of them?*

A: *I think you mistyped. Any tips for getting rid of **him**? That's what you meant, right? You don't need me to tell you that you deserve better, but here it is anyway: You deserve better. At the very least, you deserve someone who wants you and respects you enough be honest. Or, at the very, very least, someone who cleans up after himself. Or just uses some tissues for God's sake. It's not that hard. But for now, tell him to use cold water and Oxyclean. Blot, don't scrub. Then kick that scrub to the curb.*

Simon wakes before his alarm the next morning to a wiggly warm body across his chest and a wide wet tongue licking at the arm he has stretched back under his pillow.

"Walt, we seriously need to have a talk about your armpit fetish." Simon grunts, shoving the dog away until he jumps off the bed, then runs back and forth from the bedroom to the front door until Simon finally drags himself out of bed. He yanks on sweats just as his phone gives its first cheery wake-up call.

Outside, the city hints at new life and new beginnings; trees are dotted with green buds, birds chatter from electrical wire perches, fresh flowers grow in window planters and are offered for sale on carts parked on the sidewalk. He turns onto Second Avenue toward Stuyvesant Square Park. Walt, his ears flapping and tongue lolling from the side of his mouth, tugs at his leash as Simon dodges people and darts through traffic.

After a quick stop for coffee, they make it to the dog run, where Simon can let Walt loose to chase butterflies or roll in excrement or whatever Walt likes to do to get his day started off right. Simon sits on the bench and catches up on emails, pages through some of the questions submitted for this week's column and sips his mocha.

"Is that a pit bull?" An older woman, who has one of those tiny yappy dogs tucked under one arm, sits down next to him.

"He's a mix, actually. But yeah, mostly." He shuts off his phone and pockets it with a sigh. No messages from Andrew. Several *Ask Eros* submissions that can be boiled down to someone's asshole boyfriend being an asshole. Suddenly two shots of espresso are not nearly enough.

"Aren't you worried about how dangerous he is?" The woman whispers, as if Walt will overhear and remember he's supposed to be going on a murderous rampage.

Simon scans the park, spots Walt shoving his snout into a hole, covering his entire face in mud. "No, not really."

As a matter of fact, Simon is starting to think that Walt is the only decent living being in the entire city.

When they get back home, Walt is tuckered out and Simon is just starting his day. He eats a bowl of granola with blueberries and yogurt, then shaves and showers. When he jerks off under the warm spray, he tries to think of Andrew. Handsome, successful Andrew with his appropriately-sized muscles and classic features. But the picture in

Simon's head keeps morphing into blurry anyone-else men. When he finally comes it just feels empty and disappointing.

Dressed in a soft, thin gray sweater, skinny fit twill pants and black-and-white checked classic Vans, Simon feels more like himself. Not whatever he was trying to be last night. He gathers up the stiff dress shirt and boxy pants and tosses them into the empty clothes hamper, only remembering the flash drive when it clatters out onto the bottom of the hamper. He hesitates for a moment, then puts it in his pocket. He said he would help. And he *tries* to be honest, he really does.

A text comes in just as he's settling in at work. He drops the flash drive into a drawer as he sits in his desk chair and starts up his computer.

Tia: How did last night go?
Simon: It didn't.
Tia: Sorry :(Want to come to my office and talk about his pretentious taste in music?
Tia: Seriously, if he tells me about a 'hot new jazz dive' one more time...
Simon: No. I have to get working on my column. Cocktails later?
Tia: Like you have to ask.

Simon takes a deep breath, stretches his arms behind his head and waits for the desktop to boot up. Only it isn't making its usual wheezing and whirring sounds. The screen is blank. Just the fan running, hard and loud as it does when he's been streaming hilarious animal videos, listening to music and researching something all at the same time.

"Come on." He restarts it. Then he hits the processing unit under his desk and curses at it, as if either action will help. Nothing. He puts in a call to IT.

"Is nine in the morning too early for vodka?" Simon slumps into a chair and straightens the *Tia Robinson, Features Editor* nameplate on her desk.

"Wow, that bad?" Tia looks away from her computer screen, fingers still clacking away. He has no idea how she does that. Most of his first drafts are barely legible when he *is* looking at them.

Simon sits up a bit. "Just one of those days, you know?"

Tia watches him, then finally looks back to whatever she was working on.

"Can I ask you something?"

"I think you just did."

She jabs at the keyboard, dark brown eyes flitting to his for a brief moment. "Why am I friends with you again?"

"Because I'll take you out for cocktails at nine in the morning?" Simon offers.

"Right." She looks at him fully now and stops working, hands pressed flat to her desktop. "Why are you so hung up on Andrew anyway? He's decent looking and all, but kind of a tool, honestly," she says, which is kind of an understatement.

"I dunno, I've put so much work into it. You know I hate to leave a project unfinished," he jokes, but Tia doesn't laugh.

"A relationship shouldn't be a project." She tips her head sympathetically and purses her lips, considering for a moment before she continues. "Look, I don't want to tell you how to live your life, Simon—"

"But..." Simon cuts in, because she's going to anyway.

"*But.* I guess I'm just surprised you'd settle for being someone's backup plan."

Simon shrugs. "Better than no plan at all." He looks away to the stack of wedding magazines and binders full of seating charts, catering companies, menus, color schemes and flower arrangements. Easy for her to say, when she's getting ready to marry the tall, dark and handsome love of her life who worships the ground she walks on.

Is that what he's doing? Settling? Andrew just needs some time to figure out what he wants. Even if it sometimes seems as if he's put Simon on the back burner to simmer indefinitely, only giving him a stir every now and again to keep him going.

Simon sighs and rubs at his eyes. He has now sunk to imagining himself as a simmering pot of chili or beef stew or chicken noodle soup, just waiting for Andrew to add a little seasoning and take another taste. This is what happens when he watches cooking shows late at night.

Simon looks back up at Tia, stars popping at the edge of his vision from rubbing at his eyes too hard. "I just thought I'd be there by now. My happy ending. I'm starting to think maybe there is no such thing. Not for me."

"Hey now, maybe the right guy is just around the corner. Don't give up hope. And forget about settling for close enough, okay?" Tia looks up and over his shoulder. "Speaking of around the corner, IT is at your cubicle."

Simon wrinkles his nose. "Is it the one with the weird goat beard?" The one who smelled like pork rinds and whose nose whistled on every inhale. It drove Simon so crazy that he had to leave to get a third cup of coffee.

"No, it's the cute one."

"There's a cute one? Why was I not informed that there's a cute one?" Simon pushes up from his chair, gives Tia a look that he hopes accurately portrays his feeling of betrayal, and heads back to his cubicle.

At first glance, cute IT guy is a little scruffy looking with shaggy copper-red hair and dressed in a T-shirt and worn jeans. But as Simon approaches, he can appreciate how well the T-shirt fits his long body: strong lean muscle over fair, freckled skin; gorgeous green-blue eyes; a jawline and cheekbones that make Simon want to groan out of both jealousy and sexual frustration.

Simon's eyes drop, just a quick glance. Great ass. God, he's striking. Where has IT been hiding this guy?

A vast improvement over nose-whistling, goat-beard dude.

Simon clears his throat, manages to get a hold of himself. He has got to get laid. "Hey, you must be from tech support? We spoke on the phone earlier?"

"Yeah, I'm Benji." He holds out his hand for Simon to shake; good grip, bright smile.

"Simon." He scoots into the cubicle past Benji and attempts to turn the computer on again. "So it won't start up, basically. And yes, it's plugged in."

Benji smiles, but it's not mocking. "I'll go ahead and assume you weren't using the disk drive as a cup holder either?"

Simon presses the "on" button repeatedly and slides Benji a look. "Someone actually did that?"

"True story. Got Diet Coke everywhere, shorted out several of the computer's components. Soft drinks are surprisingly corrosive." He sits at Simon's desk chair, his shoulder gently brushing Simon's hip. Simon assumes it's the fact that his love life has settled into a barren and frigid ice age that the contact sends a thrill through his body. He moves to the side to give Benji room to work. Benji types some commands, but the screen stays stubbornly blank. Simon watches his biceps bulge under the sleeves of his worn blue T-shirt, which has a familiar emblem.

"Captain America?" Simon asks with a nod.

"Hmm?" Benji looks up, then tugs at his shirt, pulling it away from his neck and revealing the hollow scoop of a collarbone. "Oh. Yeah. I guess I've kind of had this shirt forever." He gets up to pull the processing unit out from under the desk. "I think it might be the motherboard, but I'll have to take it apart to be sure."

"Of course you will." Simon sighs. Benji gives an apologetic smile. "So, why Captain America?"

Benji stands, turning the chair so Simon can sit back down, then ducks under the desk, pulling out a tiny screwdriver from the little tool set he brought and focuses on removing the back of the unit. "Um. I guess I just liked the idea of a good guy who does the right thing just because it's the right thing to do?" He's almost completely under the desk, just his head popping out behind the CPU.

"That makes sense."

Benji gives an awkward, hunched over shrug. "And, you know. Like any nerdy redheaded gay kid I guess I liked imagining there was someone out there who would think I was worth fighting for. It made me feel like everything would be okay."

"I always kind of liked Spiderman myself," Simon muses. Benji pokes his head out again, the insides of the computer now exposed. "You do have a Peter Parker look going on."

Simon snorts. "Pre-radioactive bite, though. Like before he turns into a super stud."

Benji gives him a once over, eyes shifting blue-green to blue-gray in the shadow of the desk. "I always thought he was hotter before the bite. Too full of himself after."

Despite being a grown man who gives sex advice for a living, Simon finds his face flushing hot and something akin to a giggle escaping his mouth. That, of course, is the moment Andrew chooses to stop by his cubicle.

"Simon. Dinner." He leans against the opening, points with a raise of his eyebrows. Simon is surprised to see him so soon. Usually Andrew waits a few weeks and comes around when Simon is starting to wonder whether Andrew has found someone else. Uncanny timing, really.

Simon spins his chair, glancing down at Benji, who's hidden from view, and for the first time, he hesitates. "I made plans with Tia and then I need to get home to walk Walt."

Andrew crosses his arms over his chest. He's wearing a high-end suit that looks pretty much like all his other high-end suits. "Walt?"

"My dog. You know I have a dog, Andrew." Simon says.

"Well, the dog can wait and Tia will understand. Come on. Trendy new artisanal place. You love that stuff." He steps into the cubicle, closer and closer until Simon is trapped between him and the desk.

Andrew brushes his fingers down Simon's arm, circles them slowly around Simon's wrist.

He tips his chin and pouts, "Come on."

"Okay, fine." Simon relents.

Andrew beams, triumphant. "Great." He leaves the cubicle and heads back toward his office, but then turns on his heel to say loudly, "Did you bring a change of clothes? Because the restaurant is rather upscale." He flicks his fingers dismissively. "Never mind, I have a blazer you can borrow."

Simon stares after him and wonders why, when he opens his mouth to say *no* or, better yet, *fuck off*, what always comes out is *yes*. Why is he so hung up on him?

"Wow, Senior Accounts Manager Andrew Klaff, down here with the little people. Is he a... friend of yours?" Benji asks, still shadowed under the desk.

Simon pulls his feet up on his chair and tucks his legs to his chest, drops his head back and wonders if anyone will notice if he just climbs under his desk with Benji and spends the day under there.

"I'm really not sure anymore."

"Well, whatever he is, he's wrong. You look ho— fine. Your clothes look just fine to me." Benji looks up and smiles in a way that makes Simon's heart trip in his chest. Is he flirting? He's totally flirting.

Benji's gaze lingers, so Simon drops his feet, sets his elbows on the armrests and stretches his shoulders back, spine curved and chest puffing out. Simon knows he's more compact than brawny, but he takes decent care of his body and stays active thanks to Walt, so his shoulders and arms are defined with wiry muscles, his chest is flat and his waist is narrow. He is pleased to note how Benji's eyes follow the movement, and, oh yes, this could be fun.

"You know what else? I'm not even sure what artisanal really is."

"It's technically traditional foods hand made in small batches, though if you ask me it's been bastardized lately." He unscrews something with his brow furrowed, then clamps the screwdriver between his front teeth. Simon, suddenly flushed, pulls the back of his collar away from his neck.

"Wait, was that rhetorical?" Benji says around the screwdriver.

"No, I like that answer. Very informative."

Benji looks up with a crooked smile, and Simon should really track down whoever is cranking up the thermostat.

Benji yanks out a very important looking group of wires, holds them dangling in his hands and says, "Anyway, I think it's one of those things people are into just because they think they should be."

He sets the wires by Simon's feet, and Simon stares down at them. "I think you may be right."

ᗧᗧ Chapter Three

Ask Eros: Hanging Like a Horse.

Q: *I am 34 and recently divorced. I would like to start dating and, at the encouragement of my friends and family, I have signed up for an online dating site. So far, I've gone out on a few dates and I have to say, if this is what dating is like these days, I'd rather be single forever. Now, just getting a message from someone interested gives me an extreme sense of dread! Any tips on how to keep pushing myself out there despite terrible dates with no chemistry? I'm running out of time before I'll need to be taken out to pasture!*

A: *Let's go ahead and put the trip to the glue factory on hold. Things are not quite that dire. The problem may well be that you're putting too much pressure on yourself. Dating should feel like fun, not a periodontal cleaning. If you aren't having a good time, you are under no obligation to continue dating that person or anyone at all. Is it possible that you really aren't ready yet? It's okay to give yourself some time to heal before you head back into the show ring for another go round. In the meantime, focus on that group of supportive friends and family you've got. Something will happen for you when it's meant to, I promise.*

Andrew is on his phone, again, just vague declarations that Simon can barely make out over the pulsating electro pop and conversations being shouted over it all around them. At this point, Simon has interacted more with the cute pink-haired waitress about the house "handmade spiced tomato preserves" that would best suit his oxtail and truffle oil burger than he has with Andrew.

The table next to theirs is rowdy, probably on their third bottle of wine, and having a much better time than he is. Simon pokes at the rest of his food and seriously considers scooting his chair over the few inches and joining them. He pulls out his phone.

> **Tia:** Just got to Bloody Mary's. It's lonely without you.
> **Simon:** Does it help that the food is obnoxious and my date is ignoring me?
> **Tia:** NO.
> **Tia:** Do I need to come out there? I've got my nut-crushing stilettos on, ready to go.

The pink-haired waitress comes back with the check. Andrew finally sets down his phone and takes out his wallet to pay. "Told you this place was great."

Simon dodges an elbow thrown out in full-body laughter from the gentleman to his right. "So great," he says, then sighs and texts Tia.

> **Simon:** I appreciate it but that won't be necessary. Let's try drinks again tomorrow.
> **Tia:** But the night is still young!
> **Simon:** I know. I think I need to go home and spoon with Walt.

Andrew gets up, pulls out Simon's chair and helps him out of the blazer he insisted Simon borrow. It's heavy and thick and makes him feel like a school child playing dress up. Andrew guides him out of the restaurant with a hand resting on his arm. A quick kiss outside and he's back to his phone, not a backward glance at Simon as he gets in a cab. Simon stands alone on the sidewalk.

> **Tia:** I worry about you.
> **Simon:** Can't imagine why. I'll save some doggie kisses for you.
> **Tia:** I'll pass.

Benji is back the next morning lining up computer parts, installing circuit boards and microchips, and whatever the hell else is happening on the floor of Simon's cubicle. Simon had never before realized just how lonely and boring his little blue cubicle was until Benji arrived to dissect his processing unit.

"Favorite cartoon?" Simon asks.

"*Ren & Stimpy*." Benji sits cross-legged and hunched over to remove and replace parts. He's just so sweet, easy to talk to. No bullshit posturing. Today he's wearing a black shirt with narwhal who have lightsabers instead of horns.

"Oh, that's a good one. I was gonna say *Sponge Bob* but, no, that's better."

"Okay. Best Power Ranger."

"Jason. Red," Simon says without hesitation.

"Over Tommy the sexy smooth Green Ranger? Come on."

"He had a ponytail," Simon argues.

Benji blinks up at him. "Exactly."

Simon laughs and moves closer, accidentally kicking something that looks sort of important. Benji moves it.

"Favorite Disney movie?"

"Actually," Benji snaps something in place, takes out something else. Simon has given up trying to figure out just what he's doing. "I never really watched them. My older brothers always put on like, *The Terminator* or *Jurassic Park* or *Die Hard*."

"Ah. The benefits of being an only child: I got to watch whatever the hell I wanted to."

"True," Benji says. "But with siblings there's always someone around to annoy you. Plus the joys of sorting through worn out hand-me-downs."

"Hmm, good point," Simon concedes and goes back to working in comfortable silence. He writes some notes in a yellow legal pad, stealing glances at Benji from time to time. There's something about watching him move so confidently, so comfortably himself. *This is me, all of it. Take it or leave it.* Simon would be terrified to put himself out there like that.

"Hey, what are you doing after work?" Simon asks, with a sudden uptick in his heart rate.

"If I say a *Star Wars* marathon at home, will you judge me?" Benji looks up with wide eyes, computer parts scattered around him like a ritual sacrifice to the digital age gods. Simon turns, opens the decrepit old laptop he's being forced to work on for now and starts a blank word document. "Oh, definitely."

Bloody Mary's is the sort of basement dive bar Simon would have never set foot in if not for Tia telling him to stop being a slack-jawed tourist and try living in the city for real. It's dark and dank with a wooden bar stretched across one end and a scattering of sticky round tables marked with the rings from thousands of drink glasses and pints of beer. A pool table and some dart boards are tucked in the back.

It's nothing like the sleek, flashy bar near work where he first saw Andrew outside of the *Ravish* offices, where Simon hooked up with Andrew: a one-night stand that turned into an empty bed and promises of something more, something that Simon is still waiting for.

"Simon!" Tia calls out from a green pleather-topped bar stool as he comes down the stairs. Benji follows, eyes bright with excitement, studying the Irish-themed decor on the walls as if the vintage Guinness beer signs are the most amazing things he's ever seen.

"Hi, you look gorgeous." She's shed her work blazer and traded her sensible flats for red heels. A silk white camisole contrasts beautifully against her dark skin. A pencil skirt hugs her curvy hips and thighs.

Simon kisses her cheek and slides onto the stool next to her. "This is Benji from IT. Which is probably not his full name."

"I know Benji. McGee, right?"

"Close. McHugh." Benji spins a coaster on the bar top. "And you're Features Editor Tia Robinson of the perpetually sluggish Internet."

Tia sips her drink. "I swear my office has some kind of voodoo hex on it."

"Damn, I was hoping you wouldn't find out about that," Simon says.

Tia scoffs. "Just for that, you're buying the next round."

Simon orders and the bartender slides the order down with a "Here ya go."

"Play darts with me," Tia says, setting down her empty glass with a decisive thunk and tugs him away.

"Since when do you play darts?" Simon asks, pulling a red-winged set from the hole-riddled board.

Tia snags one, throws it in a perfect arc at the board and nearly hits a bullseye. Simon gapes at her. "Since I needed to talk to you about the man candy you brought. I didn't know you were into carrot tops."

"I'm not," Simon replies. He takes a dart and misses by a mile. "He's just... nice. I enjoy being around him, and he wasn't doing anything, so." He shrugs.

Tia glances back at the bar, throws another dart that hits just a little farther off. "Good."

One more round and they see Tia off in a cab, sending her home to her fiancé. She gives Simon an eyebrow waggle from the backseat. Benji's place turns out to be on the way to Simon's subway stop, so they walk there together in the night that's turning thick with the first humid hint of summer.

"This is me," Benji stops in front of a building, shoving a hand in his pocket to get out keys. "I had fun. Thanks for inviting me out."

"Yeah, me too."

Then Benji's hand is on Simon's arm, and he looks amazing in the soft light spilling from a street lamp. It would be the easiest thing in the world to just kiss him. But Simon hesitates, unsure of what Benji wants or what *he* wants, and maybe he has to protect his heart, maybe that's what the whole mess with Andrew is. Maybe he can't take Benji looking at him the way he is; as if *Simon* is the most amazing thing he's ever seen, because how does he protect himself from that? The moment stretches on, until Benji clears his throat and steps back.

"See you on Monday, Simon."

When he gets home, he's greeted by an enthusiastic Walt and the shredded remains of a boot. Simon cleans it up with a sigh. Maybe doggie day care isn't as ridiculously indulgent as he thought.

Simon finds a rope to play tug of war with. A message from Andrew about *doing lunch* pops up on his phone as he sits on the floor and pulls with Walt at the other end.

"Drop it," Simon commands, and Walt does, plopping on his haunches with ears perked and tail whipping back and forth. Simon throws the rope down the hall and the dog charges after it. Then he reaches to get his phone from the coffee table.

Andrew's text is at the top of his list of messages. A winky face from Tia next. A couple from his mom. After that is a new number: Benji's. Simon presses his lips flat, finger hovering over his options.

> **Simon:** I'm considering growing a handlebar mustache. Think I can pull it off?

Walt returns with the rope, drops it in Simon's lap and waits.

> **Benji:** Totally.
> **Benji:** But you should know I have thing for guys who look like silent film villains.

Simon grins, tucks his phone to his chest and throws the rope again.

⌐◯─◯ Chapter Four

Ask Eros: For the Love of God Keep It in Your Pants

Q: *So I know this is a women's magazine and you're a gay dude, but since you're still a dude even with whole gay thing and an expert on women, I'm coming to you. I like this chick. Don't know if she likes me. I want her to. Should I send her a dick pic?*

A: *You didn't include your name, so I'm just gonna call you Chad, okay? Okay, Chad. Listen to me, Chad. Do not send a dick pic. Not just because it's sexual harassment. Because it is, Chad. It is. But also because this is not how you get to know a woman. You talk to her. Show a genuine interest in her life. I am not actually an expert on women, Chad, because there is no such thing. I do try to treat them like individual people and not hive-minded enigmas. By the way, I appreciate you thinking I'm still a dude, despite 'the whole gay thing.' I'm truly honored.*

Tia offers to spend the day with him and keep him occupied with last-minute wedding planning, but he declines. He's just not sure he's up to helping her decide on fondant versus buttercream for an event that he feels is less and less likely to happen for himself.

He needs to officially end things with Andrew. He needs to stop clinging so desperately to something that is just not what he wants it to be. He also should really clean the bathroom.

What he's doing instead is spending his entire Saturday watching a *Will & Grace* marathon on Lifetime.

"Believe it or not, this show was really groundbreaking for its time," Simon says around a mouthful of cold shrimp lo mein. Walt is unimpressed. Simon shrugs and scoops more noodles into his mouth.

"You have to at least admit the hairstyles and clothes have held up surprisingly well. Timeless, really."

Walt yawns, ends it on a whine, then rests his head on Simon's knee.

"Oh sure, Jack wore baggy cargo pants sometimes, but it was the nineties, you know? Everyone was wearing baggy cargo pants." He chews, scoops another mouthful and slurps a stray noodle into his mouth. "Not me. Well, okay, yes. But in my defense, Mom bought them for me."

His phone buzzes on the coffee table. Simon uses a chopstick to pull it closer and presses the end of it on the home button.

> **Andrew:** Come have drinks.
> **Simon:** Thanks, but no thanks. Lots to do.

Walt licks a noodle off his leg, and Simon realizes that he should maybe get out of the house for a bit. First a shower. He scratches at his chin, prickly with stubble. Shower, shave, then attempt to be a slightly less pathetic human being. He types another text. When the reply comes in Simon jumps up with so much newfound pep that Walt chases after him down the hall, tail wagging happily and ears perked.

Simon makes it there within an hour, his hair still damp from his rushed scrub-down. He jogs up the steps and into the main entrance of the Museum of Natural History. It's crowded, but not too terrible.

A large tour group wearing matching soccer jerseys and backpacks heads to the hallway on the right, so Simon heads left.

Simon: Where are you?
Benji: Dinosaurs.
Simon: Why am I not surprised?
Benji: Because dinosaurs are awesome?
Simon: Yeah. That must be it.

Benji sends back a picture that he set up to look as if he's being impaled by the massive horns of a triceratops skull. Simon heads up to the fourth floor.

"So this is how you spend your Saturdays?" Simon finds him in front of a T. rex, looking more gorgeous in old jeans and a dancing hot dog T-shirt than anyone has a right to.

"Not always," he says with a shrug, "There was a special exhibit on pterosaurs this weekend so you know..."

"Totally," Simon replies, sarcastic, but Benji just smiles, genuinely happy to be among dinosaur bones, regardless of what Simon thinks. Or what anyone thinks.

"So, this guy is pretty impressive." Simon steps back, takes in the massive head, huge sharp teeth, the imposing attack stance.

"You know, some scientists think that *Tyrannosaurus rex* was actually a slow and cumbersome hunter, due to its size. Me, I've always been partial to velociraptors. Cunning. Fast. Stealthy. They're easy to miss. Not like these monsters here."

"Who knew the dinosaur world was so cliquey?"

Benji looks over, laughs and tugs Simon by the hand. "Come on, I'll show you my second favorite part."

He's been to the museum before, of course, just after moving to the city. The front hall was so packed with school groups he could barely get inside. He'd been trying so hard to act like a native, he'd wandered the halls as if it was some task to be checked off a list. He hadn't returned since.

Too bad, because he'd forgotten how much it seems like an oasis in the center of the city's chaos. The rooms are gently lit and it's quiet enough that people's shoes echo through the halls. Down on the first floor, they chat and stop to look at displays. Benji comments helpfully on the dioramas with their stuffed animals and reimagined tableaux of life long, long ago. It's soothing. Peaceful.

They walk side by side through the dark entryway of The Hall of Ocean Life, the chatter from the crowd adding to the swell and fade of the piped-in ocean sounds. It makes Simon think of home, makes him feel even more aware of being lonely and drifting.

"I grew up near the ocean. Florida," Simon says.

Benji leans against the railing on his forearms and looks up at the gigantic blue whale hung on cables from the high ceiling with blue skylights bathing it from above.

Benji turns, smiles, and something about being here—the sense of home, the muted light and the way Benji looks in it—makes Simon's stomach flip.

"I've only ever been to Florida once on a trip to Disney World," Benji says.

Simon shrugs. "You didn't miss much."

"I don't know about that. I haven't even spent much time at the ocean, and coming here is still just so..."

"Peaceful?"

"Yeah."

Simon is in danger of getting seasick with all the stomach swooping, so he props on his arms, too, and looks up to the belly of the beast.

"Big," he says, suave as ever.

"Biggest animal on earth," Benji replies, turning back to look as well, shoulders lightly touching as they crane to see. "Their hearts are as big as a car." Benji is quiet for a minute, then says softly, "I think you're like that. I can tell."

Simon drops his head, slides his gaze to Benji's shadowed profile. "Are you calling me fat?"

Benji laughs and looks over, and Simon doesn't miss the way his eyes keep going, down Simon's body, lingering just enough. "Not at all. I actually meant your heart. It's... big."

Simon swallows and breathes out and it hits him how all this time he's been drifting along, blending in and fading away. Being whoever he needed to be at the time instead of just himself, and somehow Benji still looks at him like that, as if he really can see Simon's heart.

"Maybe," Simon finally says. "Maybe too big." Maybe that's part of his problem, loving too easily, too much.

"No," Benji says with a shake of his head. "No, I don't think so."

It's too much, too intense for how little they know each other. It hasn't taken long at all for Simon to sense that things with Benji are just so comfortable and right, as if they've been best friends for years. How easy it would be to fall for Benji's sweet smile and genuine nature. It cannot possibly be that simple. So Simon pushes back the wave of feelings and locks it up tight. *Too soon. Not real. Not real. Not real,* he tells himself.

"Okay. I want to hear everything you know about blue whales," Simon says, and, given the way Benji's face lights up, Simon is pretty sure he can safely ignore his feelings for a good long time.

ᴕᴖ Chapter Five

Ask Eros: Is This Thing On?

Q: *I am in a wonderful relationship and our sex life is great. Or, at least I think it is. My man is so quiet in bed, it's difficult for me to tell how much he's really enjoying himself. And since he is such a committed and generous lover, I'd very much like to return the favor. But how am I supposed to know what he likes when all I get in response is silence? Any advice on how to get him screaming my name, or at least a moan every now and again?*

A: *Are you sure you aren't just blowing his mind so much that he's unable to form even the most basic primal noises in the face of your sex goddessness? I bet that's it. But a quiet partner is a little frustrating. Like playing Marco Polo with no response, just flailing around the pool wondering which end they want you in and eventually just diving in blindly. Maybe instead of forcing the issue, you could gently coax out some noises. Ask questions. Do you like that? Right there? Marco? Tell him how much it turns you on when he gasps and groans. Try to pay attention to other more subtle clues. Hitches in breaths. Jumping thigh muscles. Fingers twisted in covers or hair. And really, if his response is to enthusiastically get you off, then he's most likely having a great time. Jump on in to that deep end.*

"God, it's gorgeous out." Benji sits on the desktop, hands planted behind him and feet swinging just off the ground. Simon spins in his desk chair, knees bumping Benji's calves with every rotation, accidentally at first. Not so much now. They've completely given up any pretense of working; Simon's computer is still in pieces, his old laptop taunts him with an unfinished column.

"Sometimes I wish I could work for myself. Freelance." Turns again. Bump. "But I like buying groceries too much."

"I hear that." Benji groans and arches his back, his chin tipping up to catch the beam of sunlight coming in from the high windows above the cubicles, his pale neck stretching long, his hair glowing like fire.

Simon spins again and makes a half-hearted attempt to type a sentence that he'll probably have to go back and delete. "Did you always want to do IT support?"

"Oh, yes. Fulfilling my lifelong dream of people yelling at me because visiting *Hot Cheerleader Moms XXX* gave their computer a virus."

"First of all that's awful," Simon laughs. "Second of all, is there a *Hot Cheerleader Dads XXX*? I need to know for, uh, research."

Benji drops his head back down with a laugh. "I would assume so. I guess I always figured I'd do something with computers. Tech support isn't really my first pick, but I enjoy it. I'm good at it. I don't think I could sit at a desk and code all day." He tips his head to the side and flashes Simon a grin. "I get to meet new people."

Simon watches him just a beat too long then turns away to work, unable to focus even halfway. He minimizes his document and opens his email again.

> **From:** *Ravish* Mag
> **To:** All staff
> **Subject:** Party Time!
>
> It's that time again! Spring has sprung; *Ravish* has survived the winter. Time to celebrate! All staff are strongly encouraged to attend our annual summer party. This is a chance to honor

all of our hard work and have some fun! 8 p.m. on the summer equinox. Dress is casual. Hors d'oeuvres and drinks will be provided.

"How about you? Did you always want to be a writer?"

"Yeah. I think I did." He finally gives up on work completely and closes the laptop. "I mean. I guess what I write about is kind of pointless, but I wanted to be a poet once upon a time, so I guess it could be even more pointless," he jokes.

Benji's eyebrows knot. "It's not. Why would it be pointless?"

Simon gives a humorless laugh. "I mean, I write a sex column for women. Not exactly moving prose or hard-hitting journalism."

Benji scoots over little on the desk, sitting with his legs so close to where Simon is sitting low in his chair that he can smell Benji's crisp laundry detergent and citrusy soap. He suddenly has to fight the urge to move a fraction to the left, press his nose to the inside seam of Benji's jeans and breathe him in.

"You listen to people. You remind them that they're valuable and worthy of love and respect. How is that not important?" Simon is struck speechless, chest tight and breath caught. Then Benji claps him on the shoulder and hops off the desk. "Come on. Let's go have lunch."

It's crowded at Benji's lunch spot, too, but in a completely different way. People meander by, some alone, some coupled. Joggers pass smoothly, kids shriek and laugh in the open grassy field and a group gears up for a game of ultimate Frisbee on the hill behind them. Paddle boats laze across the pond, and Simon cups a hand over his eyes to watch a group of ducks bob in the shallows near their bench.

"I can't believe I'm eating a hot dog in Central Park. It's like the worst tourist cliché."

Benji smiles around his bite. "Want to go to the Statue of Liberty next?"

"You know, I kind of do," Simon admits.

"I never really understood the whole business of not doing something just because a lot of other people do it. Some things are popular for a reason."

Simon finishes his hot dog and leans back on the bench, relaxed and comfortable. He's right. Nothing wrong with the well-loved, time-tested things. Maybe he should just not try so damn hard. Fun. Simple.

"So, Tia's wedding is next weekend and I need a plus one. Would you be interested?"

"That depends," Benji replies, stretching forward to toss the ends of his hot dog bun to the ducks. "Is there an open bar, and do I have to wear a suit?"

Simon laughs, breaks off a piece of the bun and gets it all the way to the ducks in the back who keep missing out. "Yes. And no."

Benji turns back, eyes as bright and blue as the cloudless sky. "I'd love to."

From: Andrew Klaff, Senior Accounts Manager, *Ravish* Magazine
To: Simon Beck
    Are you attending office party? Need to see you.
    -Andrew

☉☉ chapter Six

Ask Eros: All Aboard the Meh Express.

Q: *For most of my dating life I have been a relationship drama junkie. Every single person I dated ended up being a train wreck, and every time I'd just hop onboard the next disaster that came my way. I finally wised up, grew up and got out. The problem? The steady, mature, solid relationship I'm in now is boring me to tears. I keep waiting and waiting and yet that spark just won't come. It's been months. Is this just what a real relationship feels like?*

A: *Given your past as the conductor of the drama train, I'd normally advise you to hang in there and give the mature relationship a chance. It is true that solid relationships take work and commitment and don't, in fact, involve much in the way at all of staring into each other's eyes and taking romantic moonlit walks on the beach. They take work. Work is boring. Blah blah blah. But the thing about real relationships is, you don't mind the work. Because you're with someone who makes filing joint tax returns and sending out thank you cards and negotiating dish duty seem not so bad. Fun, even. Because you genuinely enjoy their company. I think the problem here is you've swung from one extreme to the other. Yes, there should be a spark. No, that spark should not set all of his clothes on fire on your front porch after you caught him sleeping with* *your best friend. You're on the right track here, but it may well be time to disembark this particular trip.*

> **Group MMS**
> **To:**   **Tia, Benji & Mom**
> **Image IMG_0778**
> **Simon:** We're ready for the wedding!
> **Mom:**   Awwww :) <3 lol
> **Tia:**   Simon I swear to God. If you bring that dog as your date I'm having you committed.

Walt does a whole body shake and scratches at his very fetching bowtie. "Alright, alright." Simon slips it off, then removes the matching one looped loose around his own neck, and puts them back on the little rack before the owner of the tie kiosk notices.

> **Benji:** Hey, handsome.
> **Benji:** You look nice too, Simon.

He sends Benji his address, and continues the walk into Central Park.

Benji shows up bright and early on Saturday morning.

"Okay, you get first pick for music," Simon announces, slamming the door of the sensible Zipcar Toyota he'd picked up earlier that morning. Walt pants on the back of his neck. The entire backseat is dotted with short brown fur, and both back windows are slimy with nose prints.

"Your phone is already plugged in, so I'll pick something from your music." Benji pulls the phone from one of the cup holders between the seats and scrolls through the options before Simon gets a chance to protest.

Simon wrinkles his nose, releases the break and pulls away from the curb, then pushes his way into the traffic. "I have no idea how all of that One Direction got on there. Must be an iTunes conspiracy."

Benji laughs, scrolling as they slowly make their way out of the city. He's wearing a thin blue V-neck that makes his eyes look more green than usual and black shorts. He has just the slightest bit of coarse copper scruff on his chin and cheeks and upper lip. Simon has to make a concerted effort not to stare at his bare calves and instead concentrate on the dinged-up bumper of the station wagon in front of them.

The jangly opening electric guitar riffs and iconic vocals of *Help!* fill the sedan, and Benji settles back in his seat. "You know, The Beatles were the original boy band."

Simon makes some complicated lane switches, and Walt picks that exact moment to ram half of his body between the two front seats, nearly making Simon miss the exit. He shoves him away with an elbow, and Benji hooks him around the neck and rubs at his ears. "Sorry buddy, you aren't old enough to drive a rental yet."

The highway opens up a bit, and Simon feels slightly less like he's one split second away from sideswiping every asshole on the road. "Keeps miserably failing his written test, too."

"Walt. What are we gonna do with you?" Benji tips his forehead against the dog's face, earning himself a sloppy lick on the ear. Simon tries not to laugh too hard as Benji wipes his ear off.

"Maybe we should open a window for him," Simon offers, once he catches his breath. The morning is warm and clear and wide open with a perfect breeze rushing into the car ruffling his hair and pushing up the sleeve of Benji's shirt when he sticks his arm out the window.

Walt scrambles to the window behind the passenger side, sticks his head out and opens his mouth—the very definition of joy—and stays that way until they reach the kennel.

"*Camp Pup*," Benji reads on an etched wooden banner atop two thick totem pole-style logs at the entrance.

"It had five stars on Yelp," Simon tells him as Walt sniffs the ground, then lifts his leg to mark one of the log poles. "*It's not just a kennel, it's an experience.*"

They walk to the office to check in; it's a rustic log-cabin type structure. The kennel is on ten wooded acres for the dogs to enjoy, with their own plush sleeping quarters, individualized food service and scheduled playtime with a human of their preference.

It's completely overindulgent, and Simon knows it. But a tiny metal kennel with a concrete floor in the city costs just about the same, and he couldn't get out of his head the image of Walt romping around the woods with that happy-dumb face and flopping ears. Which is exactly what he's doing now as he's led away.

"I don't think he'll even miss me," Simon says on the way back to the car.

"Of course he will!" Benji replies immediately. "I mean. Maybe? A little bit for sure."

Simon drops into the driver's seat, closes the door and buckles the belt. "Just put on One Direction. I need comfort music."

By the time they hit Middletown, New Jersey, Benji's arm is burned from the beaming early afternoon sun and Simon's hair is so thoroughly wind-swept it looks as if he was the one who stuck his head out the window the whole way. They sing along to classic rock and cheesy pop music and talk about their families and their childhoods and boy band crushes past and present.

"Working class family from Queens, my dad was a security guard and Mom stayed home with us. Two brothers, typical jock types, you know," Benji says, as Simon takes a smaller road off the Parkway, just so they can see the ocean in the distance on the way in. "I even came out after Mass one Sunday," Benji says with a small laugh. "But they really just kind of took it in stride. I guess they figured I was already weird, so just one more thing to add to the list."

Simon sniffs the air, the hint of salty sea air swirling subtly around them. "It was just me and my mom and she—" Simon considers. She not only took it in stride but started a PFLAG group for his school and organized a GayLesbAll at the local rec center his junior year. "She's worked her ass off to make sure I can be or do anything I want."

He can see it then, gradients of blue on blue against the horizon. It's been ages since he went to the ocean, not since he left for college. He'd forgotten how soothing the unfathomable power and depth of the ocean could be.

"I feel like I spend a lot of my life trying not to let her down." Simon glances at Benji, who squeezes at his kneecap. Simon swallows back the thrill at that, nods to his phone again and, instead of what he really wants to, says, "Can you grab that and map the address from here?"

Benji pops the center console and hunches over, tilts the screen of Simon's phone away from the glare of the sun. "Uh," he says, passing the phone to Simon with his face twisted in irritation. "You missed some messages."

Simon slows the car, pulling to the right hand lane. He's paranoid about texting and driving, mostly because his mom tends to harass him about it whenever he has to rent a car for something. It's probably the kennel. Part of the package is frequent updates and pictures.

Andrew: Did u get my email?
Andrew: Are u coming to party?
Andrew: Pls Simon I need you
Andrew: Miss u baby

Chapter Seven

Ask Eros: Existential Ice Cream

Q: *How do I know if he's the one?*

A: *You don't! Fun, right? Take away my sappy romantic membership card if you must (it's behind that expired free Blizzard punchcard—no, the other one.) I just can't get onboard with the idea that we're all drifting through life just waiting around to find our other half so we can live happily ever after. Be a whole person. Look for other whole people and, if you're lucky, you'll find one you love that loves you back. If you're really lucky, you'll find one you like that likes you back. And then you'll choose each other over and over again, because you want them and you keep wanting them. Sounds like work? It is. Man, I could go for a Blizzard now.*

The rest of the drive, Benji is quiet except to guide Simon on the roads of the small seaside town where The Glass Lake Inn is located. They head down a long narrow gravel drive that leads to the stone masonry buildings of the inn, chapel and banquet hall.

Simon's room is on the top floor with a lake view and, despite his last-minute invite, Benji is in the room directly across the hall. He's glad Tia found some time between work and planning a wedding to help his chances at getting some action. True friendship.

But Benji goes into his room and stays there, even though they have hours until the ceremony. Simon spreads out across the Amish quilt covering his king size bed and stares at the ceiling, then over at the shimmering sun on the lake, before relenting and looking at his messages again.

It's not lost on him, the fact that the more he ignores Andrew the more desperately Andrew seems to want him. Two weeks ago, he would have been thrilled, then plotted for ways to make this new information work to his advantage. But being here, with Benji, he just doesn't seem to care as much anymore, as if Andrew were a constant dull itch in the back of his mind that he couldn't scratch and couldn't ignore. Now, it's just sort of gone.

Simon: I'm out of town. I'll message you when I get back.

He slips off his shoes and hauls his suitcase onto the bed, then takes out his clothes to iron them for later. White chinos, breezy button down; dressy casual, as per the invitation. His phone buzzes and he wants to ignore it, but knows he can't.

This time it is the kennel; a picture of Walt and a huge Labrador carrying the same stick along a dirt path in the woods, vibrant green trees and red-berried bushes blooming behind them. Simon smiles down at the screen and decides to go for a walk around the lake.

He heads out the back way and down the path to where white chairs are being set up in rows beneath the low sweep of weeping willow branches. A latticed arch twined with vines and white flowers stands at the edge of the lake. The shore is lined in thick-leaved trees with tiny pink-petaled blossoms. Past those sturdy oaks make up a dense forest that isolates the inn from the outside world.

He walks back to the inn and goes up the outside stone staircase he'd spotted from across the lake. He finds Tia with her thick dark hair braided into an elaborate updo and makeup on, wearing yoga pants and camisole and smoking a cigarette.

"You know I adore James, but if we need to hightail it to Mexico, you just say the word."

Simon sits next to her on the step. She blows out a line of smoke and fans it away from him. "No, I'm fine. Just needed a moment."

"Understandable. I'd just like to point out that you don't smoke." Simon watches her take another drag as if she's been chain smoking since middle school; the cigarette end glows orange in the dusk. "Are you sure you're okay?"

She breathes in, drops the cigarette and stamps it out with her sandal. "I came out here to check on everything and saw one of the catering staff smoking. I was about to yell at her for doing it so close to the food. That fucking bourbon-and-maple-glazed ham with croquettes bullshit was not cheap. But then I thought, James would fire her on the spot. He hates smoking. And the next thing I knew I was bumming one from her."

Simon stretches out his legs and looks back at the wedding arrangements coming together down the hill. "One last hurrah, hmm?"

"I guess so." She stands, pulls Simon up with her and grins. "Fuck, I'm getting married."

Simon laughs and hugs her close. She reeks of hairspray, her mother's overpowering perfume and cigarette smoke. He's so, so happy for her. "Yeah you are. Now go. I'll see you at the altar."

Chapter Eight

Ask Eros: Do the Hand Jive

Q: *I like sex, but it's painful. I can't seem to get comfortable with any sort of penetration. It hurts and I try to just get through it but that only makes it worse. Is there anything I can do about it?*

A: *Lube. Lube. Did I mention lube? Okay, but first let's talk about reasons it might be painful. If we're talking vaginal penetration, STDs and infections can cause pain, so get that checked out if you think that might be the case. Your partner may be hitting your cervix battering ram style, and that can hurt. Try different positions or ask them not to go in too deep. For anal: lube, relax, go slow, communicate. And that's the most important bit: lube. I kid, I kid. Communicate! The best sex is the kind where you talk about what you want and don't want, what's working and what isn't. Be honest! Be open! And, if nothing else, there's lots of fun to be had without any penetration at all.*

Simon fidgets in front of Benji's room. He's freshly showered, shaved and dressed in the wrinkle-free clothes he ironed three times. He takes a breath and lifts his fist to knock when the door suddenly swings open.

"Oh." Simon says, for lack of ability to say anything else. Benji is in a slim-fit black button down, which accentuates the broad inverted triangle of his torso, and perfectly fitted slacks. His hair is combed down and away from his face; his skin is clean-shaven and soft looking. "You look. Really great."

"Yeah, I guess I clean up okay. Shirt's itchy though. You look nice." It's curt and a little strained, but he smiles. "Did you, uh, get your messages sorted out?"

He closes the door, and they walk together down the narrow hallway; the plush carpeting mutes their footsteps and voices. Simon presses the down button for the elevator. "Oh, um. Yeah, the kennel sent some updates. Walt's having the time of his life. Wants me to stay in Jersey forever."

The elevator is wood paneled on the bottom and vintage gold and turquoise damask wallpapered on top. Benji leans against the handrail in the back, pulls his bottom lip between his teeth and seems to be working up the nerve to say something. But the elevator stops and dings their arrival; the doors slide open to the lobby. They file out and join other wedding guests in walking out the door and down the little footpath to the lake.

The sun is setting, drifting down below the treetops: huge and golden and reflecting on the smooth surface of the water. The trees are wound with fairy lights; the footpath is lined with flickering luminaries. Everything feels soft and hushed and tremulous, as though if Simon were to reach out to touch it would all shimmer and slide and drift away.

They take their seats on the bride's side as the music swells. Tia's mother dabs her eyes when Tia starts her walk down the aisle with her father and continues to sniffle throughout the ceremony.

Simon's eyes blur and his throat closes tight. Benji leans over while Tia's sister sings a dedication. "You okay?"

Simon chuckles wetly. "It's just weddings. I'm fine."

He's happy for Tia, he *is*. But some small, petty part of him is jealous. Jealous that she's getting this and he isn't, which he sort of expected. But he's also jealous that Tia now has a best friend who will always be at her side, will always choose her, and it isn't Simon. It *shouldn't* be Simon. But it still seems as if he has to let go of one more thing, one more person, one more little part of himself.

He's being ridiculous and dramatic and overly emotional, and he doesn't usually tear up at weddings. Thank God it's dusk, and no one has to bear witness to his blubbering. But then Benji slips his hand into Simon's, fingers interlacing, and there it is, that feeling of being anchored, even though he and Benji are still just getting to know each other.

So he squeezes Benji's fingers tight, watches his beautiful friend say *I do* and chooses to not think about what holding hands might mean.

The banquet hall is similarly dim and strung with twinkling white lights. There are linen-covered tables and chairs, a dance floor at one end and a DJ at the other. Simon has barely sipped his drink—"It's a Scotch kind of night," he says to Benji and sighs—when the newly wedded couple is announced.

They're seated with some friends of Tia's from college, making polite conversation over the bourbon-and-maple-glazed ham and croquettes—worth every penny as far as Simon is concerned.

They watch the cake cutting. The first dance. Simon downs two more Scotches and is finally feeling pleasantly numb when Benji stands up.

"Come on, let's go make fools out of ourselves on the dance floor."

They do look ridiculous, Simon is sure, but he doesn't care. He doesn't care what he's supposed to do, or be or want. He doesn't care that Andrew would scoff and straighten his tie and call *The Electric Slide* juvenile and gauche. He gets in place and follows along with everyone else, laughing when he and Benji stumble into each other. He wraps an arm low around Benji's waist, rocks his hips against him when the music switches to the pulse of something dirty and thumping with bass. He doesn't care. Not tonight.

A slow song comes on and Benji is there, chest to chest, arms wrapped around Simon's shoulders. He smells even better up close than Simon imagined, and he can't seem to help himself when he nuzzles his nose up and down the column of Benji's neck, his lips following in just a teasing brush.

Benji's fingers tighten across the splay of Simon's shoulder blades and he sucks in a sharp breath.

They stay like that for three more songs. Simon is so warm from his drinks and Benji pressed up against him that he feels as if he's combusting from the inside.

Then Benji's mouth brushes his ear. He's shaking, and his heart thuds against Simon's chest. Simon's eyes roll back as he whispers, "Do you want to go upstairs?"

The elevator ride seems endless, but Simon doesn't mind, just lolls his head against the wall and looks at Benji. And grins and grins.

"So you're a happy drunk. I'll keep that in mind," Benji says with a bemused smile.

"I'm not that drunk," Simon replies as they finally reach their floor. "I'm just happy."

They barely make it into Simon's room before Benji has him pressed up against the door, eyes darker than Simon has ever seen them, muscles all coiled tight, heart beating wildly.

Simon goes for Benji's belt, fumbling the buckle with a clank and rattle, but Benji cups his face, gently tugs his chin up, tilts his head and closes his eyes, mouth so close that, when he takes a steadying breath and licks his lips, it tickles Simon's parted mouth.

Then they kiss, and Simon's breath is stolen right from his lungs.

It's nothing like Andrew, nothing like any of the guys before him, either. Simon moans and opens his mouth wider to suck and lick and nibble at Benji's lips. He undertands chemistry and passion and, theoretically, feeling as if the earth is shifting and falling away at his feet. He understands connection. But this. This is something he doesn't understand at all.

"So long," Benji mutters into the stretched out skin of Simon's throat, leaning in to suck kiss after kiss down the tendon on one side, and back up the other. "I've wanted this since the moment I saw you."

Simon's head thumps back against the door, and he shivers with pleasure. He's overwhelmed and so shocked by the intensity between them that he deflects, just to keep himself from drowning. "Wow, you really have a Peter Parker thing, huh?"

Benji pulls back, lips red and wet, cheeks flushed. "I have a 'you' thing."

It's a total line, but it doesn't feel like one, not when Benji is looking at him with stark, unabashed desire. Simon lunges, kisses him deep and hard again, shoves his shirt up and pulls away with a grunt to unbutton the damn thing enough to actually get it off.

He's gorgeous: broad, lightly defined chest, flat tapered waist, soft pale skin and lean sinewy muscles. Simon runs his palms from the jut of his hipbones up the expanse of his ribs and circles his thumbs over pink nipples. Benji hooks him by the belt loops and backs them up to the bed, sealing their mouths together again as they fall together onto the quaint hand-stitched bedspread.

Simon shifts over him, his chest pressed to Benji's as they kiss. He yanks open Benji's belt, finally, then eases the button open and pulls the zipper down with a soft hum. He wants to see more of him, all of him. Touch every inch of him. But Benji flips them suddenly, kicking his pants away, his long body pressed flush to Simon's.

"You're so hot," he groans, pupils huge and dark, fingers working open Simon's shirt, his pants. He places soft kisses down the length of Simon's torso, around the dip of his belly button, then noses down the line of coarse hair and stops just above the waistband of Simon's briefs.

"Really?" Simon's cock is a long, hard line against the fabric of his underwear revealed between the open flaps of his pants. Benji gives a choked-off little groan and cups him, cheek turned to rest on Simon's belly.

"God, yeah." He squeezes once, and just that is enough to make Simon's hips churn and blood rush hot through his body.

It's not as though Simon thinks he's ugly, or undesirable. He's okay. He does all right. But he's never felt wanted the way he does right now. Benji kneels, legs wide astride Simon's, his hard cock pushing against the fabric of his purple briefs. He slips Simon's pants the rest of the way off and helps him wriggle out of his shirt. When he skims his fingers across Simon's collarbones, down his chest and stomach, then strips him naked and gasps, Simon feels worshiped.

He hooks a hand on the back of Benji's neck and pulls him down for a kiss that's mostly lips pressed hard together. "God—I need—" Simon grits out against his mouth, legs spreading and bending, pushing against Benji's ribs.

He doesn't have to clarify. Benji just knows. He slips a hand between them and grasps Simon's cock, giving a few experimental tugs; fast and loose, hard and quick, then tight and twisting. Simon's back bows and he moans into the hush of the room. Benji settles on a steady pace— exactly the way Simon likes it—and Simon can feel the tightening in his groin and balls already.

He shoves both hands down the back of Benji's briefs to distract himself, but it seems to make things worse; his ass is tight and round beneath Simon's grip, perfect taut muscles that shift and clench when Simon rubs a finger between.

"Oh," Benji breathes, his hand losing its pace and hips coming down to grind against Simon's thigh. Simon tugs at his ass to shift him, then moves one hand around to the front, wrist pushing the elastic down and Benji's erection shifting hot into his hand. He tucks the waistband under the heavy hang of his balls, then presses his fingers into the small of Benji's back to guide him down.

He settles, so solid and so hard, between Simon's legs. "Yeah. Just this." Simon turns his head, mouth brushing the flexed knot of Benji's bicep as he holds his torso up enough to move against Simon, their cocks rutting together.

It's amazing and perfect and grounding, as if Simon hadn't realized just how untethered he was until Benji's weight pressed him into the plush give of the mattress. He grips his ass again, pulls and pushes and shoves Benji against him over and over, faster and faster, until he's whimpering and thrashing. Benji leans down and catches Simon's lips between his own and whimpers high and thready. That's what does it. Simon cries out and spills between their bellies.

The world goes pleasantly fuzzy, as his body falls limp and tingling with pleasure. He breathes, can hear Benji grunting and panting, thrusting wildly through the mess pooled on Simon's stomach. Simon has the pleasure of watching Benji's face go slack, his mouth parted and eyes unfocused. *He's really beautiful,* Simon has just enough time to marvel, before Benji gives one last shudder and falls to the side.

"Mmmm," Simon hums happily, tucked behind Benji and mostly cleaned up with a perfunctory swipe of a pillowcase. He had too many pillows anyway.

"My thoughts exactly," Benji replies and wiggles in closer, his back pressed to Simon's chest with curve of his ass settled against Simon's soft cock.

Simon is loose-limbed and giddy and clearly lacking even the most basic of filters, because he tucks his face between the sharp angles of Benji's shoulder blades and says, "I think I'm bad at this."

"Are you kidding?" Benji shifts in his arms and moves back enough so that Simon can look at him without going cross-eyed. "You're incredible." He drops to his back, with the sheet twisted around his legs, and throws an arm over his eyes. Simon licks his lips and starts working up to round two.

"No, I mean. This whole one-night stand thing." Simon leans in to kiss him again, but this time Benji is stiff and unresponsive. "I'm probably not supposed to ask you to spend the entire weekend in my bed, right? Like isn't it a hit-it-and-quit-it sort of thing?" Simon dips down again to kiss him again, only Benji turns his head and sits up.

"I should go," he says, already gathering his clothes and pulling on his underwear.

"What? Benji, I was kidding. I don't want to quit it. Not yet." He grabs for him, but Benji moves away, yanks on his pants and heads to the door.

"Yeah. I'm, uh, just tired." He fidgets by the door, shirt and socks tucked against his chest, pants still undone and hanging off his hips.

"So stay," Simon implores, patting the bed next to him with what he hopes is an enticing grin. Benji heaves a breath and rubs a hand over his face.

"I... I think we want different things, Simon. It's okay. But I need to not be here now."

And then he's gone; the door closes with a quiet click behind him. Simon stretches out on his bed. The sheets have already gone cool without Benji there. Outside the sky is dark and brimming with stars. He'd almost forgotten what the night sky looked like without the bright lights of the city.

Crickets chirp and the trees rustle with the caress of a breeze, and Simon looks out the window, watches the faraway moon and feels completely and utterly alone.

⌒⌒ Chapter Nine

Ask Eros: So There's This Girl...

Q: *For years I've been comfortably dating men and women, secure in who I am and what I like. My family is fine with it, if sometimes confused. My friends are totally accepting. However, all of my serious relationships have been with men. That's how I always saw my life going: marrying a guy in the church I grew up in, having a couple of kids, a minivan, the whole boring nuclear family deal. But there's this girl. I can't stop thinking about her. She makes me happier than I ever thought possible. I am head over heels in love with her, but I still can't let go of that dream, that life I saw for myself that will never happen if I give myself to her fully. I feel unworthy of her, like I should let her go for someone who will love her the way she deserves. Should I?*

A: *Here's the thing about that fantasy life you're so attached to: It's safe. Perfect fantasy husband won't hurt you. He won't reject you. He won't leave you. He will love you always and never ever notice any of your faults and shortcomings because he is not real. And that's a hell of a lot easier than putting your heart on the line for someone who maybe, just maybe, won't love you the same way you love her. That's terrifying. It's a huge risk. Things might go wrong. But, from where I'm standing, it sounds like she's absolutely worth it. Be happy now.*

The morning dawns bright and clear and warm. A hope flutters in Simon's chest when he leaves his room to check out: Maybe Benji will be fine with things in the light of a new day. But the housekeeping cart is parked outside of Benji's room, the door is propped open and a vacuum is running inside. He's already gone. Simon's stomach drops, and regret twists through him.

No wonder his love life is a mess. He either tries to have relationships with guys who don't want one, who lead him on and only care when Simon starts to get a clue and moves on, or he tries to have a fling with a guy he really, really likes, but is too afraid of having something real with.

The drive home seems longer; it's too quiet, too empty, until he makes it to the kennel. Walt is so happy to see him he jumps up against Simon's chest and leaves muddy paw prints all over his shirt. "Hey, buddy. Did you miss me?"

"He had a great time, but I think he's ready to go home," says the kennel owner, a curvy woman with long brown hair and cat-eye glasses.

Simon bends down to get both arms around Walt's wiggly body, his tail wagging so hard his whole bottom half dances back and forth. "You and me both."

Walt starts to lick his face so Simon stands, takes the paperwork and receipt and folds them into his pocket. The owner hands over the leash and says, "Make sure you tell his other daddy how much fun he had!"

"Oh." Simon twists and twists the leash around his hand to get a good grip before Walt decides to bolt. "We're not. I mean. He's a friend. A good friend."

He doesn't have time to decide if the look on her face is disbelief or amusement, because Walt has had enough and takes off for the car. Simon pulls back so Walt doesn't get loose and run off. The last thing he needs is another abandonment. Even if he deserves it.

Walt jumps into the back seat and waits for Simon with his ears high and snout resting on the passenger seat.

"He's not here," Simon says, then gets in and starts the engine and sighs.

Walt tilts his head. Licks Simon's ear. Simon presses the button
for the back window and lets Walt ride the whole way home with his
head out the window.

He doesn't see Benji at work on Monday or Tuesday. Still no Benji
for days after that. Simon's life settles into gray monotony. He gets a few
texts and phone calls from Andrew, but it's like getting birthday wishes
on Facebook from high school acquaintances he barely knew even
back then: nice to know someone cares, but ultimately meaningless.

He's at home in his pajamas at six thirty in the evening on a Friday;
a pizza box with a half-eaten pizza is open on his coffee table. Walt is
at his side begging for another piece of pepperoni. Simon picks one
from a greasy slice and tosses it over. Walt catches it in his mouth.
Simon wipes off his fingers and picks up his phone.

He thinks about calling Andrew. Andrew is familiar. Andrew isn't a
risk because Simon isn't putting anything on the line, and, if Andrew
leaves, well, it's not as though Simon ever really had him in the first
place. Andrew is not his happily ever after, but they could be happy
enough. Simon could make it so, if only Andrew would let him.

And then there's Benji, who is nothing like the glossy posed pictures
of happily ever after Simon had in his head, and yet is somehow everything Simon has ever wanted. Benji, whom Simon can't seem to hold
at a distance. Benji, whose absence makes Simon's chest feel hollow,
with an empty space he never meant to leave so vulnerable and open.

His fingers hover over the contacts icon.

FaceTime call from: Tia R.

He accepts the call, and Tia's smiling face is a soothing balm for his
aching heart. He tells her as much.

"I've been gone for five days, Simon. What did you do?"

"I fucked up," he says. Then adds, "You look amazing right now."
Her dark skin is glowing and dewy, her eyes are bright and her smile
is radiant. Her hair is done in tight island-style cornrows, and she's
completely pulling off the look.

"I know! I'm thinking about getting married several times just for the honeymoon." She flips her hair and the tiny bright beads clatter happily. "So, I called to see if you could water the plants in my office and to show off a little, but clearly you need my help."

Simon tilts the phone, sees his frown reflected in the little window. "It's fine."

Tia rolls her eyes, and, in the background, he can see James in swim trunks, hovering. "Come on, I'm going on a boat to a tiki bar that's on a private island, and then I'm dancing all night with my husband." She smiles at that, warm and soft, and it makes Simon so happy. And so, so sad.

He takes a breath. "I really like Benji. A lot. Like this could actually be something real, and I pushed him away. Now he won't talk to me. I should have just stuck to pining after Andrew, because at least no one got hurt then."

"Except you. Even though you've convinced yourself otherwise," Tia says. James mumbles something behind her, and she flaps her hand at him. "I know you try to spend all of your time making other people happy and helping them figure out their stuff. But sometimes you need to figure out your own stuff, honey. Take a chance on Benji and maybe keep a little happiness for yourself."

Simon presses his mouth into a line and tosses Walt another pepperoni. She's right, and that's what would he tell himself if he were one of the people writing to him for help. Go after the thing that makes you happy. Life is too hard and too short for anything else.

"If I've been wrong about Andrew this whole time, and so thoroughly screwed up my own love life, then how can I possibly give anyone advice? I'm just a hack and a liar." He should forget the writing career and become a pharmacist as his high school guidance counselor suggested. They make good money, pharmacists. Good, safe living. He could do worse.

"Simon," Tia says, and she's moving now, the picture of her on the phone jarring and swooping dizzily. "Nobody needs you to be perfect. They just need you to give a shit."

After they say goodbye, he droops to his side on the couch. Walt rests his head on the cushion by his face, tail sweeping slowly against the floor.

"I'm all out of pepperoni," he says. Walt's ears go up and he licks Simon's nose. "Should I go talk to Benji? You like him, huh?" Walt puts his ears back, then up, tail *thump, thump, thumping* on the floor. "Yeah, me too."

He puts in a call to IT first thing Monday morning, not just to see Benji, but because his computer is still in pieces. He's just about had enough of dealing with a laptop that can barely load an email without timing out.

Near the end of the day they send up an IT guy who is not Benji at all: short and stocky and barely speaks more than one syllable the whole time he's there, despite Simon's attempts at small talk and his clever yet probing questions about Benji's whereabouts.

"I dunno what he's doing; he just told me to go up here." The guy says, his first full sentence in the entire hour he's been there. "Okay, you're all set. Just plug in the external hard drive and you should be up and running."

Simon spins his chair around. "Wait, you're finished?"

The guy stops outside of his cubicle and shrugs. "Yeah. It was just a blown fuse. Not that difficult."

For a week and a half, Benji was constantly popping in and out of Simon's cubicle, tinkering with his computer whenever he had the chance, on a job that would have taken a couple hours, tops? Now that he thinks about it, Benji saying he was waiting for a flux capacitor was pretty suspect, but Simon had never really stopped to consider that he was stalling, he was too pleased with having Benji's buzzing bright presence around as much as possible.

Simon bites his lip, bounces in his chair a bit and starts to feel something like hope bubble up, and maybe, just maybe, he still has a shot.

He starts the fixed computer; the welcome-chime and bright screen only add to his giddiness. He opens the drawer to find the back up hard drive so he can get all of his documents and data restored, searches past some notes and a box of paperclips and a flash drive.

He pulls out the flash drive Andrew gave him at the hotel; he hadn't really thought about in weeks. It's small and blue and cool in his hands. He plugs it into a port, watches it download, then hits save. It's late, and he wants to get home. He's behind on work and correspondence. He could just tell Andrew to get someone who is qualified to read spending reports to find any issues. But he figures may as well, and then he can tell Andrew that not only is that done, but so are they. Maybe he will go to that work party after all.

Simon: Find me at the party. Need to speak with you.
Andrew: K. I'll be there.

Chapter Ten

Ask Eros: Let's Not Get Freaky

Q: *I'm graduating college soon and I've only been with one guy. I just can't seem to get comfortable with casual hookups or even the three-date rule for sex. I want to have sex, but I can only ever see myself doing it with someone I really care about and plan on being with for a long time. I don't even like masturbating that much. Am I a freak?*

A: *So I've recently been getting an education in the wide wacky world of oft-forgotten superheroes. Turns out there was this one: Arm-Fall-Off-Boy who, get this, had arms that fell off. He used them to bludgeon nefarious super villains. That guy? Kind of a freak. (Sorry Arm-Fall-Off-Boy. Godspeed, RIP, we hardly knew ye, etc.) Someone wanting to have sex in the context of a committed, loving relationship? Not a freak. And if anyone tells you differently, just yank your arm off and smack them upside the head.*

The party is at a swanky rooftop venue in Midtown. He settles on slim-fit dark wash jeans cuffed at the ankle, a dark green short sleeved Henley shirt and black Converse high tops. It's warm and clear out; the humidity is fading as the sky grows darker. Simon stands near a cascading fountain lit up with a spotlight in the center; a margarita sweats in his hands as he looks around anxiously.

He gets roped into a conversation about juice cleanses with a photo editor named Rainbow, which then turns into a discussion about environmental toxins, which then becomes, inevitably, a rant about politicians.

"I'm just gonna get another drink." Simon takes a step back, holding up his still mostly full drink with its festive pink umbrella and strides away before she has a chance to notice his lame excuse.

The rooftop isn't huge, but is set up to accommodate a large gathering: long and L-shaped with narrow benches stretching across and the bar along the back corner. He has to do some impressive dodging and weaving to get to the far corner balcony. It's really too bad his mom wouldn't let him play football for fear of head injuries—and that he hadn't had the slightest interest in playing football.

"Hey, I could've played football. I'm agile," Simon defends to no one in particular.

Tia lifts an eyebrow, looks him up and down. "No."

Simon waves her off. "Whatever. Have you seen Benji?"

"Not yet, sorry."

"What does he look like?" Speaking of football player types, James leans against the railing, one arm propped behind him and the other around Tia's shoulders. He looks imposing: He's six foot five and solid as a linebacker, but is, in fact, the softest, cuddliest teddy bear. James stands to his impressive full height and scopes out the crowd.

"Um," Simon stretches to his tiptoes, tries to see what James is seeing. Side-parts and bald spots mostly. "He's thin but strong, you know? Lean. Wiry. Broad chest. Beautiful eyes. Oh—and his shoulder to waist ratio is like, perfect. And his cheekbones—"

"Redhead," Tia interrupts. "Tall skinny redhead." Simon scowls at her. He is not. "Really cute, tall skinny redhead," Tia amends with a wink.

James purses his lips, looks back and forth across the rooftop. "Oh yeah, I think he's here. I don't see him right now. But someone else is headed your way."

Tia cranes to see, then raises both brows, gives her drink a shake so the ice tinkles against the glass and takes a long sip. "Andrew."

"Hello, Tia, you're looking well." He shakes James' hand, then places his palm on the small of Simon's back, leading him towards the stairs that will take them off the rooftop and back inside the building. Simon's instinct is to squirm away.

He's wearing a full suit and tie, despite it being a casual function. Despite the temperature easily being in the eighties. Despite no one else being dressed up. Andrew comes off like a complete douche.

"Simon, can I see you for a moment?"

There's a set of bathrooms just outside the door to the stairs and, past that, a long marble hallway and the elevator. Their footsteps echo as they move to face each other. Andrew stands closer than Simon would like and the smell of alcohol on him is almost a physical force in the small space between their bodies.

"So, did you download the spending report yet?"

Simon crosses his arms and leans back. "Is that seriously all you wanted to talk to me about?"

Something flashes across Andrew's face then, and he visibly changes tactics; lowering his eyes and moving even closer. "Of course not. I just. I just thought you could help me out, and then I can help you out." Andrew's hand drifts to Simon's belt buckle, one finger looping inside and giving a tug.

Simon moves his hand. "All this time. You knew how much I wanted to be with you. You had me dangling on a hook and now, now I'm off your hook—now you're ready?"

Andrew cocks his head. "Timing is everything, Simon."

"I'm not a fucking business transaction!" Simon's voice bounces angrily around the empty hall.

Andrew presses in, looks down at Simon's lips and back up to his eyes. Licks his own lips. "I'm sorry. I was just afraid of how much I feel for you, baby. But I want you. I'm ready." His voice drops, gruff and heated. "Let me make you feel good."

Simon's trapped between the wall and Andrew's pushing body as Andrew's hands wander to his ass and between his legs. Simon grabs Andrew's wrists to make it clear that his advances are unwelcome. When that doesn't stop him, Simon twists, changes tactics and grips Andrew by the shoulders to shove him away. He has his hands wrapped tight around Andrew's arms, and Andrew's hands are groping high on Simon's thighs when the door to the stairs bangs open like a gunshot and a group of people spill out.

In the front, looking happy and gorgeous, is Benji. Simon freezes, and Benji stares. Then Simon realizes exactly what the situation looks like. He shoves Andrew away as the elevator beeps its arrival and the group files on.

"Benji!" Simon runs to get on before the doors close, leaving Andrew slumped against the wall swearing under his breath. "Hold the door. Wait!"

It slips closed in his face. He presses the down button over and over to no avail.

"Fuck it," he finally decides, then tears off for the stairs.

When he makes it down onto the street, he's doubled over, out of breath and with a pain in his side., He gets several dirty looks as he blocks people's progress, but cares even less than he usually does.

He doesn't see Benji or Benji's group. He starts in the direction of Benji's apartment, then realizes they were probably headed somewhere else and turns back without any real sense of where he's going. He turns over conversations in his head, remembering how Benji is a simple, straightforward guy who likes beer and comic books and classic rock. What sort of bar would he go to after a work party?

Simon stops at a crosswalk with his hands on his hips and waits for the traffic to clear. The city is too big, too busy. Too many options. Not to mention that he might be guilty of low-level stalking at this point.

He goes home.

"Oh, Christ." Simon's keys dangle from his fingers, and he stops dead in the outside hallway in front of his door. There's a huge bouquet of two dozen roses and baby's breath, a generic *I'm sorry* balloon and a huge box of dark-chocolate sea-salt truffles.

Simon opens the door, kicks the whole lot into the entryway and isn't sure if he's more impressed by the speed of the delivery or of Andrew's sudden, insistent desperation.

Walt greets him with a head bump to his knees and an enthusiastic tail wag. He sniffs the flowers and chocolate with interest.

Groping the dark wall for a light switch, Simon feels the beginnings of a headache forming at his temples. He'd thought that he could just go home and regain his bearings and try again. But he feels claustrophobic. His small apartment feels even smaller, as if the walls are pressing in. The rattle of the window unit pulses in his ears as though it's been cranked to max volume. His jaw clenches and his head throbs.

Walt shoves his nose against the box of chocolates, making the bottom of the box scrape against the floor. "Leave it," Simon snaps. Walt slinks away.

He needs to think. To get out. Some fresh air.

Walt jumps up when Simon opens the door again and he feels a sick twist of guilt. He just doesn't have the energy to deal with leash pulling and pigeon chasing and trying to make friends with everyone right now. He hold his hand up—"stay"—and leaves for a walk alone.

◻◻ Chapter Eleven

Ask Eros: The Human Torch

Q: *I'm in love with my best friend. We're both single, we get along really well, we're perfect for each other. I've tried so hard to talk myself out of it or ignore it or let it go, but I just can't. I'm so afraid of complicating things. Should I just be grateful for what I've got?*

A: *Consider this: It's already complicated. You're carrying a torch for someone while trying to just be friends. Like it or not, things are tricky now. Continuing to ignore it isn't changing that. You need to be brave, you need to let them know how you feel, but, most importantly, you need to understand that they don't owe you anything because of that. They might be in love with you, too. They might not. But once you've done the very courageous act of being honest, you can work on what to do next. Like best friends should be able to.*

"Hey, it's me again. Sorry for sort of hanging up on you earlier. And then the message of me breathing, that's not creepy. Oh god, I'm hysterical. Never mind.

"I'm sorry. I know you don't want to talk to me but Tia's not answering her phone and I don't know what else to do. I'm freaking out. He was just lying there. I don't know what I'll do if he leaves me and it's my fault. It's my fault if he leaves, and I keep hurting people I care about and—I mean. Not that he's a people. Person. No, this message is worse than panicked breathing. I'm sorry."

Simon crouches against the rough brick wall, holds his pounding head in his hands and then rubs the heel of his hands against his eyes. He swallows past the lump in his throat and takes a deep breath. Dials one more time and waits for the call to go to voicemail. Again.

"Hi Benji. Walt ate some chocolate and I'm at the vet near my house and I—I don't know if he's gonna be okay, and I thought you might want to know."

The waiting room is sparse this time of night, just a young couple with a dog having emergency surgery and a woman whose cat is undergoing dialysis.

"He's eighteen years old and mean as a rattlesnake," she tells Simon. "And he's the love of my life."

Normally he'd scoff at having twice-weekly dialysis for an animal clearly ready to pass on, but right now he gets it. He'd do anything to make Walt be okay. Anything to erase the image of him curled into a ball, shaking and whining and covered in his own vomit with the remains of the two-pound box of chocolates in shredded bits around him.

He doesn't know how long he was like that before Simon got back from his walk of self-indulgent moping. He should have just brought him along. He should have thrown the balloon, the flowers and the goddamn imported chocolate in the dumpster on the way out. He should have told Andrew to leave him alone a long, long time ago. He should have let go of Andrew a long, long time ago.

The magazine across his lap, from which he hasn't absorbed a word, is hazy in his vision. The theoretically calming light-green walls of the waiting room doing nothing to make him feel better as the time passes and passes with no word from the vet.

"Simon."

He's out of breath and his face is blotchy and red. He's decked out in his baggy pajamas printed with a Superman emblem pattern and his hair is an absolute disaster. Simon has never been more happy to see anybody in his life.

Simon bolts up and hugs him before he can stop himself, buries his face in his neck and just lets his body melt into his arms. "Benji."

"There's like, six veterinarians near your place. And they all think I'm a lunatic. God, the people I've yelled at... Are you okay? Is Walt okay?"

Simon releases him, though he doesn't want to at all. Doesn't want to stop feeling Benji's arms around him, ever. But he makes himself sit down and regain some sense of calm. For the dialysis cat lady's sake. She's clearly under a lot of stress.

"They took him back a while ago. If they can get it all out of his system in time..."

Simon sits at the edge of his chair, fingers twisting and knees jogging. Benji takes his hand and gently slips their palms together and gives a squeeze. Simon feels as if he can breathe for the first time since he found Walt hours earlier.

The dialysis lady leaves with her cat growling in its carrier, and, a little while after that, the couple goes back to see their dog. Then it's just them, with loosely held hands and a palpable quiet between them. The clock *tick, tick, ticks* away on the wall, and finally Simon has to say something.

He pulls his hand away and fiddles with the bunched seam at the bend of his knees. "I'm sorry."

"You don't have to keep apologizing. I knew going in that you and Andrew are... whatever you are," Benji says with a casual shrug that Simon doesn't quite believe.

"Andrew and I aren't—" Simon starts, but Benji shakes his head.

"It doesn't matter. And I'm sorry for icing you out." He shifts in his seat, flashes a crooked half smile and a gaze that doesn't quite meet Simon's. "I'd love it if we could be friends still."

Simon doesn't want to be just friends, not at all, but God, it's better than nothing and far more than he deserves. "I'd like that." Simon breathes out and tries to smile.

"Mr. Beck?" The vet tech calls from the doorway. "You can come back now."

When he opens the exam room, there's Walt on his side on the paper-covered exam table. Simon's heart jumps into his throat, and then Walt's skinny tail gives a sad thump of a wag.

"Hey, buddy," Simon whispers, scratching behind his ears as Benji rubs his belly. "I was worried about you."

The vet comes in, middle-aged with salt and pepper hair. "Well, you'll need to monitor him as closely as you can for the night as there's still a chance of seizures. But I think he's going to be just fine. Weak and tired for a while. But fine."

They get instructions about making sure he gets water and, later, food. Simon wonders if he'll be able to muster the extra adrenaline-fueled strength to carry him again back to the apartment, but, while the vet talks to them, Walt starts to perk up little by little. He manages to walk home on a thin nylon vet-issued leash.

"Free gift. Score," Benji says as they wait for the elevator to arrive in the lobby of Simon's building. Walt leans against Simon's leg with his eyes half closed, drained from the quiet walk home.

The elevator arrives, and they drag themselves on. "Yeah, free leash with every chocolate poisoning. Offer available while supplies last. Irresponsible dog owners only."

"Hey," Benji says softly, nudging Simon with his hip.

"It's my fault," Simon says, then sighs and leads the way down the hall to his apartment.

"So you made a mistake," Benji leans against the doorframe, teasing grin at the corners of his mouth. "You are just a people after all."

Simon breathes out a sort of sob-laugh, gently leads Walt the last bit until they're inside, then kicks the door closed. He feels lighter, as if a weight has been lifted from his burdened shoulders. He's home. Walt is okay, and watching Benji help Walt settle on the couch, talking soothingly and getting him fresh water feels... right.

Simon shoves the flowers and the balloon under the sink with his plastic bag collection, spray bottle of Windex and jug of bleach while Benji throws away the wrappers and what's left of the box of chocolates.

Finally, Simon takes a breath, ready to say what he means and what he wants, as he watches Benji lower himself on the couch and start to scratch Walt's ears and under his chin and pet carefully down his flank. Walt's eyes droop closed, and Simon says, shaky, "Will you stay? Just a little bit?"

Benji catches his eye and replies immediately, "Of course."

▭▭ Chapter Twelve

Ask Eros: Rizzmic Is for Lovers

Q: *There's this guy at the gym that I'm crushing on. He's really cute and nice and we end up being at the gym at the same time a lot. We're even taking a Rizzmic class together! He makes a point of standing next to me or spotting me or finding two machines together so we can talk while we work out. He's always smiling and saying really sweet things and talking about how very single he is. I think he likes me, but I don't want to embarrass myself by making a move if he doesn't. Do you think he's into me?*

A: *I know men can be confusing sometimes, what with all the weird body hair and belching contests and repressed emotions and football and backwards baseball caps. But I sense you've been convinced somewhere along the line that men are constantly playing a high-stakes chess game with women's emotions and that, if a man shows possible interest in you, then you have to write up a thesis and present it to a panel of your peers for academic review. Do you see what I'm saying? Yes. He likes you.*

"Okay, here we go," Benji crosses his legs beneath him and puts the remote down on the coffee table so Walt can settle his head on his lap. *Harry Potter and the Sorcerer's Stone* starts its opening credits and music as Simon curls up on the opposite end of the couch. Benji throws him a smile, and says. "I'm so happy you have all of the movies DVR'd. That should get us through the night."

Simon tries to ignore the excited flutter in his chest as he pats Walt's rear and scoffs, "What kind of person doesn't have all the Harry Potter movies?"

"No one I'd like to know," Benji mutters, then settles in.

They both make it through the first one just fine, commenting on the movie: the differences from the books, how well each of the actors aged and, of course, how vitally important Dame Maggie Smith is, not just to film, but the world at large. When Simon admits his favorite character is Ron, Benji makes a smug sort of sound and Simon is forced to throw a pillow at him.

Maybe he does have a thing for redheads.

Halfway through *The Chamber of Secrets,* Benji slumps over, and his head lands on the arm of the couch. His body is still curled around Walt. Simon watches his eyes grow unfocused and heavy, and he struggles to keep his own open. Walt sleeps on, chest rising and falling gently, ears or legs wriggling slightly in sleep, but nothing out of the ordinary.

The last thing he remembers is pressing play on the third movie, and then he's blinking his eyes against the bright morning sun, jolted awake by someone shouting outside as a car horn blares.

The TV has turned itself off; the cable box is on sleep mode with a blinking blue light. Simon sits up and moves his neck from side to side. He's stiff and achy from falling asleep at an awkward angle. He stretches with a groan, back cracking.

Then he remembers why he was sleeping on the couch. As his head whips over to make sure Walt is okay, the muscles in his neck seize painfully. "Shit. Ow."

Benji makes a sleepy grunt at the outburst, still curled up in the same position but with Walt spooned behind him. Simon's heart squeezes like a clenched fist inside his chest at how Benji looks for all the world as if cuddling Simon's dog on Simon's couch is exactly what he was always meant to do. And this is exactly where Simon was always meant to be. But Simon missed his chance. He screwed up.

"Mmm, hey." Benji stirs, opens his eyes and stretches his arms above his head so his shirt bunches up on his stomach. He looks unfairly beautiful in the morning: eyes heavy and ocean blue, hair sleep-mussed, cheek criss-crossed by lines from the folds of couch fabric. He's relaxed and unguarded and unassuming, as he always is.

"We fell asleep," Simon tells him, just for something to say, because this is perfect. Benji is what he wants, where he belongs.

Benji sits up suddenly, twisting around to see Walt, who lifts his head and yawns. Benji slumps back against the pillows. "Oh, thank God."

Walt drinks a whole bowl of water, eats a little and then happily takes a short walk to a patch of grass and flowers optimistically called a park not too far from Simon's apartment. Simon expects Benji to be gone when they make it back, but he's still there, sitting at Simon's tiny table by the window between the kitchen and living room in his pajamas, still all sexily rumpled. Simon feels a rush of want, but ignores it, feeling hot and itchy under his skin as he asks, "Are you hungry?"

Simon scrambles some eggs, divvies them up onto two plates, grabs two forks and steps over Walt who is doing his very best sad-puppy face. "Sorry. No people food for you right now."

"Just us peoples." Benji grins.

"Very funny. Mock the hysteria of my darkest hour." Simon sits and takes a bite of eggs.

"I'll get tired of it eventually," Benji says and digs in as well. "Seriously though, are you all right?"

Simon tips his head back and forth while he chews and swallows. "Yeah. It was just—kind of everything."

Benji searches his face, then looks down at his plate. "Yeah."

"Thank you for coming to the vet. And staying over. You didn't have to."

"Sure I did." Benji reaches out, grabs Simon's free hand and gives it a pat. "Besides, I'm really looking forward to taking the subway home in my jammies in broad daylight."

Simon laughs. "I've seen much worse than jammies. But you can borrow something if you want."

They finish eating, and Walt gives up on scoring leftovers, trotting off to stretch out in a sunbeam. Simon finds a loose-fitting shirt and some sweatpants that are a little too long on him for Benji and gives him first dibs on the bathroom. While the shower runs, he brews a pot of coffee and checks his phone for messages and emails. Nothing. Benji comes out smelling like Simon's soap and shampoo with Simon's pants snug and short on his body and T-shirt stretched tight across his broader chest. Simon feels weak with how much he wants Benji. How much his body aches for him.

"Looks good," he manages to croak, clearing his throat and handing Benji a travel mug with coffee. "Um. Cream and sugar on the counter, if you want."

"Thanks," Benji smiles sweetly, his fingers brushing Simon's as he hands over the coffee. Simon can only stare at the slow sweeping of his eyelashes; strawberry-hued and almost translucent in the sunlight.

"So, I'll see you soon?"

"Yeah, yep," Simon replies. The urge to kiss him is a tug at his belly, a physical force he pulls back against as Benji leaves.

Simon releases his breath after he's gone, sinking onto the couch with a groan. "Ugh, Walt, I am a mess."

Walt stretches on the floor, sprawling out on his back in the sun. He doesn't disagree.

⬯⬯ Chapter Thirteen

Ask Eros: Listen to Oprah

Q: *I started dating this guy several months ago and, at first, things were great. Then, after a few dates, he started pulling away: canceling plans, ignoring my calls. A couple weeks will pass after I've tried to forget about him, and he'll call saying he misses me and apologizing for being a jerk. He says he has commitment issues, but he likes me so much that he wants to keep trying. I'm so confused. What do I do?*

A: *You listen to him. He told you he has issues and that he's a jerk. Believe him. I understand wanting to give him chances and hoping you can get some of that early magic back, but you're stuck in an ugly cycle that's only going to get uglier. Stop taking his calls. Forget about him. Focus your energy on dating someone who isn't screwing with you just because they can. You have the power to end it.*

Now that his decent computer is fixed, Simon has some writing to catch up on. Not just his column, but the annual *Good Sex* feature for the website, one of many special features that he's a contributor for. He doesn't get to work as early as he'd like because Walt is more enamored with the world than usual and has the added thrill of extra squirrels in the park. Simon fires up the computer, puts his head down and gets to work.

He's just stopped to stretch a bit and adjust his chair higher when his phone buzzes on the desk.

Tia:	Sorry your dog was sick! Everything ok?
Simon:	He's fine thanks. I spent the weekend making it up to him.
Simon:	Extra belly rubs. Went to all his favorite places.
Tia:	Such a good dad.
Simon:	Minus the whole near-fatal poisoning thing.
Tia:	Happens to the best of us.
Simon:	He tried to steal my brownie last night. Starting to think he's just a masochist.
Tia:	Only wants what's bad for him. Sounds familiar.
Simon:	Yes well. I never claimed to be a fast learner.
Tia:	What are you up to?
Simon:	Buying dildos. Want one?
Tia:	I have a new husband. I'm good.
Simon:	Sure, sure. Rub it in.
Tia:	Oh he has.
Simon:	TIA! I am scandalized.
Tia:	Says the man who is buying dildos at this very moment.
Simon:	*Professional* dildo buying
Tia:	Mmhmm. Hey, you get your carrot top back yet?
Simon:	Working on it.
Tia:	Just don't work too slow okay?
Tia:	Have fun with your dildos.
Simon:	I always do.

He's finishing up his online shopping for the vibrators he, and anyone he can get to volunteer, will be trying soon. Just for fun, he's adding one that looks like a cupcake, when Benji stops by, draping himself over the top of Simon's cubicle.

"How do you feel about burritos?"

Simon's stomach gurgles; he hadn't even realized it was lunchtime. He clicks the button for checkout and finishes up. "I am pro burrito."

"Great. Because some food trucks are parked outside."

Simon stands; his chair spins behind him. "I'm in."

Summer seems to have fully settled in; the sun glares, and the air is thick with the sour smells of New York City summertime. Some of the other members of the IT team join them, including nose-whistle goatee guy, who turns out to be named Ari and is actually pretty cool. Everyone is friendly and welcoming, if not chatty.

They find seats in a courtyard between two buildings where people are lounging on the wide edges of planters and the metal and concrete steps that run along the sides of the buildings. Benji snags a picnic bench when a group gets up and sits down at the end. Simon sits across from him; Mark, the IT guy who finally fixed his computer, sits next to Benji.

Simon squints at Benji in the sunlight.

"What? Do I have guacamole on my face or something?"

"No, just—" Simon leans in. "Your freckles are really noticeable now."

Benji touches his nose and cheeks where the light smattering of freckles has grown darker and more numerous, spreading to his forehead and chin. He grimaces. "Ugh. I know."

"No, I like it. I'm into it."

Benji's cheeks flush a pretty pink, and Simon is pleased that he can still make him do that.

"I'm, um, gonna get a drink." He sets his food down and stands, brushing crumbs from his hands. "Simon, you want anything?"

"Just water? My food is kind of spicy." The five-alarm salsa has turned out to not be an exaggeration at all.

"Sure. But eat some chips in the meantime. They'll absorb the capsaicin." Benji heads back over to the closest food truck as Simon snags a handful of his tortilla chips from the little cardboard basket.

"Wait, you're Simon?" Mark says, surprising him.

"Ah, yep. That's me." Simon crunches his chips and wonders if Mark has a relationship or sex question. That happens sometimes when people figure out who he is and what he does for a living. One of his mother's friends from the church soup kitchen where she volunteers every Sunday night once called him for advice about open relationships and avoiding STDs.

"Oh, Benji talks about you all the time." Mark frowns. "I thought you'd be taller."

"Yeah, join the club," Simon sighs. "Wait. Benji talks about me all the time?"

Mark bobbles his head a bit, shrinking to the side.

"As in, *talks* about me present tense or *talked* about me, past tense?" Simon drops the chips, grips the edge of the table and leans across. Mark shrinks back even more. "Mark, this is very important."

Mark has the face of a man with many, many regrets, but he stutters out, "This—this morning he—"

"What did he say? I'm gonna need an exact quote." Simon can see Benji returning with a can of soda and a bottle of water. He's running out of time. He needs to know. "Mark, I will buy you all the burritos you can eat for a week, just please, what did he say?"

"He—" His mouth flaps without sound and he looks left and right, then down at his food and mutters in a rushed monotone, "He told Cassidy that you look really cute when you first wake up."

Simon wiggles happily and claps. "Excellent. Thank you, Mark."

Benji sits, plunking down Simon's water. "What did Mark do?"

"Nothing." Mark stands, and Simon motions to the burrito truck and signals a thumbs up. Mark makes a hasty retreat.

Benji narrows his eyes and tips his head. "What was that about?"

"Oh, you know Mark." Simon laughs, waving a hand in the air.

"Hah, yeah. He is kind of a weird guy." He pops the can open with a snap and a hiss, and drops of Pepsi sprinkle onto his fingers. He lifts them to his mouth and licks off the droplets, and Simon chugs half his water in one go.

"Did you know"—Benji tilts his soda can in Simon's direction—"that capsaicin has numerous health benefits?"

Simon abandons his food, rests his chin on his fist and happily listens to the ramblings of his own pretty weird guy.

Later, the office is quiet and semi-dark with just some desk lights still burning. The cleaning crew runs vacuums and floor polishers somewhere near the fashion department as Simon sends off one last group email asking for help with his sex toy reviews.

He runs his hands through his hair, twists the kinks out of his back and starts to close down. As he's exiting his documents folder, the spending report Andrew gave him catches his eye. He considers it for a moment, then figures he may as well give it a quick look.

Only it's not a spreadsheet or spending documentation, but a scanned series of receipts. Simon squints and glides his chair closer; his eyebrows pull low as he studies the information on the screen. Some of the lunches and dinners they went to together are on there. As well as the hotel room Andrew was staying at when he gave Simon the flash drive. Other hotel stays, drinks and dinners. Even some spa out in the Arizona desert.

But why did he give Simon this info? And what exactly is he supposed to do with it? He stands, deciding to worry about it another day when he isn't totally wiped from working overtime. He needs to get home before Walt uses the rug as a bathroom. Then he sees it. His own name on every receipt. Not just the places they went to together, but all of them. All of the spending on this account charged to Simon Beck. And that's so wrong. He couldn't charge all that, mostly because he'd be living in a cardboard box under a bridge and drowning in debt.

"Oh my God." He shoves away from his desk, shock and anger buzzing through him like a live wire. "Oh my God."

☐☐ Chapter Fourteen

Ask Eros: Slip and Slide

Q: *So you talk about the importance of lube and taking things slow and foreplay, but what lube? How much lube? How slow? How much foreplay? What kind of foreplay? I'm new to sex and it's still really intimidating!*

A: *Oh dear, now you've got me all worried that I talk about foreplay and lube all the time. Am I dropping it into casual conversation without realizing? Someone asks about this crazy weather we've been having and I just shout, "Water-based lube!" and monologue about hand stuff? It's possible we're both overthinking this. Look, sex is this amazing, fun, wonderful thing, but it takes some practice to get it right. So try to focus on enjoying it, and not getting it perfectly right the first time. Or the first few times. It's okay to make mistakes. It's okay to learn. It's okay to mess up and try again. Hopefully you've chosen to be with someone that you trust enough to still be there with you through it all.*

"Walt, come on. You've peed on this tree hundreds of times. It cannot be that interesting." Walt pays him no mind, sniffing and snuffling and winding his way around the tree on the sidewalk close to his building. It's where Simon takes him when he's in a hurry and phoning in a walk. He bounces on his toes, tugs at Walt's leash impatiently. "Come on, come on."

The clouds above start to swirl, bloated and gray and just on the edge of a storm. The wind whips cool, and the air feels charged and ominous. And still Walt sniffs.

"Screw it," Simon mutters, dragging Walt to the edge of the sidewalk and stretching up on his toes to watch for a cab. It's never easy flagging down a taxi with a pit bull at his side, and today is no different. Fat drops of rain start to plunk on rooftops and awnings and car hoods as round, wet splotches dot the sidewalk. Simon hunches over, trying to cover his head with one hand and wave with the other while still holding tight to the leash.

Walt leans close to his side, and Simon moves them under the spindly branches of the tree they'd abandoned. When a cab finally rolls to a stop in front of them, they're damp, but not too wet, so Simon pulls Walt forward, only to stop and wait while he pees on a parking meter.

It's a downpour when they make it to Benji's building. Simon tips generously, hoping that and Walt's mostly good behavior—there was the one brief ear lick—will encourage the cabbie to continue to stop for people with dogs. They run to the call box and Simon mashes the button, pressing up as close to the building as he can, but it doesn't make much difference. By the time they're buzzed in, Simon's clothes are soaked and Walt's coat is drenched.

Benji opens the door to his apartment, only to be bowled over by a very excited Walt freed from his tether and Simon who all but shouts, "That asshole is trying to make me his patsy!"

Benji's face scrunches in confusion, and it's adorable, but Simon really doesn't have time to dwell on that. "All this time," he throws his hands up and marches in without giving Benji a chance to react at all. "I am such an idiot."

Benji puts his hands on Simon's shoulders and starts to reply, but Walt chooses that moment to shake the rain from his fur, spraying drops of water all over Benji's cramped entryway.

"Oh, crap. Sorry."

"It's okay. Just stay there."

He disappears into one of the rooms to the side of the living area and comes back with two towels: one fluffy and royal blue, one threadbare and tattered with a *Teenage Mutant Ninja Turtles* graphic on it. Simon takes one, rubs his hair and arms and face with it as Benji dries Walt with the other.

"Sorry, I only have the one *Ninja Turtles* towel," Benji says, rubbing Walt's ears with it while the dog wriggles happily. "Now. What the hell is going on?" He releases Walt, who runs around the room like a greyhound on amphetamines a few times before settling into an armchair.

Simon blinks, everything is so comfortable and warm, no wonder Walt settled in so quickly. But he's in a crisis here. He needs to focus.

He spins back to Benji with the towel still draped over his head. "Andrew. He's been taking funds from the magazine for personal use and he's trying to set me up to take the fall. No," he whips the towel down. "Trying to get me to voluntarily take the fall. That's why he was suddenly so interested in me. And I was too involved in having some idealized fake relationship that I couldn't see it and completely screwed up something real with a guy I'm totally crazy about!"

He flings his arms out and the end of the towel collides with a coat rack in the corner, knocking down a ball cap and sweatshirt. Benji gently takes the towel as the corners of his mouth twitch with a grin, and says. "Take your clothes off."

"I—Huh?" Simon stutters.

"You're soaked," he points out. "I'll dry them for you."

Simon hesitates, looks down at himself, then strips awkwardly, his shirt plastered to his arms and head as he struggles to get it off. His jeans get caught up at his ankles so he has to kick at them and step on them until he's finally free. When he stands in the living room in just his socks and underwear, Benji looks him up and down, gaze hot. Simon shivers anyway.

Benji gathers up the clothes, and takes them to a closet in a corner of the kitchen. There's the sound of a metal door being slammed closed and the whir of a dryer.

Simon quickly takes in the small room. Next to the armchair Walt is in there's a couch, a red Ikea standard model and a black coffee table with video game controllers and a headset. A tall bookshelf against the far wall is stacked to the brim and then some with books and DVDs and even some tattered VHS tapes of childhood classics; *Ren & Stimpy, ThunderCats, He-man and She-Ra, JEM*. Action figures stand on display in front of those, and a LEGO replica Millennium Falcon is proudly featured at the very top. Some generic black and white nature photos are hung: leaves, waterfalls, clouds. On the edge of the coffee table is a picture of a younger Benji with three dark-haired men, two young and one older and plump, and a tall woman with red hair. All of them have the same sweet smile and aquamarine eyes.

"So are you going to do something about it?" Benji says from the kitchen.

Simon crosses his arms and rubs his biceps for warmth. "I'm thinking I'll write an exposé. Make him pay publicly."

Then Benji is right there, moving close and leaning so his nose bumps Simon's and his chest presses against Simon's arm. "I meant the other thing."

Simon swallows, wets his lips and draws in a shaky breath. He looks at Benji's mouth cross-eyed as he whispers, "You mean the thing about how I'm an idiot? Or about how I'm crazy about you and terrified that I ruined it for good?"

"You're not an idiot." Benji leans in, finally brushing his lips against Simon's. It's gentle, warm, a questioning press.

Simon breathes harshly through his nose, drops his hands from his own chest and wraps them low around Benji's waist. Benji's mouth opens; he catches Simon's bottom lip between his own and sucks. He passes his tongue across it. "Say it again," he breathes, pulling back, eyes still closed.

Simon can count every individual freckle on Benji's face, see the auburn tint of his eyelashes and the darker rust of the stubble on his face. His lips are moist and pink and waiting, open and wanting. "I'm crazy about you," Simon says, then grips his neck and kisses him with the force of every moment of pent up waiting and wishing and hoping on his lips and tongue and fingers.

They stumble and trip down the hall, turn into a room and fall onto a bed, shedding Benji's clothes and Simon's underwear and socks on the way.

"You're kind of intimidating," Benji says, his mouth sucking little wet kisses onto Simon's neck. Simon's leg is hitched over Benji's hip, and one of Benji's legs is slotted between his so Simon can ride it underneath him with tiny, aborted thrusts. It feels amazing, and Simon is pretty sure he's been moaning nonstop for the past ten minutes.

He catches his breath and laughs, but Benji lifts his head, his gaze fixed on Simon's throat , his swollen rosebud lips frowning, serious. "I mean it," he says.

"I am not intimidating." Simon runs his hand up Benji's thigh, over his ass, up along the long muscle on the side of his torso, then sinks his hands deep in Benji's hair and stretches his own neck out long, hoping Benji will take the hint. He doesn't.

"You are," he insists, finally flicking his gaze up. "You're like, this sex and relationship expert and you dated, or whatever, this hotshot upper management guy. You have these glamorous, beautiful friends." He looks Simon over as best he can with their bodies twined together and sighs. "You're gorgeous. And smart. And funny."

Simon's ears and cheeks feel hot. He scratches at Benji's scalp and feels flushed all over with affection for him. He has to close his eyes and take a few deep breaths to gather his thoughts. "First of all, thank you. Second of all, what Andrew and I did could barely be called dating. Third of all, well, actually, Tia is amazing, isn't she? But honestly, if these last few weeks have proven anything, it's that my expertise is theoretical at best. Total bullshit at worst."

Benji drops his head to Simon's shoulder and huffs out a gust of air. "You sound like you know what you're talking about."

Simon hums. "Ah, the secret to successful journalism. Always sound like you know what you're talking about. Actual knowledge unnecessary." Benji starts mouthing hotly at his skin again, and Simon's focus starts to go hazy. But he needs to be clear. "I felt safe going after Andrew, because it was never really anything. Abstract, hypothetical relationships—those I can keep at arm's reach. Those I can deal with. I do it all the time. With you it was real from the very beginning, and I didn't know how to cope with that."

Benji lifts his head again, and he looks so taken aback that Simon has to kiss him, has to hold him close and rock their bodies together.

"I run away when things get difficult. I'm not like Captain America at all," Benji blurts, just as things are starting to get heated. "I could never be a superhero."

Simon shifts them so he can nudge Benji flat on his back and hovers over him. "Is that a life goal of yours?"

Benji rolls his eyes. "I mean it. If Walt hadn't gotten sick, I probably would have just awkwardly avoided you for the rest of my life."

"I wouldn't have let you." Simon says immediately. Because it's true. He's a slow learner, but he does manage to puzzle out his shit eventually.

"Good." Benji's legs open so Simon can settle in, but then he thinks better of it, pushing up onto his elbows until Simon sits back. "Can I—" Benji slides his eyes away again and seems to be working up the courage for something. "I um. I have condoms if you want…"

Simon grins. "I really do."

☌⊃ Chapter Fifteen

Ask Eros: Paging Richard Gere

Q: *What happened to romance? To being swept off your feet? Why can't I find that thrilling grand love affair like the romantic comedies I've been watching since I was a little girl? Is it so wrong to refuse to settle for a guy that can barely be bothered to text me now and again? Or asks me to send him pictures of my boobs? Or thinks microwaved pizza bites is fine dining? Is it all hopeless?*

A: *Wow that's a lot of questions. Where to start... First of all, let's leave pizza bites out of this. They've done nothing wrong. The big question, is it all hopeless? That depends on how good you are at managing your expectations. Is it wrong to want a sweeping, storybook romance? Of course not. As long as you remember that real people are complicated and imperfect and probably not following the script you wrote in your head at age eleven when you saw* Pretty Woman *for the first time. Be open, is what I'm saying. And also, Richard Gere in* Pretty Woman. *Yum. I've gotten off track. So, the part of the movie where they've overcome society's obstacles to find their happily ever after, or the girl realizes that she can have love and a successful football career (that's what Jerry Maguire was about, right?) Then they run through JFK in the pouring rain, and the music swells, and they kiss and it's so beautiful and you cry and the* *credits roll? It stops there because watching the happy couple argue with the ticket agent about getting a refund and trying to dry off with the hand dryers in the airport bathroom doesn't make for great cinema. And that's more what a relationship looks like. So, romance? Yes. Unrealistic ideas of what a relationship actually is? No.*

Benji moves around the room, sliding the curtains closed, shutting the door on Walt who has come to check out the bedroom. The dog whines for a few minutes, then gives up.

"You don't have to do that," Simon tells him, hands tucked behind his head and sheet pulled up to his chest. Benji flicks a match to light a candle on his dresser.

"I'm setting the mood. Just go with it."

Simon smiles, and not just at the way Benji's long, lean body glows in the flickering candlelight. But because it's so sweet. Because Simon has never had anyone go to the trouble of lighting candles for him before.

"Is that a cookie-scented candle?" Simon sniffs the air, and Benji kneels onto the edge of the bed, a clear bottle in one hand and small foil packet in the other.

He tosses them next to the pillow. "Christmas cookie. I got it in the office secret Santa gift exchange." He frowns a little, and he's close enough now that Simon can touch him, so he does. "You don't like it?"

"I like it." He rubs across a hip bone, up to the definition of Benji's abdominals. "It's kind of making me hungry, though." Benji waggles his eyebrows, then gives Simon a saucy sort of grin in the low light. Simon pokes his belly. "If you're about to reply that I can eat something on your body, I'm leaving."

"No, you're not."

"No, I'm not."

Benji leans down, one hand planted on either side of Simon's head on the pillow, and brushes his lips with just a gentle slide, then a tug, before moving down to his jaw. He sucks hard where Simon's pulse is speeding up, hammering against his skin.

Simon hears the snick of a bottle being opened, and Benji licks into the hollow of Simon's throat before settling to his side and lifting the sheet away. His fingers bump slick against Simon's hard cock on the way, making Simon hiss. It's cold, and he wants Benji's hands on him already, wants him inside now. Benji's fingers rub and coax him, gentling him open, so Simon relaxes his body and lets his knees fall to the side. Then two slick fingers press in.

Simon inhales sharply; his knees bend. He tosses his head to the side as he gets used to the stretch. His breath catches with every inhale. It feels so good and yet not enough. He needs more. He grips at Benji's arms and can feel the muscles flexing and working. Simon encourages him to go deeper, stretch wider as he slides in and out, then back in.

"Okay?" Benji pulls out, presses the tips of three fingers, and Simon can only nod and swallow and moan.

As Benji pushes back in, he ducks down to lick broad and flat and rough against Simon's nipples. Simon's cock twitches and lifts from his belly and he stutters out a groan. He twists his fingers in Benji's hair as Benji moves down, down. When he presses deep inside with three fingers, he takes Simon's cock in his mouth.

Simon makes a choked-off strangled noise because he can feel everything drawing up tight and breathless, as if Benji is sweetly and gently coaxing every spark and rush of pleasure from Simon with his tongue and fingers and lips.

Simon tugs at Benji's hair and stutters out, "C—Close. Fuck."

Benji pulls from his cock, removes his fingers and kneels up to lean over the side of the bed. He grabs the condom and tries to rip it with one hand and his teeth, and it's taking way too long. So Simon stretches forward and grabs it, tears it open and fits it over the swollen tip of Benji's cock. He rolls it down the shaft—hard and hot and velvety—then squirts out more lube to slick him.

Benji's hips twitch forward and his eyes close, his face lax with pleasure as Simon strokes him. He'd love to watch him fall apart, just like this, be underneath him when he spills over the edge, but not right now. They'll have plenty of time, more chances. Simon is sure of it.

Instead, he tucks his hands back behind his head, bends his knees back and hooks his feet around the backs of Benji's thighs to tug him forward. Benji shuffles on his knees, hikes Simon's legs up and settles them in the humid crooks of his elbows. He holds his breath, grips his cock at the base and slowly starts to push in.

Simon breathes slow and deep as he gets used to the bigger stretch of Benji's cock. Benji freezes, in just past the tip, eyes so hooded they're barely slits. He shudders and blinks and looks up Simon's body with pupils lust-blown to black.

"God. You're so—" He swallows and pants and visibly struggles to get ahold of himself. "If I come in, like, two seconds please don't write an article about me."

Simon laughs, and the movement makes Benji's cock go deeper. They both moan.

"I won't. I promise."

Then he's in all the way and he's so big, and Simon feels so full, finally. He rakes his fingers down Benji's back and sides to tell him he can move. He holds tight as Benji starts a steady thrust, pulling most of the way out and back in, dropping down to cradle Simon's head and kiss his face and lips and neck.

"You feel so good," Simon breathes against Benji's temple. He crosses his legs over Benji's back, uses his heels to encourage him to go faster.

His thrusts pick up speed and heat sparks up Simon's spine, buzzes low in his groin, in his balls. "I need—" he grunts as Benji's hips snap, making the headboard thump against the wall.

Benji pushes up off Simon's body, sets his knees wider for leverage and pushes Simon's legs back. Simon's knees bump against Benji's side with every thrust. Simon arches his back, reaches to stroke his cock but Benji gets there first, wrapping his fingers around it so the jolting of his hips pushes it through his tight fist.

Simon watches the straining of Benji's torso for as long as he can, watches the flexing of his thighs as he works his hips hard and fast. Watches his own cock slip through the channel of Benji's hand over and over until he can't hold off anymore, has to screw his eyes closed and scrabble to grip the headboard. Every muscle in his body pulls like an archer's bow and he's crying out, gasping and moaning as his cock throbs and gushes and his body buzzes with pleasure.

Benji pumps his hips a few more times then spills into the condom with a gasp and collapses, breathing hard, his skin slick and his body heavy.

"Oof," Simon grunts, rubbing across his shoulders.

"Sorry, all of my limbs stopped working. Gimme a moment." He smiles into Simon's neck, nuzzles his nose against the damp skin and hums happily. "Okay."

He grips the base of his softening cock, pulls out carefully, then stumbles off the bed to remove the condom and throw it into a trash can next to his dresser. Simon shifts and wriggles and scrunches his nose. It's always a little weird, the aftermath.

Then Benji is back, snuggling up close to his side and tugging the covers up over them, lazy and warm and happy. It's probably the endorphins talking, but Simon doesn't care. It doesn't matter, because, in his arms, Benji feels right. He feels good. He feels like... his.

So when Benji rests his lips at the top of Simon's head and asks, "Will you stay?" Simon doesn't need to think about it.

"Of course."

He can feel Benji's answering smile. Benji wraps his arms around Simon tighter, sighing in sleepy contentment.

"One problem though," Simon continues. "Walt won't sleep alone. Someone has to let him in." He gropes on the ground for his underwear and hopes Benji has a toothbrush and washcloth he can use. "Also he's a bed hog. And he drools."

ᴗᴗ Chapter Sixteen

Ask Eros: The Best Laid Planners

Q: *I planned on losing my virginity in college, but it just didn't work out that way. It feels like everyone I know is trying to set me up with someone so I can "just get it over with," and that's not what I want. I'm beginning to think I'll never meet the right person. Should I hook up so we can all forget about it?*

A: *If you feel like you're ready and that's what you want, sure, go for it. That is your call and yours alone. Don't let other people make you feel like you have to do anything you don't want to. I'll be the first to admit that plans don't often unfold the way we wish they would, but that certainly doesn't mean that you have to let go of something that means a lot to you. You are allowed to wait for the right moment and the right person for as long you want.*

Simon had made plans before falling asleep. Sexy plans. Plans that involved waking up before Benji and slipping beneath the sheets to bring Benji to slow, sleepy awareness with his mouth. Plans that did not at all involve fifty-six pounds of gangly overgrown mutt bounding onto the bed and stomping his dew-moist paws all over him.

"No, *why*," Simon groans, drawing out the vowels and covering his head as Walt tries to bathe him with his tongue. He shoves him away, then grabs him around the chest and gives him a thorough belly rub. Walt whips his tail against the comforter with his mouth open and tongue flopping. He smells like grass clippings. "Did you take him out?"

Benji plops down next to him and pats Walt's ribs with a dull thump. "I set an alarm. Otherwise, I probably would have stayed in bed with you forever. I happen to be fond of my carpeting, so, you know."

"You could've woken me up." Simon stretches and yawns.

"It's okay." Benji leans over for a kiss and Simon offers his cheek; it's a little early on in the relationship for morning-breath kisses. Got to save some mystery for later. "We had fun. Peed on sign posts. Chased some pigeons. Barked at a skateboard." He sits back up with a grin. "I guess Walt did some stuff, too."

"So, are you trying to impress me?"

Benji looks down, ears red and adorably bashful. Simon is so onboard with this staying in bed together forever plan.

"Yes," Benji admits.

"Good, because it's working."

Simon pulls him down for a kiss before remembering he has morning breath and that Walt isn't the only one who needs a bathroom trip. So he groans and stretches again, pushing up out of bed, and checks his phone. He missed a call from his mom—that's two—she's probably freaking out. He fires off a quick, *I'll call you later.* There's a text from Tia who was with James at some fancy party. Three calls from a blocked number.

He uses the bathroom, washes his face and comes back to his dry but not actually clean clothes folded on the bed. He has to leave soon so he'll have time to stop at home and drop Walt off, shower, change and make it to work. But, as he heads into the living room, he's struck with how wrong it will feel to go home without Benji. As if he's forgetting something important, leaving part of himself behind.

"I made breakfast," Benji chirps, sitting cross-legged on his couch with two bowls and two spoons, a carton of milk and a bright red box of cereal on the coffee table.

Simon bites down on a grin and sits next to him, so close that their knees bump. "Fruity Pebbles?"

"It's part of a complete breakfast!" Benji defends.

"Sure, as long as your breakfast is also all of the other major food groups." He picks up a bowl and spoon anyway.

Benji pours cereal for both of them, then drowns it in milk. "It gives me a cheerful start to the day."

Simon looks over at Benji crunching his artificial rainbow-colored sugar flakes happily and says warmly and softly, "Yeah, I get that."

Simon starts to eat, and he has to admit they *are* good and he *does* feel awfully cheerful.

Walt sits on the floor between them, eventually resting his head on the couch and flicking sad, round eyes at whomever he thinks will take pity on him.

"Haven't you had enough people food?" Benji snickers at that, and Simon pokes his side. "I'll feed you when we get home."

"I fed him," Benji says. "I stopped at this pet boutique on the way back. I got him some treats because he kept making that face." He nods at Walt's sad-puppy show.

"Oh," Simon blinks, and he's overwhelmed for a moment by a rush of affection.

"Sorry, is it too early in our relationship to be spoiling your dog? I'm not just trying to impress you, I swear."

"No, no. It's—" Simon crunches a mouthful of cereal just to give himself a moment. "It's really sweet of you."

"Okay, whew." Benji sets his bowl aside and rubs Walt's ears. "I always wanted a dog. My brothers are allergic, so the most I got was a goldfish."

"We had a little yappy miniature poodle. She enjoyed biting ankles." Simon finishes his cereal, drinks the sugary milk and stacks his bowl inside of Benji's. Walt inches his head closer to them. "Leave it," Simon commands, and Walt backs off with flattened ears.

"After I moved to the city, I kind of resigned myself to not having one. Just seemed like a lot of hassle."

"It is," Simon confirms. "But in a good way? Like it forces me to get up and out and enjoy the world, when I'd usually be lazing in bed or watching television. I never really planned on having a dog, so I'm grateful I sort of wound up with him by accident."

Benji takes their bowls to the kitchen, Walt trotting at his heels and sitting on the little kitchen mat at Benji's feet as he washes them. "What kind of accident?" he calls over the spray of the faucet.

"Oh. Well, when I was still freelancing and just taking whatever writing jobs I could get: travel websites, how-to articles, stuff like that." He wanders over to the book shelf and moves the little plastic Superman figure to link arms with Luke Skywalker in his orange flight suit. Cute couple. "I got a gig for an online magazine for pet owners who live in big cities. Regular column, decent pay. Only problem was, I didn't have a pet."

Benji and Walt return, Benji sidling up behind Simon and Walt getting comfy in the chair he seems to have claimed.

"I was going to get a cat," Simon continues. "But, first, I walked through the dog area just to see. Most of them were either barking and lunging or else cowering in the back of their cages, all hunched over and defeated. Not that I blame them, mind you."

"Must have been sad." Benji's hand comes to rest on his lower back, thumb stroking and starting an unfurling of heat in Simon's belly. He really, really should get going.

"Yeah. Yeah, but then I saw him. Just sitting behind those metal bars on the cold hard floor. Watching me and wagging his tail with that big dumb happy face. There's this Whitman quote that popped into my head when I crouched down to say hi to him. *I think I could turn and live awhile with the animals... they are so placid and self-contained, I stand and look at them sometimes half the day long.* And I just—" He turns then, to see Benji's eyes bright and clear in the morning sun. "I guess I just knew."

"Yeah," Benji says, before kissing him, and it doesn't take long before Simon is getting lost in it despite the very insistent, very annoying voice of responsibility nagging at him.

He puts his hands on Benji's chest, distracted just feeling the definition of his pecs before he remembers again. "I should get home; I need to shower and change."

"I have a shower," Benji replies, voice gruff, fingers twisting the hem of Simon's shirt. "And clean clothes."

"What about Walt?" Simon protests.

"He can stay. I don't mind." Benji tugs him in; their hips bump and Simon can feel the line of Benji's cock starting to harden. He remembers his sexy morning plans, pleased that he may be able to see them through after all.

Simon breathes out and nods. "Okay, but hide your shoes. He'll eat them. The left ones in particular."

When they finally make it out the door and outside into the sunny morning, Simon isn't sure what was the sweetest: the Fruity Pebbles, Benji's smile, or tasting him for the first time, Simon on his knees behind him in the hot spray of the shower with Benji's moans and gasps and the rush of water echoing like music. Whatever it was, he could get used to starting his mornings like that.

ᴗᴗ Chapter Seventeen

Ask Eros: The Grass Is a Metaphor

Q: *I met this guy on a dating site, and we hit it off online right away. Then we met in person and had great chemistry and liked each other a lot. He's everything I've been looking for, and we're ready to make it official. But, for some reason, every time I go to delete my dating profile, I just can't do it. It's still there, and I got a message from another guy recently. I don't want to end things, and I don't really want to date other people. So what is wrong with me?*

A: *You've got a bad case of "the grass is greener syndrome," and I'm afraid the only cure is to stop looking at the messages other grass sends when you're already grazing on the grass you've been looking for. This is guy is great, and you're happy, but could you be even happier? Who the hell knows? Commitment is always a risk, for both of you. However, if you spend your life gazing over the fence wondering what if and if only, you will miss out on the amazing guy you already have.*

"Okay, I have a confession to make."

Simon gives him a look, but, before Benji can answer, the elevator stops and the doors slide open to let a cluster of people get on. Simon is forced even closer to Benji. He can feel the soft hair on his arms brushing his skin and smell the soap that Simon has now had rubbed all over his body.

They finally reach the *Ravish* floor, walking together past reception and the expansive glass-walled office of the editor-in-chief. Its blinds are closed, as always.

"I figured out it wasn't the motherboard on your computer that first day. I didn't really need all that time to fix it. All I was doing was taking things out and putting them back in while I worked up the nerve to ask you out." His face is twisted with guilt, as if this ruse has been eating him alive. Maybe he has more in common with Captain America than he realizes.

Simon decides to cut him some slack. "I know. It's very endearing. Don't worry about it."

They turn the corner, past Tia's office and toward Simon's desk. Tia looks up as they pass, tips her head and glances at his borrowed outfit, then slides him a sly, knowing smile.

Simon waves her off as Benji asks, "How did you know?"

"Mark told me. He also said that you talk about me all the time and that you think I'm cute first thing in the morning."

"For someone who doesn't talk much, Mark sure is a terrible gossip," Benji says.

"Oh, I bribed him." Simon tells Benji and then greets the other writers and editors in his cubicle cluster.

They reach his desk, and, as he starts his computer up and swivels his chair, Benji admits, still hovering in the doorway, one elbow propped on the low, cloth-covered wall, "I wish I'd just asked you out right away."

"Yes well, I wish I'd pulled my head out of my ass right away, but I think we figured it out okay."

Simon wants nothing more than to drag Benji into his lap, but Andrew's constant reminders of being "discrete and mature" as a convenient excuse for keeping Simon at arm's length bubble up unpleasantly. So he just smiles and starts to turn to his work when Andrew himself comes waltzing up as if Simon summoned him just by sparing him a passing thought.

"You've been ignoring my calls." He pushes past Benji, and stands inside Simon's cubicle with his arms crossed over his Italian-suited chest. The cloud of Armani cologne makes Simon vaguely nauseous.

Simon pretends to be working on something, clicks at random icons on his desktop and glances back to look past Andrew to Benji, who is hunched over and looks uncomfortable and awkward.

"I should go," Benji announces, then skitters away. Great.

Simon faces Andrew. "Please leave."

"Simon, if you'll let me explain. I know how terrible I've been to you. If you'll give me a chance..." He holds his hands up, comes closer, then narrows his eyes. "Are you wearing a shirt with a robot cat on it?"

Simon smooths his hands over the shirt that's just a little baggier than he likes, the pants cinched tight with a belt and folded over twice at the ankle. All of Benji's clothes are so soft and comfortable, though.

"Robocat."

"I—Excuse me?"

Simon huffs in annoyance. "Not *a* robot cat. *Robocat*. And anyway, did you really come in here to criticize my clothes again?"

"No, I'm sorry." Andrew sits at the edge of his desk and Simon finds himself scooting away to give himself space. He actually feels sorry for Andrew. The more contrite he looks, the more Simon does want to help him, despite everything. It's one of the pitfalls of spending so much time caring about other people's problems. "I know it looks like I'm trying to set you up, but it's not like that," Andrew continues. Simon just sets his jaw. "It's only because you're the most compassionate person I've ever met that I came to you in the first place. I need help, Simon."

He does this thing. This soft-eyed, pouted lip thing that should be ridiculous and off-putting, and Simon knows he does it when he's trying to get his way like a spoiled child. It always worked on him. Always.

Simon scrubs at his face, shakes his head a bit then replies, "What do you want from me? What exactly did you hope I would do? Take the fall for you out of the goodness of my heart? "

Andrew's face breaks out into a grin, the one he gets when he knows he's won, and Simon hates it.

"You know they'll go easy on you. Slap on the wrist. Tia's in your corner. Daisy loves you. Your column is hugely popular. " Simon can just picture the headline for his next column. *What To Expect When You're Embezzling: Indictment, Community Service, and Beyond!.* "You're an asset," Andrew continues. "They'll understand that people like you and me, we're free spirits. We need indulgences and decadence to feed our souls."

"And you can't just tell them that yourself? That you had to stay at a luxury hotel for a month to feed your soul?" Simon presses.

Andrew scoots closer, closer, until Simon can feel his body heat in waves. "They don't know me. Not like you. You're the only one who's ever really known me."

He reaches out, tentative, searching, so unlike him. He rests his hand over Simon's, gives a gentle squeeze and then leaves.

Simon blinks after him, bewildered, but not by the pleading touch or doe eyes. But that Simon could be the person who knows him best. Simon, who doesn't really know him at all. That Andrew spends so much time and effort being some false version of what other people expect from him that no one knows him. Not even Andrew himself. And one of the saddest things Simon has ever realized is that he came so close to being exactly the same.

He opens his email and starts a new message.

From: Simon Beck
To: Daisy Martinez, Editor In Chief, *Ravish* Magazine.
Subject: For Your Info
One attachment

* * *

"Hey."

Simon jumps, yelping and banging his knee on the underside of his desk. He had no idea Benji was behind him.

"Benji." Simon presses his hand over his thundering heart. "Didn't notice you there."

"Working hard, huh?" He sits on the desk with one hand tucked behind his back. He smiles and Simon's heart seems to be having some trouble slowing down.

"I could make a few innuendo-laden jokes right now, but instead I'm just going to say 'yes' because I am on fire with this." He reads over what he's written so far. He's rusty at this sort of thing after writing an advice column for so long. It's not bad, though. Not bad at all. "The problem is, I just don't have enough proof," he mutters, mostly to himself.

"I was hoping you would say that," Benji says, whipping out a small stack of papers from where he had them hidden, only to lose his grip and accidentally fling them to the other side of the cubicle. "Crap. That was supposed to be smoother."

Benji hops off the desk to pick them up, bending over to gather the scattered papers into a pile. Simon cocks his head and lets his eyes drift low to the rounded curves of Benji's pert ass, not really minding the lack of suaveness.

He plops the papers down on Simon's keyboard. "While Andrew was in here being a creep, I snuck into his unlocked office, got into his not-password-protected computer and printed out the Internet history he apparently never clears."

"Benji!" Simon widens his eyes at him, then scans the printouts. "You deviant."

"I know, I know. But sometimes for justice to be served, drastic measures must be taken."

Simon looks down the list, and, at first, there's nothing of major interest. Andrew seems to waste a lot time on Damnyouautocorrect. com and Facebook and Reddit. But then he spots the spa that was charged on one of the altered receipts. The booking site for the hotel.

Searches for some of the restaurants and bars whose names look familiar.

"God, you're are a superhero. For justice to be served... Did you just make that up?"

"I did! Well, I tried out a few different things first." Benji crouches down. "Can you bring up the receipts he gave you?" Simon clicks to his documents to open the images. "That's what I thought. This an obvious photoshop. You can see how the name was altered. God, he didn't even bother to switch out of the default font! Like an actual receipt would use Calibre. Please."

This is it, everything he needs to bring Andrew down. He just has to finish his article and submit it to Daisy. He's flushed and buzzing with the rush. It's been so long since he's attempted any sort of investigative reporting, not since his college newspaper.

"I feel like Batman and Robin right now. Like we're a crime-fighting duo. We should grapple up a building and do some roundhouse kicks or something." He turns to Benji, feeling a little manic.

Benji's eyes darken and he licks across his bottom lip. "I want to make out with you so hard right now."

Heat gathers low in his belly, but Simon ignores it. "First the article, then the burrito truck, then making out."

Benji whines a little, nuzzles into his neck and kisses his shoulder as he stands. "Burritos again?"

"Oh, yeah. I bribed Mark with burritos. Did I not mention that?"

"Uh, fine." Benji heads back out to leave Simon to his article. "But if Mark sees things he can never unsee, it's his own fault."

⬯⬯ Chapter Eighteen

Ask Eros: Stuff a Sock in It.

Q: *During some totally hot sex I blurted out "I love you" to this guy I've been seeing. Not once, but twice. I mean, I like him. I'm just not in love with him, or at least my rational mind doesn't think so. So why am I shouting it at the top of my lungs? And how do I take it back?*

A: *I suggest a ball gag. Quiet fun for everyone. Okay, so. It's out there now. You may as well own it. What's probably happening is you're expressing how you feel in that moment, and there's nothing wrong with that. Telling a guy that he's so amazing in bed you can't think straight is likely to go over fairly well. You were caught up. You said some stuff. It happens. Something to ponder in the meantime though: Is it possible you do love him and it takes really letting your guard down to realize it?*

Everything in Daisy's office is crisp, clear, organized and intimidating. In the center is her glass desk with razor-sharp corners. The chair Simon waits in is made of scrap metal twisted and bent and reclaimed into furniture. The book shelves are stacked with massive reference materials, the floors are gleaming tile and in front of him is the blinding brightness of a view of Columbus Circle and Central Park. Even the white flowers on the desk seem to be reaching out toward him, bending and stretching their stems like grasping fingers—

"They call that the Zen bouquet." The door opens and closes, and Daisy's heels clack across the floor. She sits at the desk, wrists set on the clear surface, one knee snug over the other. "Is it working?"

"No, not really." Simon uncrosses his own legs so his feet are securely on the ground; his arms are set on the hard armrests.

She tips her head to the side, her black glossy hair shimmering and her dark eyes wry and calculating as always. "It's good to see you, Simon. Feels like we're always just missing each other lately."

Simon releases a breath he hadn't realized he's been holding. "Good to see you too, Daisy."

She smiles briefly, and then says, "Let's get right to it, shall we? First, I appreciate you bringing this matter with Andrew to my attention. The article was very concise and convincing."

"Thank you."

She nods. "But you know we can't run it."

"So he's just getting away with it?" Simon pushes forward to the edge of his chair, ribs pressing against the laser-cut edge of the desk.

Daisy holds up a hand. "He will be dealt with, I promise. Internally. This is not that kind of publication, Simon. We run articles about celebrity gossip and make-up tips and whether or not skorts should make a comeback this summer."

"They shouldn't," Simon cuts in.

She smiles again, but this time it lingers. "You probably already know that your column is one of our most well-read and popular features. So, I'd like to offer you a chance to write more of whatever you're interested in. Within the parameters of the publication."

Simon sits back, arms over his chest. "Are you bribing me?"

"I am offering you an opportunity. And asking you to let me deal with Andrew. I promise you, he will be dealt with. I am giving you a chance..." She drums her fingers on the desktop. "To be done with him once and for all. Isn't that something that interests you?"

His decision tugs at the back of his mind the rest of the day. He wants to talk to Benji about it, but he's on calls all day away from his desk, and it's as if Simon can't settle it in his mind until they talk it through.

He's at home after a long, confusing day, and it's well after dark before he gets a chance to call. When the ringing stops and Benji picks up, there's some sort of shoot-out going on in the background. Someone yells. A bomb goes off.

"Is this a bad time?" Simon collapses on his couch, kicks his shoes off over the edge and whistles for Walt.

"Nah, just playing *Call of Duty* with my brother. Hold on, I'll get rid of him." There's a muffled, muted protest and Simon guesses Benji must have him on speaker over the game's intercom system.

"Is that Simon? Lemme talk to Simon."

Benji sighs. "Brandon says hello."

"Hi, Brandon."

"Simon says hi," Benji repeats. Then the tinny voice on the intercom responds, "Does he know if the orange carpets match the orange drapes yet? Ask him Ben—" And then the game and the voice both go silent.

"Brandon says goodbye."

"Aww, I was gonna tell him that you wax everywhere. Just as smooth as a baby seal." Walt finally trots over for a head scratch, satisfied that the toy he was chewing has been sufficiently decimated.

"That's not even true."

"Yeah, but think of how impossible it would be for Brandon to get that image out of his head."

Benji laughs. "I think my family might end up liking you more than me."

"So... Can I meet them soon?" Simon flops one of Walt's ears up and down and grins to himself.

"Definitely. Speaking of, how did the meeting with Daisy go? Are they running the article?"

Simon stretches his arms out; he's so tired all of a sudden. Benji's low voice in his ear is like a lullaby.

"No. I mean, I knew it was a long shot going in so I guess I can't be too disappointed. However, she did offer to give me more opportunities to take the lead on other projects." Benji *hmms*, skeptical. "Honestly? It's kind of a relief. I'm just done with him and all of that fake bullshit, you know? Now I can get back to helping people get semen stains out, navigate dating sites or even find the male g-spot."

He can hear rustling, as if Benji moved suddenly. "Wait, that's a real thing?"

"Oh, Benji. Sweet, sweet Benji." He drops his voice and purrs. "Want me to show you?"

"Um." Benji audibly swallows. "Maybe after, uh, our date on Friday."

"What and skip frozen yogurt?" Simon tuts.

"After yogurt too, of course. I still can't believe you're dragging me to a musical based on *50 Shades of Grey*."

"It's my new favorite musical, and I haven't even seen it yet," Simon gushes. "Can't wait to see it. And you."

"Mmm, me too." Benji yawns, which makes Simon yawn and stretch again, which makes Walt jump up onto the couch and settle heavily across Simon's legs. "Okay, sleep, then work, then date."

"Kay," Simon replies, muzzy and distracted, wishing he didn't have to take Walt out again and could just pass out on the couch, cricks in his neck be damned. "Love you," he says, and hangs up the phone. He rests his eyes for a moment, then bolts up so fast he launches Walt right off of his lap.

Simon quickly spirals into a panic while Walt looks on, mildly affronted. Maybe he didn't hear. Maybe he did, but he'll let it slide. Maybe he heard and he's trying to figure out how to break up with him gently. Or not gently. Or maybe—

His phone buzzes, and Simon reaches out with his pulse pounding and terror still clutching at his chest. He does love him. He meant it. He just hadn't meant to say it quite yet.

Benji: Love you too

When he takes Walt out, Simon feels as if he's walking on air, as though sunbeams will follow his footsteps and bluebirds will perch on his shoulder and sing. They don't. But an alarm wails somewhere in the distance, and the streetlamp Walt relieves himself on flickers and zaps. It'll have to do. Because he's in love.

He changes into pajamas, brushes his teeth, washes his face and settles into bed with his dog.

Simon: I'm in love
Tia: I know. Glad you figured it out
Mom: CALL ME
Benji: :) Good night
Benji: Sleep tight
Benji: I love you

◡◡ Chapter Nineteen

Ask Eros: Say Goodbye to My Little Friend.

Q: *I recently moved in with my boyfriend, and, during the unpacking, he found my vibrator. He was upset, saying he didn't understand why I still need it. He feels betrayed, because it means I'm saying he doesn't satisfy me. He wants me to get rid of it. Should I?*

A: *Moving in together is a big deal and a huge adjustment for everyone. It means compromise. It means working together. It means accepting that black-light posters and a completely out of hand Star Wars action figure collection is going to find a home in your new office, and you'll have to make your peace with it. Ahem. But it does not mean you give up everything. You are allowed privacy. You are allowed orgasms that are just between you and your battery-powered buddy. But here's the thing. It doesn't have to be that way. Show your live-in lover how you can both benefit from ol' BOB. He can use it on you, you can use it on him. You can hang it on the wall and pretend it's the latest trend in modern art. The point is, you guys are a team now. Work it out together.*

"How do I look?" Simon stands in the hallway, with his arms outstretched, in his new rust-orange corduroys and plaid button-up.

Benji is busy luring Walt into his oversized crate in the corner of the dining area. "I don't think they care what you look like."

Simon frowns. He even tried something new with his hair: a little coiffed swoop up front. He happens to think he looks pretty great. "I want to make a good first impression."

"A good fi— Ha!" Benji successfully secures Walt in the crate and slides the lock across. Walt looks confused, then dismayed, then settles with a sigh on the plush microfiber pillow. It was Benji's idea to get the crate. Not only does Simon now have several pair of shoes still intact, right *and* left, but it's cut down on Walt's anxiety when they're out for longer than usual.

Simon touches the top of his hair, watches Benji grab his keys from the new key hook by the door and wonders if he should just wear a beanie and be done with it.

"Hey. Wait. Lemme see." Benji tugs him by the elbow as Simon turns away to open the door. "I like it. You look comfortable, yet trustworthy. And, not that it matters to them, but—" He brushes a kiss to Simon's cheek. "So hot."

"Maybe they do care," Simon replies, tugging on a sweater and waiting outside the front door. "Maybe hotness is their number one requirement for applicants."

Benji closes the door behind them, locks it and quickly smacks Simon on the ass. "Well, we're all set then aren't we?"

They spent months considering all their options, taking longer to decide this than they did on their apartment, though they did luck out with a great place close to work. That was a big deal, moving in together, but this feels bigger. This is choosing a future, ten to fifteen years or so down the line.

They had talked about breeders, about rescues. About the nicer no-kill shelters. But as they take the subway to the rundown barebones animal control center where he'd found Walt, Simon knows it was the right choice. The train slows to a stop at their station, and Simon presses their legs together before standing and offering Benji his hand to hold. This is it.

Simon fills out the forms and talks with the volunteer at the front. Benji looks around with his hands in his pockets and his nose wrinkled.

"The smell takes some getting used to," Simon tells him, handing over the clipboard so Benji can sign his name next to Simon's.

Nina, the front desk volunteer, leads them back to the cat room with row after row of cages stacked in a concrete-walled room. Some of the cages have several cats. One has a mother with kittens still nursing and not quite ready to be homed.

They split to opposite sides of the room, automatically skipping any cat that has *NO DOGS* written on the cards clipped to the cage doors. Simon passes several found strays, then an owner surrender and two huge white male cats who were found in an abandoned home.

He finally makes it around to where Benji has stopped at a cage with one cat standing stoic in the dark corner; yellow moon eyes watching them, all black save for a tuft of white on her chest. Her card says she's approximately four years old, spayed, a stray. Okay with kids. Okay with dogs.

"Black cats are statistically the least likely to be adopted," Benji says, crooking his finger inside one of the square openings between the bars.

She blinks slowly at it, considering, before reaching out and tapping his finger with one paw. Benji smiles and makes sweet little tutting noises with his tongue to entice her closer. Simon glances wistfully at the fuzzy, round-bellied gray kittens.

"We could call her Emily. Or... Maya?" Simon suggests, threading his fingers into the cage. She's close enough now that he's able to stroke some of the silky fur on her side.

"How about Peggy?"

Simon tips his head. He likes it. "That's some sort of nerd reference I'm not getting, right?"

Benji sighs. "Peggy Carter?" Simon narrows his eyes, purses his lips, shrugs. "Badass military intelligence officer? Steve Rogers' love interest? Honestly Simon, it was a major blockbuster film."

"Right, yes. Of course. Peggy." Finally, she seems to trust them enough to come right up to the wire door of the cage, rubbing her body along the metal, then nuzzling her face into Benji's knuckle. He baby talks her a bit and Simon's stomach does that warm swooping thing. "Not after Black Widow or Catwoman, though?"

Benji tsks, "That's way too obvious."

"Yes, how silly of me." Simon replies, sarcastic, but Benji either doesn't notice or doesn't care. He's too busy cooing at and petting the cat, telling her that she's coming home with them, that she's gonna love their apartment and Walt too.

Simon leaves to fetch Nina the front desk volunteer so they can post bail and spring Peggy.

Walt loves Peggy from the moment they open the door to his crate; shoving his sturdy, strong body past their legs, sniffing at the cat carrier so hard that Simon worries he might snort up half her fur. Simon sets the carrier down and peers in. She's crammed in the corner again, hunched over and wide-eyed with her fur standing on end.

Benji pulls Walt back by the collar. "Walt, buddy, you gotta give her some space. Don't come on too strong. Play it cool okay?"

Simon laughs, opening the door of the carrier just enough so Peggy can push it open when she's ready to venture out. "That's some smooth advice."

"I can be smooth."

"Uh-huh." Simon gives the cat some space and gives Walt a warning look. He's settled down on the floor, tail still wagging but waiting patiently. Simon goes to the shelf in the closet where they stashed all the cat supplies.

Benji comes up behind him, kisses the nape of his neck and says, "I got you, didn't I?"

Simon tucks the canvas bag against his chest, turns and presses up against him. Crowded in the tiny hallway of their new apartment, he really wants to continue their mission to christen every square inch of it. But first, "Can you get her some food and water, maybe put it by the carrier, and see if she'll come out?"

Benji takes the bag with a grin, settles down cross-legged and pours some food. "It took some coaxing to get me to come out, too."

Simon takes the water bowl with a shake of his head. "How long have you been sitting on that one?"

"I just came up with it! See? Smooth."

Simon sets down the full water bowl and sits next to Walt to keep him calm. After several minutes Peggy slinks out, looking around the room with her ears flat and body low. Walt's tail picks up speed, and he whines. Simon touches just at his ribs. "Wait."

Eventually, she's comfortable enough to sniff around the apartment: the walls, behind the couch, the food. She struts past Benji and lets him rub her head briefly before jumping up on the windowsill to stare outside.

Walt watches her the whole time, and Benji talks soothingly and moves slowly. Simon doesn't know her past, but she's here now. Earlier this morning, Simon wouldn't have thought that anything was missing from his life. He felt satisfied. Happy. As she silently tracks something moving on the street below, Simon realizes how easily she fits. Just another piece of the puzzle he spent so long trying to cram together with mismatched parts.

"Okay, Walt." Walt lifts his head, scrabbles to his feet and trots off to the window. Peggy's tail swishes as she regards him warily before turning back to the sunlit window. Walt rests his head next to her and, together, they watch the world go by.

"Hey," Simon stands up and offers Benji a hand to pull him up and into his body. "Wanna play *Mario Kart*?"

"I was really hoping you were about to offer something else." He leans down for a kiss, and Simon obliges him with a quick peck.

"Later. After the kids go to bed."

Benji turns on the game console and tosses Simon a controller. "Okay, but we are not calling them our kids. We will not be those people."

The tinkly opening music for the game starts. They sit on the couch, shoulders and hips and knees snug together. "I don't know what you're talking about." Simon picks a course, a character, a vehicle. "Oh, we do have to dress them in their matching sweaters and send my mom a picture."

Benji groans and drops his head to Simon's shoulder.

"I love you." Simon tells him.

Benji presses his lips to Simon's shoulder and Simon takes the opportunity to run him off the track.

"I love you too, you jerk."

ᴏᴏ Chapter Twenty

Ask Eros: Glad You Came.

Q: *Dear Eros, I've been sexually active for ten years and have never had an orgasm. I enjoy sex, but I just can't seem to let go and relax to get there. Is something wrong with me?*

A: *First, I think it would be wise to go see a doctor and get anything physical ruled out first. But aside from that, sex is inherently about making yourself vulnerable to another person. You will never be more bared—mentally and physically—as you are during intimate moments. I would encourage you to spend some time focusing on what makes you feel good, putting any expectations or shame aside. Try a vibrator, fantasize, show your partner what makes you tick. And the value of a good lubricant cannot be overstated.*

Simon:	I was organizing the movie shelf after you left.
Simon:	You have a lot of movies.
Simon:	And "The Broken Hearts Club" really?
Benji:	That is a heartwarming classic.
Benji:	Also Dean Cain.
Simon:	Fair enough. Anyway, combined we now have the original VHS *and* DVD releases of "The Labyrinth,"

the two-disc special edition DVD with bonus features and the fully restored Blu-Ray edition.

Simon: Which one do you want to keep?

Benji: Sorry I don't understand the question.

"Look out, Daisy's on the warpath." Tia steps into his cubicle and
hands him a to-go coffee while craning her neck to look down the hall.

"What? Why?" Simon takes a sip. It scalds his tongue, so he takes
the lid off to let it cool a bit; tendrils of steam curl out of the top.

"Well…" Tia leans close as she always does when there's juicy gossip. "She fired Andrew. After haggling with HR for months, she
finally got the chance to toss him out on his ass. Apparently, she
had this whole backlog of people that needed to go. Trimming the
fat, she's calling it. And now she's got the green light to fire anyone
she pleases."

Simon frowns and sips. "Shit, that's hot."

"How's cohabitation going?"

"Good," Simon chokes out. "Great. He keeps his toothbrush in
the refrigerator."

Tia arches an eyebrow over her coffee cup. "Okay."

"He's paranoid about roaches. I think it's cute." He finds most
of Benji's little habits cute, as a matter of fact, but he'll spare Tia the
details. He knows it's all still new, and they're settling in to not just
living together, but being in a committed relationship. For the first
time, Simon is with someone he genuinely likes. And the stuff he
doesn't like just seems to not really matter.

"Oh, here she comes. Just pretend to be working, and she'll leave
you alone."

"Or I could actually work. Which is a thing I do."

Tia waves him off, scurrying out of his cubicle on her killer stilettos,
leaving behind the faint trace of cocoa butter moisturizer and a cold
rising panic in his chest. Simon puts his phone on silent and gets back
to writing his response to this week's question.

"Simon, just the man I wanted to see."

His stomach drops and he freezes. Would she really fire him? He's the one who told her about Andrew in the first place. Or is that why? She's firing him for being a snitch, and now he'll have to go back to writing copy for travel agents. Crap.

He turns slowly in his chair. "Hi, Daisy. Are those new shoes?"

She snaps at him, "Don't."

"All right." Simon sits up straight and folds his hands over his stomach. "What can I help you with?"

She grins, and the twist of it gives Simon little zap of ice down his spine. It's not as if she's ever been anything but kind to him. Or that he has any reason to be afraid of her. It's just that she has the air of someone who should always be feared. He's pretty sure that's exactly what she's going for.

She slinks over to his desk, sits and crosses one leg over the other so the fabric of her skin-tight skirt stretches over her toned thighs, and places her red-taloned hands over her knee. She peers down at him like a bird of prey, her sharp, dark eyes calculating and intense.

"Have you decided on the article I proposed? The series about spicing up your sex life?"

"Uh. Oh." Simon replies, caught off guard. Honestly, with the "Good Sex" edition of the magazine and the column as well as moving in with Benji occupying his personal hours, he'd almost forgotten about it.

Before he can tell her that, Daisy cuts in. "I'm prepared to make you an even better offer. I think this could be a huge hit for us."

Simon has learned a thing or two about playing hard to get from Peggy. If he had a tail he'd flick it back and forth noncommittally. But he, sadly, is not a cat, so, instead, he leans back in his chair and crosses his arms snugly over his chest.

"I'm listening."

He skips lunch with Benji to mull over the offer on his own. He also gets started on next week's *Ask Eros* question for the magazine's website.

He's intrigued by Daisy's offer, and if it were just him, he'd probably be all over it. But he and Benji are partners now, and he needs Benji onboard with sharing some of their most intimate moments.

He's on the couch playing video games when Simon gets home that evening. He feels like the sappiest person on earth because, every time he comes home to Benji, every time he wakes up next to Benji, Simon feels like bursting into song. Which is *not* a thing he does.

Benji tips his head backwards for a peck. Walt is curled up with him on the couch with Peggy perched on the arm.

"Good day?" Simon asks after grabbing cold fettuccine Alfredo from the fridge. Walt wags his tail against Simon's leg and shifts so Simon can scratch at his belly.

"Mmhmm." Benji presses a series of buttons on the controller and something blows up on the screen. "My parents want to do brunch."

Simon makes a face and swallows. "Your dad doesn't like me."

"He doesn't like anybody." Benji stares at the screen, the tip of his tongue pressed to the corner of his mouth.

"That doesn't make me feel better."

Benji's mom loves him. Benji's brothers like him. Benji's cousins and various loud and often drunk aunts and uncles love him. Benji's dad has said maybe five words to him in all the family dinners he's attended, and three of those words were a variation of *bye*.

Benji sets the controller down. "When I came out, he didn't say a word. Nothing. I had no idea how he felt about it, and I was terrified. Then I started getting some shit at school from a teacher, nothing major. Honestly, it probably had more do with this thing where I answered questions in class like Yoda. First and only time I got detention. Anyway." Benji smiles, that soft, sweet smile that makes warmth settle in Simon's chest. "He went to the school, never told me when or why. To this day, I have no idea what he did, but someone made sure that I was never bothered again."

"That's nice." Simon sets down the plastic container and drops his head to Benji's shoulder.

"Yeah. He's a softie, deep down. Deep, deep, deep down."

Simon laughs. "I think my father was a blackjack dealer. That's all I know about him."

Benji's arm circles around his back, he tugs Simon in closer. "Sorry."

"I don't miss him." He presses his nose into Benji's neck, breathes him in and runs his bottom lip against the hinge of his jaw. He really was planning on asking Benji about doing the series of articles together, but he's so warm and he smells so good.

Benji's thumb strokes the exposed skin low on Simon's back and Simon is, once again, reaching the point where words have lost all meaning.

They hold hands and walk to the bedroom, past the office/guest bedroom and the bathroom with an almost garden tub and the extra hall closet. This apartment feels like home, finally, and Simon is pretty sure his life is perfect.

He knows the honeymoon phase can't last and that relationships are not all sex, video games, getting a cat together and commingling media. But when Benji pushes him up against the closed door and fucks him right there, Simon finds he doesn't care about any of that.

▬▬ Chapter Twenty One

Ask Eros Special Feature: Spicing Up Your Sex Life, Field Tested for Your Pleasure.

There is no shortage of articles with tips on how to bring some excitement to the bedroom. From the vague—"Spend time together!"—to the woefully misguided—"Nibble on his scrotum!" (Please don't ever do that.) But how many offer guidance beyond a handful of tips and an alarming level of enthusiasm while bandying about words like "scrotum"? Well, dear readers, I am here to offer you my experience, expertise and the weekly sacrifice of my dignity for your benefit. Up first: a little food, a lot fun and one willing partner.

They're in SoHo for brunch: Mr. and Mrs. McHugh fresh from Mass in their Sunday best. Simon dressed up for the occasion in a new tie that was pressing too tight against his throat; Benji in his usual T-shirt and jeans with the addition of a hooded sweatshirt. He had given a one-shouldered shrug when Simon asked him if he was overdressed.

"It's just brunch," he'd said, and Simon wishes he'd listened to him.

He isn't so much overdressed as he is suffocating.

The place is beautiful; small and intimate with dark mahogany tables and bouquets of imported out-of-season flowers centered brightly on top. Soft classical music plays over low chatter, and the waiter leads them to a four-top by a window. Benji's mother Bethany and his father Bruno are seated across from each other, as are Benji and Simon.

"Nice place," Simon ventures. Mr. McHugh scowls down at the menu.

"Too fancy," Bruno says. Across from him, Bethany sighs and rolls her eyes. Bruno ignores her. "Creme brûlée brioche French toast? Clove and cinnamon spice crepes? What the hell?"

"Clove and cinnamon have been used to enhance the male libido for centuries," Simon blurts without thinking. Benji grins at him. Benji's dad narrows his eyes. Benji's mother searches her purse for her hot-pink-framed bifocals. Simon orders a mimosa.

After they order, Bethany catches Benji up on church gossip. Simon has no idea who any of the people are, so he fiddles with his silverware, then orders a second mimosa.

"Amy Fitzgerald is getting married! Long after her mother had given up hope," Benji's mother says. Benji nods vaguely and eats his chocolate chip pancakes. Simon feels something rub against his calf and jumps, nearly knocking over his water.

Benji's father raises his eyebrows.

"Thirsty," Simon tries, voice too high. He chugs it down.

"Anyway. It made me think, maybe I shouldn't either. I mean, Brian and Brandon. Well, you know your brothers. I'd given up hope on all of you, then I remembered: The gays can marry here now!"

Simon freezes with his glass against his lips. Bruno stares at him. Simon swears this place has moving walls. Are the walls moving?

"Mom, we talked about that. Don't say *the gays*."

"Well, what should I say? Everything is offensive these days!" Bethany jabs her fork in Benji's direction.

"Something that doesn't make us sound like a zoo exhibit, maybe."

"Fine. You and Simon can get married, that's all I'm saying! My optometrist has a gay son, and they rented out Carnegie Hall. Can you imagine how beautiful that would be?" She looks at Simon, her pink-lipsticked grin hopeful and sweet. She looks a lot like Benji. Or, he looks like her: tall, thin, fair, freckled and pretty.

Benji could protest that it's way too soon for them to be talking marriage, but he takes a sip of orange juice and says, "Actually, did you know that you can elope in a helicopter as it flies over Niagara Falls? Or even under the falls themselves. Just get completely soaked while you say your vows." He smiles over his juice glass.

She turns to Simon. "Is he teasing me?"

"I don't know," Simon tells her. It's not really like Benji, trying to get a rise out of someone for fun. Now he's back to happily eating pancakes and both of his parents are staring at Simon. Simon's tie is so tight against his throat, *he can't breathe*. He sets down his glass, takes a deep breath and announces, "I have to pee."

In the bathroom, he considers finding a window and making a quick escape, but he does really have to pee first.

The bathroom is empty and quiet save for the dining room music being pumped in through speakers in the ceiling. Maybe he'll just stay in the bathroom until brunch is over.

Then the door opens, and Bruno enters and takes the urinal next to his. Simon's entire life flashes before his eyes. He finishes, zips up and washes his hands in record time. He nearly crashes into Bruno as he heads to the door.

"Sorry," Simon says, backing away with his hands up.

Bruno orders, "Wait a second," and starts washing up. "Moving kind of fast aren't you?"

"Um, I don't want my crepes to get cold."

"Not that. You and Benjamin. Moving in together? A cat? Marriage?" He shuts off the water, pulls down a paper towel and waits.

"Uh. Well, we weren't the ones—" Simon stutters out.

Benji's father is right around Simon's height, round faced and round bellied with thinning gray hair and bright blue eyes. He's shrewd and set in his ways and impossible to read. "Look. Benjamin is a smart boy. A good man. But he's always been so softhearted. I just want to know what your real intentions are here."

That was not what Simon had expected. A rant about young people these days. Maybe an awkward discussion of what sort of relationship his son wants with another man. Or possibly some fun and fascinating Bible quotes. It turns out Benji was right, his dad is a softy deep down.

Simon looks at him right in the eyes. He needs him to know how very serious he is about this even as his voice shakes a little. "I know it's fast, but what I feel for Benji? It's the real thing. I'm serious about him. Getting a cat serious. And I know it's real, because I used to spend a lot of time faking it. Loving Benji is the most honest thing I've ever done."

Suddenly, the claustrophobia lifts, and Simon isn't worried about what kind of impression he's making. What matters is what he and Benji have and nothing else. The helicopter wedding sounds kind of awesome, as a matter of fact.

Mr. McHugh throws away his paper towel with a *humph* and a slam of the lid. He stares at Simon long enough for prickling heat to gather around the stiff collar of his shirt.

Then he nods. "Okay then," and leaves the bathroom.

"So, cloves increase libido, huh? Do we have any of that? Or did you get enough with your crepes?" Benji asks with a smirk after they make it back home and release Walt from his crate.

"I panicked when the waitress came okay? And like you need any help with libido, groping me while I'm sitting next to your father." Simon strokes Peggy as she walks back and forth on the counter, purring and bumping her cheek against his hand.

"I touched your leg with my foot, Simon!" Benji protests.

"Next to your father, Benji!"

"Oh, he doesn't care."

Peggy hops down from the counter and walks over to where Walt is chewing a bone. "I know. I think he likes me," Simon says.

Benji comes closer, craning over the counter to give Simon a gentle peck. "How could he not?"

Simon grabs his shirt before he can move away, kisses him harder. "I do have something in mind, if you're interested in learning more about food and sex."

"Cloves?" Benji says, nose scrunching in confusion.

"No. Chocolate."

Simon opens the fridge, pushes aside milk, juice, takeout containers and a jar of pickles to find the handmade ganache he bought from a cute local bakery. He kicks the door closed.

Benji peers into the jar skeptically, eyebrows high and mouth thin. Walt clamors up from his spot on the living room rug and plants himself at their feet to beg.

"Do you ever learn?" Simon asks him. He wags his tail. "Not for you," he tells Walt, and to Benji he says, "Bedroom."

"So romantic," Benji mumbles, but heads down the short hallway off the kitchen anyway.

"Sorry," Simon follows and closes and locks the door behind them even though Walt can't work a lock. Peggy, maybe. "May I please slather your naked body with chocolate?"

"Yes. So much better," Benji laughs, undressing mechanically then sitting down on the bed with his arms and legs pressed tightly to his body and his jaw set.

"So," Simon starts, taking in Benji's anxiety. "We can just try this for fun. I'd like to write an article about it. An ongoing series. But I don't have to write anything if you don't want me to."

Benji nods with his face tilted down at his naked lap, worries his bottom lip with his teeth and says, "All right. We can try."

Simon undresses, stops briefly at Benji's back to rub his shoulders. Then he swings one leg over Benji's hips and leans down to press a soft kiss to Benji's waiting lips. Benji lifts one hand to tangle in the back of Simon's hair and brings him down again.

"Mmm. Thank you for doing this." Simon smiles against his mouth and flutters his eyes closed. He's a little emotional because Benji trusts him enough to go outside of his comfort zone. He needs

Benji to feel how much that means to him, how much Benji means to him.

Benji finally relaxes, flashes his open, easy grin and leans back, offering himself to Simon with his head tipping up and arms flinging wide. "My body is your canvas."

Simon's belly twists with heat as he reaches to the little side table that's stacked with their laptops, some tissues and piles of magazines and comic books

The ganache is thick and sticky, and Simon hadn't really come up with a plan of action after *get Benji to agree*. So he swirls a finger through it, tilts his head and allows his eyes to roam over Benji's skin: the pull of it over his neck and how it's stretched taut on the sharp edge of his jaw; down to the curve of clavicles and the hollow scoop at the base of his throat; broad, flat planes on his chest and his peaked nipples; pale skin flushed pink at his neck and chest; muscles of his abdomen pulled tight; all of him long and angled and hard.

He looks up to meet Benji's eyes, which are patient and waiting. Simon's cock throbs where it's resting on Benji's belly. Beneath him, Simon can feel Benji's cock stirring and swelling.

"Okay," Simon says, mostly to himself. He pulls his finger out and drips of dark chocolate land on Benji's ribs. He jolts.

"Cold."

"I know, sorry." Simon smears it across one nipple, crosses Benji's chest with a dark trail of sticky sweetness and covers the other. He considers the remnants still on his hand, shrugs and licks it, the sauce dark and rich and decadent. He sucks his finger into his mouth, then pulls it out with a pop. Benji swallows and licks at his bottom lip, his cock now pressing more insistently along Simon's ass. Emboldened, Simon tips forward, ducks his head and presses his tongue flat onto Benji's chest, licking up the chocolate with long strokes.

He sits back again to swallow the thick sweet-bitter mouthful. Benji's chest hair is matted with chocolate and saliva in swirls and streaks. It's messy and sticky and too sweet. Simon considers dashing off to the kitchen for a glass of milk to wash it down, but swallows again and scoots down Benji's body to soldier on.

Simon dips two fingers in the bowl. The chocolate oozes down his wrist and arm and onto the old afghan covering the bed. He coats the underside of Benji's cock from the base to just under the head, then across the tip and down the other side. Then he grips Benji's thighs without thinking, and a smear of chocolate covers the tender skin there. Benji starts to breathe heavily as Simon pushes his leg wide and sucks a path from thigh to hip to groin.

He starts with tiny licks up the veiny shaft of Benji's cock; sweet and hot and jutting up. It's thick on his tongue and down his throat when he stretches his mouth around. He pulls off to swallow the chocolate down, then dips back to lick at the salty pre-come beading in the slit, trying to chase away the choking sweetness.

It's too much.

"You okay?" Benji is flushed and straining, lifting up onto his elbows in concern.

Simon swallows and swallows, nods and chokes out, "Water?"

Benji hurries away, then Simon can hear the fridge door rattle open, a glass set on the counter, and Benji exclaiming, "Walt, what is wrong with you, cut it out!"

Simon sits back, laughs and then coughs. He tries to not be too disappointed in himself that this did not go as well as he'd hoped. Maybe he should have gone for the whipped cream. Benji returns with a glass of water in hand. Simon grins after taking a long drink.

"You are a mess." Chocolate sauce is spread across his chest and groin and stomach and still hard cock, his thigh and the underside of one arm. He's obscenely delectable. Simon touches his fingertips to Benji's abdomen, paints some of the chocolate across his hip, and runs one finger up the curve of his straining cock.

Benji lifts a shoulder sheepishly; his hips twitch into Simon's touch. "I guess I was into it."

It takes some effort to get Benji out of it; he's so lost to desire that he slumps against the shower wall with heavy-lidded eyes while

Simon scrubs him with soap. "Enjoying yourself?" Simon lathers the coarse hair at his chest, the smattering on his stomach, the thatch of it around his cock. He's been hard the whole time and Simon has barely touched him there, but when he does Benji groans so loudly it echoes off the walls.

He drops the soap and curls his hand around Benji's cock, suds running off his body and down the drain in a river of bubbles and chocolate. "You like when I take care of you?"

He drops down, pins Benji's hips against the cool tile and takes him into his mouth again, tasting only skin and salt and Benji.

Benji yelps, hands scrabbling against the slippery tile, as he's held captive by Simon's hands and Simon's mouth while he licks and sucks and bobs. He breathes deeply through his nose and takes Benji down as deep as he can go.

"Ah, Simon. Shit." He hears Benji's head thunk against the tile, and the first taste of him coming is a strange contrast to the overwhelming sweetness of the chocolate. Simon wraps his lips tight and swallows until Benji is spent and lands in a heap on the shower floor.

Simon braces himself on the tile, draped over Benji, draped to watch the quick movement of his hand on Simon's cock. He works Simon over expertly. He's tipping over the edge in no time, hips thrusting forward as he moans, stripes of come painting Benji's chest where the chocolate had been before.

They catch their breath and come down, folded together side by side. Simon drops his wet head to Benji's shoulder. Over the sound of the spraying shower nozzle, he asks, "So, can I share that or?"

Benji waves a hand feebly in Simon's direction, all goofy grin and loose limbs. "Do whatever you want."

Spicing Up Your Sex Life Tip: *Try food play for extra yummy fun!*

Good idea or bad idea: This one is a toss-up. One of us enjoyed it, one of us found it sticky and messy and not terribly appetizing. It's worth experimenting with different foods to see what works. Whipped cream seemed to go over better than chocolate (yet still too sweet and messy), strawberries were best overall (sticky, but less so). In the end, I declare it a good idea, but proceed with caution, and mind the sheets. I will say though that I personally preferred the clean up afterwards. But maybe my partner is just particularly delicious.

Chapter Twenty-Two

To: Simon Beck
From: Andrew Klaff
Subject: Please do not delete!

    Simon, I know you don't owe me anything or want to hear from me, but I needed to reach out to you and apologize. What I did and how I treated you was inexcusable, and I'm sorry. I'm figuring some stuff out, working on myself. I'd love to have lunch and clear the air.

    -Andrew

Simon dumps Peggy from his lap and brushes stray black hairs from his shirt. Benji is stretched out on the couch, reading something on his iPad. His phone is chirping with text after text that he's completely ignoring save for a tick in his jaw every time it vibrates with a new message.

"You'll never guess who e-mailed me, I can't—" Benji's phone buzzes and buzzes and chimes. Simon nods at it. "Are you gonna get those?"

"It's just Brandon being a jackass." Benji swipes at the screen, concentrates instead on whatever he's reading.

"I take it he read the article, then?" Simon props himself on the edge of the couch by Benji's feet. He knows it's less that Benji worries about being judged and more that he's just a private person. And, of course, Brandon knows exactly what buttons to push.

"Yeah." Benji says, without any further explanation.

"Well, you could ask him why he's reading a women's magazine in the first place," Simon offers.

Benji swipes again, swipe, swipe. "He claims he's learning to *decode the mysteries of females.*"

"Ah," Simon says. "Has he tried maybe treating them like actual people?"

Benji huffs and finally looks up, his forehead still crinkled in irritation. The phone finally stops buzzing and he offers Simon a wry half-smile. "He is kind of an idiot, isn't he?"

"Mmm. A lovable one, but yes." Simon squeezes at his ankle. "Ignoring him is smart."

"Yeah." Benji sighs, looks back at the screen in his lap, then quickly back up again. "Oh, hey. You said someone e-mailed you?"

"Oh! Yes. Oh my God. Andrew. Can you believe it?" Simon whacks at his leg and laughs, but something dark flickers across Benji's expression. His jaw knots, mouth pulling flat.

"And you deleted it after you told him to leave you alone right?"

"I didn't reply yet. But get this, he apologized." Simon lifts his hands, palms up. "He seemed genuine, which is quite a feat for Andrew."

Benji flinches a little. "The guy's full of it."

Simon doesn't deny it. "He wants to have lunch."

Benji jabs angrily at his screen and doesn't answer until his phone chirps again. He flips the iPad off his lap, stands and snatches up his phone. It buzzes in his hand.

"I don't want to do the articles anymore."

"What?" Simon stands, too. "Because of Brandon? Who cares what he says. Come on."

"No." Benji looks away, breathes sharp through his nose. "Because I just don't want to, okay?"

Last week, Benji was fine with it, if a little wary, but Simon thought they were in a good place. They trust each other. Or at least he thought so.

"Because of Andrew," Simon says flatly, arms crossed over his chest.

Benji's cheeks flush red, jaw set. His phone chirps again in his hand, and he tosses it down on the couch. "You know what? Have lunch with whomever you want and do whatever weird sex stuff you want, okay. Just leave me out of it."

He starts to walk away, but Simon can't seem to stop the words rising like an angry swell. "Right, because God forbid you try something different."

Benji turns, eyes flashing with anger and hurt. "What the hell is that supposed to mean?"

"I don't know, Benji. You eat the same breakfast you've been eating since you were six years old. You're on issue eight hundred something of Captain America Saves America from the Bad Guys. You've watched *The Phantom Menace* like five million times and you don't even like it!" Simon paces, throws his hands up. He's revved up and can't seem to stop; Benji's rejection hurts more than he wants to admit. He shouts, sarcastic and biting, "Whatever could I possibly mean?"

Benji's nostrils flare, eyes narrowed. He opens his mouth, closes it, then strides to the front door and leaves without a word.

Simon sinks down on the couch with his head dropped in his hands. "Shit."

Walt's nails clatter on the hardwood floor, no doubt excited by the door opening. Then his cold nose is on Simon's arm.

Simon brings his hands away from his face to pet Walt's ears. Simon is shaky and nauseated and disappointed in himself. He doesn't have much time to stew in his guilt because the door opens again.

The couch dips next to him, Walt wags his tail and wiggles around happily, and Simon stares down at his own lap. "You came back."

"Yeah, well. I ran outside and bumped into an old lady and almost kicked a pigeon and I felt terrible. Then I realized I was doing it again. Running away. So I... I came back."

Simon twists the hem of his pants and tries not to smile. "You should never feel terrible about kicking pigeons."

Benji lets out a surprised burst of a laugh, then goes quiet again. Walt settles at their feet and Benji's hand drifts over to Simon's knee. "I'm sorry."

"God, no. I'm sorry." Simon picks his hand up and tangles their fingers together. "I love all of that stuff about you. And I'll tell Andrew to fuck off."

"No. No, have lunch with whomever you want. I trust you," Benji says, ducking his head to catch Simon's gaze. Simon believes him. He knows Benji, trusts him. He's still relieved to hear Benji say it. "I just—I felt insecure," Benji continues, looking down at their joined hands and rubbing his thumb against the tender skin of Simon's wrist. "Sometimes I wonder why someone like you, so out there and adventurous and bold... Why you would even—I want to be that guy for you."

"Benji, I want you to be you. That's one of the things that I fell in love with right away. You're just yourself. No trying too hard. No faking. Please don't think you have to change for me." Benji looks at him and nods with eyes wide and solemn. Simon aches with how much he loves this man. He kisses him, soft and gentle, because he has to.

"We can stop the articles. I'll just ask for volunteers instead, like the sex toy reviews. Okay? I never want you to feel pressured or uncomfortable."

Benji leans in again and kisses Simon harder, lips parted and tongue nudging in, urgent and seeking. He cups Simon's face and Simon sighs and wraps his arms low around Benji's slim waist. "I love you so much."

"I love you, too," Benji says, pulls away with a wry little grin. "I think that was our first fight."

Simon considers this, bites his lip and raises his eyebrows. "Time for first make-up sex then, huh?"

Benji presses his parted lips to Simon's, moves over to his cheek, his ear, down the column of his neck. "Let's do it."

"Yeah, that's kind of what I was getting at..." Simon says, gasps and groans as Benji sucks the skin over his collarbone.

"No. I meant the stuff for the article. Let's do it."

Simon pushes him back with a palm flat on his chest. "Are you sure?" Benji nods, the tips of his ears and neck red, eyes blown dark; turned on and eager for it. "Okay. But you pick this time. Whatever you're comfortable with."

Simon waits at the edge of the bed as Benji rustles around in the shadows of the closet.

"I saw these after we moved in here, before all the boxes got put away and I've never... I never tried it, but I couldn't stop thinking about it."

Benji comes out with two black leather cuffs with crushed purple velvet around the inside, silver rings embedded in the outside and long black straps dangling down.

They were a gift, not something he'd used often. Simon personally finds anything with a BDSM bent to be a little too much. Unless he's with someone that he really, really trusts.

So Simon reaches out, loops a tether around Benji's wrist then uses it to pull Benji down, craning up to kiss him, hard and close mouthed. "Yes."

He gives a squeak of surprise as Benji clamors onto his lap, grabbing his face in both hands and capturing Simon's mouth in a long deep kiss, tongue dipping in and sucking hard at Simon's bottom lip. He braces his hands on Benji's hips to steady himself, then is surprised again to feel Benji already half hard and pushing against his stomach.

"Okay, clothes off." Simon taps at his side, pushing up his shirt and avoiding the chase of Benji's mouth, huffing a laugh at his enthusiasm.

Benji ducks his head, licks at his lips. "You first."

Simon undresses quickly. He wonders if he will ever get used to that stark hunger in Benji's eyes, to being with someone who wants him that much and makes no effort to hide it. He sits back on the bed, fidgeting as he waits for Benji. His own want pulses like a heartbeat through his body.

But Benji stays clothed and, instead, picks up the restraints, unhooking the tethers and slipping one cuff then the other gently over Simon's wrists.

"Do they go with my outfit?" Simon tries to joke, rubbing his hands down his naked thighs a little self-consciously.

"You look amazing," Benji replies, without a hint of teasing or lightness. "Can you sit against the headboard?"

Simon rises to his knees, shuffles forward and leans with his back against the cool wooden slats. Benji's gaze is on him the entire time. Simon can feel it trailing whisper-soft all over his skin.

"Tell me if you get uncomfortable," Benji says, looping the tether around a slat, then bringing Simon's hand up and securing it crossed over his head. "Or if you want to stop." He fixes the other in place, pauses to kiss the center of Simon's captive palm. He's so sure, so authoritative now, so unlike how he usually is, that it makes goosebumps rise all over Simon's skin.

Simon tugs at the restraints, testing their strength. He doesn't care for the loose feeling of his hands dangling in the air, so he wraps the straps around them and pulls tight.

Benji's eyes widen when Simon's biceps flex and bulge, and he presses his fingers to the swell of his own groin.

Simon swallows. "Good?"

"Simon, oh my God."

Benji kneels at the end of the bed, shoves his sweatpants and under-wear down just enough that his cock emerges, hard and thick and rosy tipped, curving up to his belly. He grips it, flicks his wrist once and grunts. Heat pools low in Simon's groin at the sight.

"Benji, come here." Simon yanks hard on the restraints, straining forward as far he can, then falls back with a gust of air. Benji shakes his head and strokes his cock, eyes traveling up and down over Simon's body. Simon whimpers in frustration. "Baby, please."

"So hot." Benji's hips jolt forward, cock pushing through his fist.

Simon tries to nudge him forward with his feet, digs his toes into Benji's calf. He just needs to touch him, needs to be touched, needs. Benji growls, low and rough, standing up and off the bed, continuing the increasingly rapid jerking of his hand.

Simon thumps his head back, pulls on the restraints again, then decides to try a different tactic. "You should ride me." He spreads his legs a bit; his hard cock bobs in the air, and a drip of moisture stretches from the tip down to his abdomen. Benji watches with hooded eyes. He kicks his pants off and away and returns to the bed, and Simon purrs, "Yeah, come on."

Benji moves between Simon's legs, bumping one knee out farther with his free hand, stroking quick and steady with the other, but he makes no movement to get lube or straddle Simon's hips, or touch him anywhere else. "Amazing," he mutters, as his hand speeds up.

Simon's back presses hard into the headboard as he thrusts into the air. He wants to clamp Benji between his legs but doesn't want to risk him leaving again. He can feel the heat from Benji's body so close, can hear every whine that spills from his throat. Finally Benji touches him, gripping Simon's knee as he groans and comes on Simon's thigh and hip, a line splashing hot across Simon's aching cock. Simon's hips thrash and he whimpers, desperate, then Benji looks up, breathing hard and with an impish grin.

"I like you like this."

"Clearly," Simon bites out, pressing his knees to Benji's sides to tug him forward. Benji pushes Simon's legs open again, tuts and brings his hand up to his mouth, laps up the come still sticking to his fingers. Simon moans and squeezes his eyes closed.

He feels Benji finally move over him. He kisses Simon and slips the taste of him onto Simon's tongue, says against his lips, "What do you want?"

"Anything. I'm close. Please."

Benji pulls away with a smack of their lips, lays his palms flat against the spread of Simon's thighs. He drops down to take Simon into his mouth and down his throat.

After a litany of swearing and praise, Simon turns his head and bites into the leather strap. When Benji slips a hand down to rub against Simon's hole, he's gone; pulling so hard on the restraints as he comes that his wrists burn and the headboard groans.

His whole body is tingling and spent. He hazily registers Benji taking off the cuffs and dotting kisses along his wrists, up his arm and shoulder. Then he nuzzles his cheek against Simon's as they slump down into the pillows.

"Love you," Simon says, pleased that he remembers how to form words.

"Oh good. I thought I broke you." Benji pulls him into his arms.

"So I won't be writing the article on how to tease your lover to the point of sexual combustion?" Simon drops his head to Benji's chest and presses his nose to the soft fabric of his T-shirt.

"You did not combust."

"Didn't I?"

Spicing Up Your Sex Life Tip: *Try handcuffs or other restraints so you can take charge or tease him into a frenzy!*

*Good idea or bad idea: With so many articles focusing heavily on "how to please your man," I want to take a moment to emphasize how important your own pleasure is. Because the truth is your partner will be turned on by what turns **you** on. (And if they aren't, may I suggest throwing them out of your bed and quickly.) There is a give and take in sex, a duality that is all too often forgotten. Trust. Honesty. Care. And now that we've gotten my deep thoughts out of the way: good idea. Buy good quality restraints, or even a silk tie or scarf or leash if that's your jam. Go over some ground rules, be aware of each other's limits, then take turns being restrained. You may be surprised by who gets turned on the most.*

ᴖᴖ Chapter Twenty-Three

Simon had long had fantasies about the domestic bliss of sleeping and waking up next to someone, the same someone, every night and every morning. Way back when, his dreams of partnership were amorphous and vague. They turned decidedly male, and, after that, blond and hard bodied and broad shouldered and with a jaw that could fracture diamonds.

Okay, they were about Brad Pitt.

The reality is different, of course, not just because Benji is less chiseled and more—Simon purses his lips and watches Benji sleep—beautiful, exquisite, ethereal.

Apparently Simon is a poet in the mornings, even a slightly creepy one, now watching Benji fast asleep for a solid fifteen minutes. On weekend mornings, Benji tends to be, well, dead to the world. Weekdays, he's up with his alarm, in the shower and out the door while Simon is still blinking dreams away and avoiding Walt's morning tongue baths.

Benji more than makes up for early weekdays by sleeping well into the afternoon on Saturday and Sunday before finally emerging like a beautiful, sweetly-rumpled zombie. Benji sleeps so deeply this Saturday that the dog barking doesn't rouse him and the cat sleeping on his face doesn't bother him in the slightest. Sirens outside make him smack his lips and turn to his stomach. Simon shoving at his leg to make him stop snoring gets only a grunt.

But Simon endures snoring and the zombie act, the early morning weekday wake ups and cold toes on his calves because he gets to fall asleep with the trace of Benji's kiss still on his lips, a laugh from their last conversation in his heart. He gets to wake up and roll over to Walt licking his face and armpits and wagging his tail and Peggy begging for food morosely. All with the most beautiful man he's ever seen next to him, in his bed, making dying bullfrog noises as he sleeps.

It's the sort of contented peace that Simon never imagined possible. Even better than Brad Pitt.

Simon watches him a little longer until his stomach rumbles and he can no longer stand Peggy's constant meowing. He pushes the covers off and steps onto the cold floor.

Letting Benji take the lead with which "spicy" item to try out next had worked so well last time that Simon had left it up to him again. He'd picked morning sex, and seemed very enthusiastic about it. So was Simon. And Simon wants to wait, not push. But he's quickly coming up against a deadline and isn't sure if he can convince Daisy that an article about masturbating in the morning while your partner sleeps in would be interesting to anyone.

He can't even convince himself, really.

So he feeds the cat, takes the dog out and eats an orange, coming up with a plan while he watches the coffee drip slowly into the carafe.

When he returns with two steaming mugs in his hands, he intends to wake Benji up and tell him to get to the seducing already, the clock is ticking. So he sets the mugs down and whisks the blankets and flat sheet off the lump that is Benji's sleeping form. But Benji had planned to surprise him, and, at some point in the night, had stripped down and slept in the nude.

He takes a moment to admire the view: the bright morning sun glowing radiant on Benji's skin from his lovely profile to his weirdly long toes. He's on his stomach so Simon trails his gaze along the muscles and tendons of his back, the narrow curve of his waist and the pale rise of his ass. He has one arm tucked under his pillow, one flung out wide. One leg is stretched long and the other is bent up at the knee. Simon climbs on the bed behind him and settles in the empty space there. He rests his palms softly on the pert round globes of Benji's ass and lets one thumb slip in, just a bit. Benji sniffs and his face scrunches up, but he doesn't wake.

Simon presses in more, down to where Benji is hot and clenching at the pad of his thumb, and he circles around it, tests the give, wonders how far he can take this before Benji wakes up. He slides his hand back to palm and knead the swell, squeezing and pushing and pulling. Simon hunches over, ducks down low to place a kiss on one indented dimple at his sacrum, then the other, tongue darting out to lick long down the seam. Benji's hips twitch back and he lets out a breathy whine.

"So you *are* awake."

Benji mumbles into his pillow, "Nuh-uh."

"Oh well, in that case, I'll just go try out that spring vegetable omelet I've been meaning to make."

Benji whines again, petulant and low this time, and hooks his bent leg under Simon's knees, making him fall forward with his hands splayed on Benji's shoulders, pressing him down into the bed. Benji groans and writhes under him.

"Yeah?" Simon asks and leans down to kiss the curve of shifting muscles between the sharper edges of his shoulder blades. "Want me to take care of you again?"

Benji says something that may have been *please*, it's hard to tell, but Simon knows anyway. Knows by the catch in his breathing, the tremble of his eyelashes, the quiver of his parted lips. Benji wants him.

Simon discards his pajamas, locates the lube, then tucks one leg under himself and sits on the edge of the bed. He strokes Benji's hair. "Just relax, okay? I've got you."

He waits until Benji's muscles give and release, until he sighs and breathes deeply once more. Simon threads his fingers into the mess of copper hair and admires Benji's features. He never can decide if Benji is more beautiful sleep-softened and peaceful, or awake, smiling and enthusiastic about life in general.

Simon stands slowly and moves back to kneel between the spread of Benji's legs, slicks his fingers and grits his teeth at the jarring squelch of the container of lube in the otherwise quiet room. Benji's eyes stay closed; his mouth is softly parted and his body loose.

He sucks in a long breath at the first finger in, but Simon presses and stretches slow, slow. Much slower than the usual rush to open him up so Simon can sink inside already, impatient and aching for him. Today he takes his time and ignores the throb of his cock, gentles Benji's restless hips. He waits.

Benji's body sinks back to relaxed; his twisted grip on the sheet unclenches. Inside, he's yielding and ready and open around Simon's fingers. Simon gets a solid grip on Benji's hips with one hand and tilts them up, coats his own cock. He lines up with Benji's hole and pushes in.

He spreads his body wide over Benji's; chest to back, thigh to thigh, fingers intertwined, face buried in Benji's neck. He bottoms out, breathes Benji in, waits.

The slightest thrust of his hips and Benji's fingers grip tighter around his, ass shoving back harder onto Simon's cock. Simon groans and nips at the nape of his neck, then he commands, "Relax."

Benji sinks, boneless, to the bed.

Simon closes his eyes and focuses on Benji: hard bone, taut muscle and slick skin, the tight grip on his cock as Simon thrusts into him in long slow strokes, pulling out to the tip and then inching back in. He feels decadent and wicked, wants to be inside Benji forever, wants to do nothing but fuck him for the rest of the morning, glut himself on sex and Benji's body the entirety of this lazy Sunday.

But his hips pick up speed when the pleasure becomes too much, and he tumbles helplessly over the edge in free-fall floating bliss. When he sighs out his release, Benji's eyes finally snap open, begging. "*Simon.*"

"Okay," Simon says, gives Benji room to work himself over Simon's gradually softening cock, tipping them to the side just enough for

Simon to circle his fingers tight around Benji's cock. It passes slick through his fingers with the snap of Benji's hips until he finally goes rigid, coming with a soft cry and a bowed back.

"Surprise," Benji says weakly, rolls over onto his belly as Simon flops onto his back and smiles up at him.

"I feel like you planned on making me do all the work."

"What? No way. I was totally gonna rock your world." He reaches over and clumsily bats at Simon's face. Simon hums, unamused, and Benji grins. "Now make me an omelet."

Simon scoffs and smacks Benji's ass. "Lazy."

"Ooh." Benji wriggles happily against the bed. "Or more of that."

"Go pick up some fresh berries for smoothies and we'll see."

Benji groans, hauls himself out of bed dramatically, stops to gulp a mouthful of lukewarm coffee and pulls a face. He grabs a towel out of the closet and heads to the shower.

"By the way, you are on the hook for next time so you better make it good!" Simon calls. The only reply is the squeak of the faucets turning on.

Simon curls on his side, pulls the blankets back up and closes his eyes. Maybe he'll just sleep a bit until Benji gets back. He's had an exhausting morning, and Benji shouldn't be the only one who gets to sleep the day away.

Spicing Up Your Sex Life Tip: *Jump start your day with surprise morning sex!*

Good idea or bad idea? Well to start, I feel that this would probably work best with a partner who doesn't most closely resemble a reanimated corpse in the mornings, but wakes up spry and ready to go. (See what I did there?) Morning quickies are fun and not a bad way to start the day, so long as you can deal with the morning breath. But if you can make the time, there is fun to be had with long, lazy mornings and long, lazy sex. Go ahead, give yourself permission to indulge and luxuriate in each other. Get some rest and sustenance and go for round two if you dare. We sure did. Good idea.

⌐⌐ *Chapter Twenty-Four*

To: Andrew Klaff
From: Simon Beck
Re: Please don't delete this
    Andrew, I can't do lunch—sort of have plans for lunch indefinitely—but I'd be willing to meet you after work. How about Bloody Mary's? I can text you the address if you need it.
    ~Simon

Tia offers to go and bring James along; the combined narrow-eyed judgmental stares from the two of them would be more than enough to send Andrew scampering away with his tail between his legs. Simon talks her out of it.

He does bring Benji, even though Benji trusts him, and Benji is okay with it. They're a team now, and he wants his partner at his side for this.

They walk into the bar holding hands. Benji's is just a little damp and gripping too tight. Andrew is at a table, and he looks—

Good. A burgundy cowl-neck sweater and tailored slacks, hair a little freer than he used to keep it. He looks rested and healthy, and he's always been handsome, easy and sure in his looks and charm. But now he's relaxed and happy with a glass of wine in his hand in the low red light of the bar. It suits him.

Andrew spots Simon and lights up with a smile. His gaze slides to Benji at Simon's side, his smile falters just for a moment before he plasters it back on. Nothing has changed. Not really.

Simon had wondered after he'd sent the email, after he'd told Benji. Intrusive moments of worry, of *what if.* What if being around Andrew again turned him around and mixed him up? He loves Benji, wants to be with Benji. He's never been more sure of anything. But being with Andrew made Simon forget what he wanted in the first place and why he ever wanted it.

But he sees Andrew, and feels nothing, and realizes that had been the issue between them all along. Trying to fill nothing with something, with anything. Believing that if he just tried hard enough, Andrew could be what he wanted him to be. That Simon could be what Andrew needed. He never was. He never would be.

Benji had always been like a sunrise, just as brilliant. Just as inevitable.

They sit, and Andrew orders three more glasses of the wine he's drinking without stopping to ask if that's what they want.

"Thanks for coming. I'm so grateful," he says, smooth and charismatic.

"Sure," Simon replies, leaning back and crossing his legs.

Benji is stiff and awkward next to him, directly across from Andrew. "The ancient Romans used to put lead in wine as a preservative," he says, tearing little pieces off the cardboard coaster. "Some historians theorize that lead poisoning was a key factor in the fall of the Roman Empire."

Andrew tips his chin, narrows his eyes and says, "That's... nice." Then sips his wine and looks over the top of Benji's head with disinterest.

Simon lifts his own glass and puts his other hand over Benji's to stop the cruel destruction of the drink coaster. "They used lead pipes for their water system too, right?"

Benji's fingers flex beneath Simon's hand and he looks up, bright eyed and beaming. "Yeah, that's right. We watched that together."

"So you guys are..." Andrew dips his head in a nod.

"Together," Benji says again. "We live together. In the same apartment. Together."

Simon twists his lips and tries not to grin too hard.

They chat about nothing much, conversation that's so irrelevant that it's instantly forgotten. Andrew leans too close to touch Simon's wrist and elbow. He smiles too wide and too hard. Simon feels nothing, not even annoyance that Andrew seems to think he would—What? Run away with him? Ditch Benji and meet him in the bathroom for a tryst?

"Again. I am so sorry. I am making amends for my mistakes, so I'd like to make it up to you." Andrew brushes Simon's wrist, and Benji excuses himself to the restroom. Simon's eyes are drawn with a physical pull to the lanky shift of his body as he walks away. Andrew continues on about righting his wrongs and repaying his debts but Simon's too busy looking after Benji to register what Andrew is saying.

"Excuse me for a moment," Simon interrupts, then follows Benji into a dark narrow hallway past the cramped kitchen, past the emergency exit and a closet door ajar with mop and yellow bucket propped next to it.

There are two bathrooms, side by side, the kind with one toilet and one sink and a lock on the door. Simon looks around, sees no one, and knocks.

"Just a sec!" Benji calls. After a moment the toilet flushes and the sink rushes on. The hand dryer roars and stops. Then the door opens and Simon pushes his way inside.

"Oh. Are we at the phase of our relationship where we can pee in front of each other?" Benji asks, after Simon pushes the door closed and presses the lock with his thumb. "Because sometimes when you take really long showers—"

Simon shuts him up with a dirty kiss.

Benji gasps and blinks his eyes open. "What was that for?"

"I just really like you."

"Oh." A pleased smile stretches across Benji's face. "Okay, then."

Benji draws him back in and kisses him again. Simon backs them up until Benji's shoulders and ass are shoved against the door.

"How gross do you think this bathroom floor is?"

Benji licks his lips, looks down and grimaces. "Really gross probably."

Simon considers his jeans; they aren't his favorite but he will be sad to see them go. He decides it's worth it; he just needs to get his mouth on Benji's cock like several minutes ago.

So he drops to his knees and tries very hard to not think about what sort of grime is now being embedded in the fabric of his pants. He pulls open the button on Benji's jeans, the zipper with metal teeth warmed from Benji's body heat, goes down, down. He spreads open the flaps and pulls out Benji's dick.

"Oh wow, okay," Benji spits out, head cracking back against the door.

Simon suckles the spongy head into his mouth as he holds the shaft between his thumb and forefinger. Benji hardens and fills against his tongue.

Simon feels devious and daring, widens his jaw and takes him deep. Benji's moan echoes off the tiled bathroom walls, and thrills heat up Simon's spine.

He bobs his head, breathes in through his nose and gets his fill of Benji's scent. Earthy, musky, sticky-bitter gushes fill his mouth as he sucks and slides. He sucks up to the crown, swipes his tongue around the ridge, swallows him back down with his tongue flat against the fat vein that runs down the underside.

Again and again until Benji is panting and whining and twitching his hips. Simon's jaw aches, his knees are numb and his cock strains against the stiff fabric of his pants.

"Ah—I'm—" Benji stutters out, just as a knock rattles the door.

"Just a minute!" Simon calls, trying to be casual but his voice comes out graveled and rough. He closes his eyes, pumps with his hand and sucks. Benji moans, clamps his hand over his mouth to muffle his own cries as he comes down Simon's throat.

He catches his breath, mutters, "Jesus, Simon," before hauling Simon up to his feet and drops down to quickly return the favor.

They try to look normal, but Simon's hair refuses to go back into place. Both of them are swollen-lipped, giggling and sort of falling all over each other. But it doesn't matter because Andrew is gone.

"Oh, now I feel bad." Benji frowns, picking up the paid bill and his half-empty wine glass.

"Don't," Simon tells him, knocking back the rest of his wine and rolling his eyes at Benji's pout. "Fine. I'll send him apology chocolates."

Benji rushes over and kisses him hard.

"What was that for?" Simon teases.

"I just. I really like you a lot."

Spicing Up Your Sex Life Tip: *Try a public rendezvous to really get the blood pumping!*

Good idea or bad idea? This week I learned two things: One, bleach needs to be added to water first to avoid ruining a pair of jeans that, apparently, did great things for my ass. Second, sex in potentially public places is very exciting, but must be approached with caution. The thrill of almost being caught is incredible. Being caught, not so much. And don't think it must be in the wide open public or necessarily devious. Start with taking the fun out of the bedroom to the kitchen table, a private beach, or even a filthy bar bathroom. All sorts of new experiences await. Good idea.

ᴖᴖ *Chapter Twenty-Five*

Mom:	What should I get Benji for Christmas???
Mom:	I got Walt a stuffed turtle.
Mom:	And Peggy a seashell collar.
Simon:	I think Benji would also like a seashell collar and stuffed turtle.
Mom:	>:(
Mom:	Simon.
Simon:	(:
Simon:	I don't even know what *I'm* getting him! You don't have to get him a gift.
Mom:	Yes I do you love him so I love him that's how it works.
Mom:	He's such a nice boy.
Mom:	He makes you so happy.
Mom:	I'll knit him a sweater!
Simon:	You don't knit?
Mom:	I WILL LEARN

Their first Thanksgiving together had been chaotic: going to another office party, feasting at Tia's swanky gourmet affair with a menu that would make Martha Stewart fume with envy, then dragging themselves bloated and sleepy to Benji's parents to stuff their bellies even more. They barely had time to put in a phone call to Simon's mom.

They'd brought turkey home for the animals, passed out on the couch with football on TV and considered the milestone a rousing, if exhausting, success.

Simon's column was doing well, very well. Benji shrugged off Brandon and Brian's teasing with a quip about them being jealous that he was the only one of them getting laid regularly. Brian high-fived him. Brandon sputtered and choked on his mashed potatoes, then looked at Simon, who gave him a saucy wink. And that was the end of that.

They've settled into their life now, walking home from work huddled together arm in arm for warmth, red nosed, with their breath billowing out in clouds as they talk about their days.

Simon takes Walt out in the mornings, Benji in the evenings. They try to find a patch of grass among the growing piles of gray snow plowed onto the sidewalks.

They have lunch dates and dinner dates and go to shows and concerts, but Simon's very favorite thing is just curling up on the couch and watching movies or dumb television shows and eating takeout.

Simon knows their first Christmas together is kind of a big deal, but he's really sort of put it out of his head. He wonders if he can go ahead and kill two birds with one stone.

"Hey, you have a *Star Wars* fantasy, right?" Simon asks, mid-toilet-scrubbing.

Benji is crouched in the tub wearing athletic shorts and ratty tank top, cleaning the tile while Peggy insists on weaving around him, leaving little wet paw prints on the edge of the tub.

"What kind of fantasy?" He sprays and scrubs, bare toned arms flexing, just a little sweaty. It's all terribly sexy.

Simon turns back to his task and Peggy hops up onto the counter above to watch. "Like. I dress up as a Jedi and you're the new recruit I have to train. But in the naked way. With frustrated angry sex and lightsaber fights." Simon raises his eyebrows a few times to make sure Benji catches his meaning.

"Oh." He stands and frowns, holds the brush and cleaner out at his sides. "Not really, no."

"Oh. Huh." Well there goes that plan.

"See, not so predictable am I?"

"I never said—" Simon protests.

"—You kind of did."

"Fine. I just assumed—You know what, let's not fight in front of the cat."

Benji laughs and steps out of the tub. He passes Simon with a kiss on his cheek, stashes the cleaning supplies back under the counter and starts to leave. "We're not fighting. The cat's trying to climb in the toilet bowl, by the way."

"Peggy, come on now," Simon mutters. He chases her away with the gross toilet brush and finishes his chore. Okay, if not *Star Wars* roleplaying then what? He's not really crazy about Santa and elf kinkiness; too close to childhood memories. Pool boy and rich homeowner? No pool, though. Cop and burglar? They've kind of done the handcuff thing though. A lot.

Simon washes his hands with scalding hot water and the slippery glycerine soap that doesn't irritate Benji's sensitive skin.

"Okay, what fantasies do you have?"

Benji is in the bedroom, shirt off and balled up on the floor, shorts riding low on his hips. Walt is curled up on the bed and the heater churns loudly beneath the ice-frosted window.

Benji purses his lips. "Well. I had this one where I'd meet this really hot guy who was also kind and funny, and we'd have amazing sex and move in together and fall in love."

Warmth blooms in Simon's chest, he can't help it. "You're cute."

Benji grins. "I know."

Simon flops onto the bed with a huff. Cute as he is, he's really not very helpful. Walt lifts his head and licks Simon's nose in sympathy. "Thanks, buddy. Benji, seriously though."

"I don't know, you pick this time. I'm up for whatever." Fingers trail over Simon's stomach where his shirt has ridden up. "I'm gonna take a shower, care to join me?"

He gets the idea while he's soaping up Benji's broad, smooth back, his earlobe between Simon's teeth and their bodies pressed slickly together as slippery bubbles swirl around their feet. Simon runs his hands over every bit of skin he can reach without moving too much. One sudden movement and they're both going down. Not in the good way.

His middle finger finds the scar on Benji's elbow from when he ran headlong into a tree on his bike his junior year of high school. He was all bandaged up for picture day, and his mom has never let him forget about it.

"You went to Catholic school, right?" Simon asks, sliding his hand around Benji's hip, dragging his palm down to his cock and starting a slow stroke.

"Mmm. You know I did. My mom showed you all of my yearbooks." His head drops back against Simon's shoulder.

"Yeah. What was with that haircut in the ninth grade by the way?" Benji ignores this, his breathing starting to get ragged, hips starting to twitch. Simon speeds up the pace. "You still have that uniform?"

"Uh. Mmm, that's good, yeah." He groans, leaning more of his weight into Simon. "Yeah, I think so, why?"

He'll explain more when Benji can better carry on a conversation. For now, he flicks his wrist, jerks him fast and says, "I think I picked."

The magazine goes on a brief winter break, and Simon spends most of that time tracking down all eighteen issues of *The Death of Captain America* story arc. There's yet another boring store party, and Benji gets another scented candle at the IT gift exchange. Benji loves it. Simon thinks it smells like fabric softener gone horribly wrong.

Their Christmas is quiet; just them and a warm apartment, dozing pets, softly blinking lights and eggnog splashed with rum.

Benji is thrilled with the comics and a new shirt with a T-Rex roaring out a rainbow across the chest. He puts on the lumpy too-big sweater with one extra-long sleeve that Simon's mom did indeed knit. Simon snaps a picture to send to her.

"It's hideous. I'm so happy." Simon laughs.

Benji's parents get them a steel shaker and martini glass set. It has Simon wondering if he spends too much time drinking around Benji's family. Then he picks up Benji's present.

"Oh my God, how?" Simon tears back the paper, to reveal the worn and battered cover of a first edition *Leaves of Grass*. He flips the cover open and squeaks. It's signed by Walt Whitman himself.

"Do you love it?"

Simon closes his eyes, presses the soft leather cover to his mouth and breathes the sweet heady scent of the book. "I love you."

Benji kisses him. "Go put it up on the shelf before you accidentally inhale it."

Simon hops up off the floor to place the book in a prime spot on the shelf, turns it this way and that to get it just right.

"Oh. I got you something else, too."

"No, no. Stop being perfect. You're making me look bad."

"It's not a gift, it's well... I'll show you." He stands up, torn wrapping paper rustling under his feet as he retrieves a plastic grocery bag from the closet. "I told my mom it was for a play that a friend of mine is doing, but I'm pretty sure she figured it out. Anyway."

Simon pulls out boxy khaki pants, a white long sleeve dress shirt and a red blazer. Also a red and yellow striped tie still tied with a crooked knot. "Naughty school boy, I'm assuming?"

Simon's pulse picks up speed. "Or...What if I was the naughty one?" Benji looks up questioningly, tracing lightly over the seams of the blazer. "And you were just that innocent, earnest private school student?"

Benji scoffs, then puts the blazer on over his T-shirt. "Dirty old man."

"That's the spirit," Simon replies, taking him by the hand and leading him to the bedroom.

Benji changes into the rest of the uniform, loops the tie loose over his neck and buttons the shirt with mismatched buttons. "Still fits." Benji attempts a smile, fidgets uncomfortably. "I feel weird."

Simon leans against the edge of the dresser and extends a hand. "Come here."

He situates Benji so he's standing between Simon's knees with his hands shoved into the pockets of his uniform slacks. "Weird like you don't want to do it or weird like you hate wearing ties weird?" Simon asks. Benji shrugs.

"Weird like—I don't know how to act like someone else?"

"Forget about all that. It's just us, okay? Follow my lead, let me show you."

Simon lifts Benji's left hand to drop a kiss to the back of his knuckles and winks. "Has anyone ever touched you before, Benji?"

Benji's eyes narrow before he gets it, sucks in his lips and lowers his eyes. When he looks back at Simon again he's dropped his shoulders, turned his face to the side with eyelashes fluttering against his cheeks and mouth slightly parted.

He looks ten years younger.

Simon's breath catches and he sits up straighter in his desk chair. How many times will Simon lead him somewhere while he's reluctant and unsure, only for Benji to shock him by embracing it completely and making Simon go weak for wanting him?

"You're so beautiful, Benji. Has anyone ever told you that?"

Benji continues to look away, gives an imperceptible shake of his head. "I've never—" He drops his head lower, scuffs the toe of his socked foot on the floor and says in a quiet, timid voice pitched just a bit higher than usual, "I've never even kissed anyone."

Simon stands and cups Benji's chin so he's looking him in the eye. "Do you want to kiss me, Benji?"

Benji's gaze flits down to Simon's lips, then snaps back up again as if he's afraid he'll be chastised for it. "Uh-huh."

Simon leans in, slowly, watching the stunned expression on Benji's face until he has to close his eyes, and presses his lips to Benji's. He thrills at finding Benji's mouth soft and pliant under his; Benji just takes it, lets Simon kiss him and nudge his mouth open with his tongue, sucking and nibbling at his bottom lip. Benji sucks in a sharp breath through his nose and grips Simon's shirt in his hands to haul him closer.

"Whoa there, easy." Simon laughs, ducking back to avoid the chase of Benji's mouth. He breaks character for a moment to wonder if he should be embarrassed by how hard he already is, pressed up obviously against Benji's hip. Innocent school boy suits Benji very, very well. "We should go lie down."

He leads Benji to the bed, stretching on his side next him while Benji leans back flat on his back and clutches the blanket as if it's the only thing keeping him from flying away.

"It's okay," Simon murmurs, keeping his own hands away for now, but kissing gently on the corner of Benji's jaw. "Does that feel good?" He dots a line of kisses from behind Benji's ear and down his neck, nosing aside the collar of the blazer to get at more skin.

"Yes," Benji breathes.

"Where else do you want me to kiss you, Benji?"

Benji's hips wiggle against the mattress, the outline of his hard cock visible just under the bottom hem of the blazer. "Everywhere."

Simon chuckles, low and dark, and finally reaches out to skim a fingertip from Benji's sternum to the button of his pants. He tugs but doesn't open it. "I'd like that. You'd feel so good in my mouth, sweet boy."

Benji whimpers and bucks, throws his head back and squeezes his eyes closed. "Simon, I—" His hand darts down to where Simon has moved to cup him gently, so gently, and takes a shaky breath.

"What is it?" He kisses Benji's cheek, the innocence of it a thrilling juxtaposition to the press of Simon's hand, the twitch of his own cock. "Don't be afraid, you can tell me."

Benji blinks his eyes open, clear and soft and doe-eyed innocent. "I want. To see. To see you. If that's okay?"

Simon just smiles, then kneels on the bed to pop open the snaps on his shirt. Benji's mouth drops when Simon shrugs it off. The clink of Simon's belt has Benji pressing his lips together and swallowing hard. When he looks up to find Simon smirking at him, Benji looks away with a blush on his cheeks.

He finishes undressing, then returns to Benji's side, stretching out languorously, smoothing his palms along his bared skin before tucking them behind his head. "You can look now."

"Oh..." Benji blinks and blinks, turns to his side and lifts one shaking hand to hover over Simon's body like he can't decide what to touch first or how. "Wow. You're so hot."

"Do you want to touch me?"

Benji responds with an emphatic nod of his head.

Simon covers Benji's hand with his own and brings it down to curl loosely around his cock. He swallows a moan and moves his hand away. "That's good. Just like that."

Benji's eyebrows pinch together in concentration and his teeth indent his lip as he starts a slow rhythm.

"Do you like it, Benji?" He lolls his head to the side, closes his eyes and focuses his attention on the slide of Benji's fingers up and down his cock; Simon gasps and arches his body, putting on a show.

"Yeah," Benji says, reverent and rapturous, as if Simon's dick is the key to the promised land. He snorts to himself, and Benji's hand freezes, eyes too big and flashing with hurt.

"No. It's not you, sweet boy. You're perfect, keep going." Benji releases a gust of breath and doubles his efforts, gripping tighter and jerking faster. Simon gives a groan in appreciation and encouragement. "What else do you think you'd like?"

"I—I want to taste you. There."

"Mmm, yeah." Simon starts to feel the tension build low in his groin, heat spreading through his veins, balls drawing up tight.

Benji's voice, soft and hesitant, says, "And—and—what you'd feel like... inside me."

"God, Benji." Simon rocks his hips, pushing his cock faster in Benji's grip. "You'd feel so good. So tight for me." Then Benji thumbs at the little sensitive spot under his cockhead, twists his wrist on a stroke up. It's technically breaking character: a trick Benji learned quickly that works every time. The wave of pleasure crests over Simon and he can't hold back. He streaks hot onto his own stomach and chest with a gasp.

Benji spreads his fingers through the mess, burying his face in Simon's shoulder. He ruts and shudders against Simon's hip as he comes.

Benji flops over, strips out of the blazer and then the rest of his clothes, lazily wiping both of them off with his shirt. "I can't believe I just did that."

He turns to look over at Benji. "It was very convincing. You sure you've never done it before?"

"No. My teachers were either nuns or ninety-five year old priests." He grimaces.

"Hey, there's an idea. What about playing priest and nun?" Simon jokes.

Benji wrinkles his nose and tucks their bodies together; interlocking parts, puzzle pieces. "Ew, pass. Hmm, football player and cheerleader?"

"I dunno. Athletes don't really do it for me. Soccer players maybe. What about pizza boy who gets a very special tip?"

Benji makes a soft noise of consideration, tucking his face into Simon's neck. "I like the handcuffs. Cop and criminal?"

"Cop and young first-time offender?"

Benji nips at his jaw and laughs. "Dirty old man."

Spicing Up Your Sex Life Tip: *Try roleplaying some naughty scenarios!*

Good idea or bad idea: There will be times in your life when you want to do something or try a new experience and that annoying voice in your head will shout, "But I'll look stupid!" This is never, ever a reason to not do something. Everyone looks stupid sometimes. Who the hell cares? So

Chapter Twenty Six

"Can you see me?"

"Yes, Mom, we can see..."

"Can you hear me? Hello!"

"We can see and hear you, Mom—Whoa, nostril close up. Just... Back, a little. There you go."

"Hi, Joan!"

"Benji!"

"Hey, Mom."

"Simon!"

Simon adjusts the screen on Benji's laptop. It's set in the middle of the kitchen table with the overhead light turned on because the afternoon is gray and the sun is buried in heavy clouds. He and Benji sit squeezed together so they can both be framed in the screen. A little over a thousand miles away on her sunny back porch, his mom smiles and waves.

"How's Florida?" Simon asks. Palm trees rustle in a light breeze around her, and spots of sunlight bounce in waves off the surface of the backyard pool. He doesn't miss Florida, not really. So it's always strange to feel a pang of nostalgia for a place he couldn't wait to get away from.

"Fine. Oh! A house exploded in Boca. They were making—" She leans in, looks around like someone might be spying on her video call with her son and his boyfriend. "*Marijuana.*"

"So, the usual?" Simon muses.

"People don't make marijuana," Benji butts in, "they grow it. Are sure it wasn't meth? A lot of the chemicals are highly volatile."

"Oh. Maybe," she replies, wide-eyed. Simon is amused that she doesn't even question Benji's drug knowledge.

They chat about work, Tia's latest exotic vacation, the weather, a charity Simon's mom is involved with that provides microloans to business women in disadvantaged areas.

"Benji, I keep getting these strange popup ads lately." Benji starts slinging computer jargon so Simon tunes out. They bring Peggy over so she can glare at all three of them. Then Walt so he can wag his tail and wiggle his ears in confusion. He races around the apartment trying to figure out where Joan is.

"Such a beautiful mind," Simon quips, and then they say good-bye. "Please tell me my mom didn't get a virus from the *MILF Cheerleaders XXX* website."

"No," Benji chuckles, closing the laptop. "She just needs to update her firewall. Your mother is not into MILF cheerleaders as far I know."

He gets up, goes to the fridge to grab a bottle of water, and Simon stretches back in his chair and asks, "Are you?"

Benji takes several long swallows, throat stretched long, the knot of it bobbing. "I know you're really asking me something else, so I'm just going to wait you out this time."

Simon stretches, up and up, twists so his back pops and cracks, crosses his legs at the ankle in an attempt to look nonchalant as he replies, "I'm asking what kind of porn you're into."

Benji caps the water, sets it back in the fridge and pushes the door closed. "I dunno. Regular porn? I don't watch it that often."

"Oh, come on."

"I don't, I swear!" Benji protests. "I have an imagination that works just fine."

"Hmm. And what do you imagine?" Simon sits up and pulls the laptop closer. "By that I of course mean: What do you imagine about me?"

"Have I ever told you how much I love your humility?" Benji sits back at the table, bumping their knees together.

"I'm just curious."

Simon opens the web browser, types in a somewhat innocuous search for romantic male-slash-male porn and follows a promising looking link. There has to be something they'd enjoy watching together.

"Your mouth," Benji finally answers. "And your hands."

"My hands?" Simon asks, hovering over a link that reads *2 strong guys fucking nice*. Pass.

"You have great hands. Long fingers..." Benji trails off, and, when Simon looks up, he's staring at Simon's fingers on the keyboard.

"Oh. Huh." Another link, *Amigos, 100% Nice*. Simon scowls at it. This website is terrible. He clicks back, tries a new site that looks a little more highbrow. "Your ass," Simon says offhandedly, still searching. "I could write sonnets to your ass, Benji. And you should know I used to write terrible poetry all the time."

These To Guys Loves Homosexual Only, Simon reads and, wow, all of these porn sites are desperately in need of some decent copy editors. He clicks back again with a sigh.

"Please be careful about what you click on," Benji warns. "I don't feel like spending the afternoon removing malware."

"I am. Okay, here," Simon says, finally stumbling on some videos with passable grammar and nothing too out there. "Long Lost Lovers are Reunited." Benji scoots in and moves the laptop between them.

"I guess that sounds okay—Oh my God." He slams the laptop shut and turns to look at Simon with alarm.

Simon lifts the screen gingerly, one eye squinted closed like it might shoot out poison or contain some kind of bomb. "'Monster Cock.' Missed that part," Simon says mildly, chest shaking with suppressed laughter.

Benji covers his face and drops his head onto the table. Simon's hand immediately comes up to stroke through his hair.

"Monster, indeed. That thing could star in a horror movie."

"Horror porn," Benji says, muffled, face still hidden. "I bet that's a thing."

Simon strokes through the soft strands, coppery shimmer threading through his fingers. He's never thought much about them, his hands, they are kind of nice. "There should be categories of porn," he says. "Victorian Romance Porn, Action-Adventure Porn, Romantic Comedy Porn, Noir Porn."

"Superhero Porn," Benji pipes up, turning his head to the side and leaning into Simon's touch.

"I would put good money on there being superhero porn, but somebody didn't want to dress up as—" Simon gasps, pats Benji's head a little too hard in his excitement. "That's it!"

"Ouch." Benji hauls himself up and away from Simon's flailing hands. "What's it?"

"The porn." Simon replies with a clap of his hands. Benji lifts his eyebrows, dubious. "We could make our own." He's up off the chair and opening the junk drawer in the kitchen before Benji can reply. He pulls a little video camera from a pile of rubber bands, pens, balled up receipts and loose change.

"Wait, seriously?"

"Sure. That way we can see exactly what we want. No surprise tree-trunk sized penises."

"Tree-trunk sized..." Benji mutters, looking vaguely off in the distance before shaking his head and standing up. "Okay. Let's do it."

Benji sets up the camera on the top of the low bookshelf in the corner of their bedroom, lips pursed as he sets it just so: facing the bed, close but not too close. Simon peers in the camera, frowns at the boring beige wall. He pulls the dark red top sheet off their bed and stands up on the mattress, wobbling a bit until Benji comes to bracket his legs. He tacks it up on the wall over the headboard. "Can you see the top?"

Benji darts away to look into the camera. "Nope."

"Excellent." He knows nothing about film making, but he's fairly sure backdrops are important. Simon hops down, then rubs at his arm, nibbles his lips. "So…"

Benji presses a button on the camera, the tinny beep in the too quiet room like a gunshot at the start of a race. Simon's pulse jumps. A red light blinks, a silent judging eye. He's starting to feel a new compassion for porn stars.

"This is super awkward," Benji finally blurts. Simon huffs, sinks down to the bed and pats the space next to him.

Benji sits, and Simon immediately leans in. Their mouths slide softly together. Simon pulls away just enough to say, "We have to forget about our audience. Just focus on us. If it feels good, it'll look good, right?"

Benji nods, pulls Simon closer. Simon shifts them down across the bed, and he knows, should anyone ever watch this video, they could see how badly they want each other. If making love to Benji looks as incredible as it feels, this will be an award winning porno.

After, Benji changes the sheets and Simon takes down the makeshift backdrop. They settle under the blankets as they wait for the video to download. Simon hides it in a folder within a folder under the name *Benji's collectibles* > *spreadsheet* > Star Wars *figurines*.

"I do not have that many *Star Wars* figurines." Benji protests, and Simon just lifts an eyebrow and presses play.

The kissing is lovely, at first. They look good kissing, lips and hands and tongues coordinating in a sort of well-rehearsed dance. It felt really good, too. Their bodies press closer and closer, in increments. Clothes are shed. Benji's fair skin and long body and constellations of freckles are a beautiful contrast to Simon's more compact body, darker skin and darker tufts of hair on his chest and stomach.

And still kissing.

Simon's mind starts to wander. The sheet is off-center, drooping on one side. He wishes they'd changed the bedspread; brown plaid isn't doing either of them any favors.

Then he snaps back to attention, feeling a flush of guilt that he isn't enjoying himself as much as he should be. Until Benji inquires, "Do you think I should shave the backs of my thighs?"

"What?" Simon says.

"I just didn't realize they were so hairy."

"Benji, your legs are a perfectly acceptable level of hairiness." Simon barely resists the urge to roll his eyes.

"If you say so. You're the one who has to look at them." He seems unconvinced, rubbing at his legs beneath the blanket.

Simon does roll his eyes then, taking a moment to blink at the ceiling before he skips ahead in the video, past the kissing. Now, on the screen, he's reaching out to the nightstand, pulling lube out of the drawer; slicking his fingers first, then Benji's.

He watches as Benji flips to his back, bends his legs and plants his feet. Simon's hand circles his cock, then pushes a finger inside him. It's incredible. Watching his fingers disappear into Benji's body; the angle perfect to watch the stretch, the way Benji's legs fall open farther, the way he just yields to the movement. Or, it's hot at first.

They flip over; Benji is stroking Simon's cock and kneeling by his hips.

"Oh no, what is that face?"

"What? Oh. That's your pleasure face." Benji replies. Under the blanket, his hand moves from his leg to Simon's.

"I look like a suffocating trout." Simon covers himself on the screen, unable to take watching himself flop around openmouthed as Benji's fist works him over.

"Are you kidding me? I love that face. You made it when we shared that pie at the bakery last weekend. I was seriously considering another bathroom blowjob."

Benji looks pleased at the memory, cheeks pinking across the sweep of his cheekbones, but, Simon turns and grips Benji's shoulders, horrified. "Are you saying I make that face in public?"

"Simon, relax." He removes Simon's hand, folds it into his own and resettles the laptop. "I mean, at least you don't look like Sasquatch from behind."

The laugh comes out in a snort, and Benji scrunches his nose at him. Simon pats his knee and tries to reassure him. This whole experiment is starting to feel like a colossal failure; his entire column this week will read: *Do not videotape yourselves having sex! Some things cannot be unseen!*

But then the Benji on the video has shifted, straddling Simon's lap as he sinks down onto Simon's cock. And sure, Simon's toes are doing this weird wiggling thing, and he's making that face again, only somehow worse. But, wow, Benji looks amazing like that; back curved in, muscles pulled tight, his strong thighs working his ass up and down. Oh, and his ass. Simon's never had such a clear view: watching as he fills him, fucks into him. It's stunning.

"I'm gonna blow you now," Benji mutters. Simon barely hears him. He's barely breathing. He sets the computer to the side, tilting it so he can still watch as Benji's hot mouth sinks over him.

He watches as video Benji takes his cock deep, circles his hips. He lifts up as Simon plants his feet on the mattress, grips Benji's waist then snaps his hips, jolting Benji forward with the strength of his thrusts.

He can't keep his head still, thrashing back and forth from the visual of Benji's head in real time, bobbing and working, and Benji's ass around him on the video. It's too much. Too much to process. Then he's gripping Benji's hair tight, watches himself buried inside Benji, hears how he cried out in a choked-off sob.

Benji swallows him down, and Simon comes hard for the second time.

"Holy fuck," Simon says, feeling as if his blood has turned to lead. Benji whines, waiting impatiently on all fours between Simon's legs, his cock hanging full and heavy, untouched.

Simon forces one hand into a sloppy sort of grip, steadies the other on the back of Benji's fuzzy thigh, scratches at the hair and catches his eye with a grin as Benji thrusts into his fist.

"Not funny," he grunts, face twisted up tight. Simon just keeps smiling, slips his fingers up higher to press two at the still-slick stretch of Benji's hole. Benji's mouth opens and he spills across Simon's legs, the bed, low on Simon's groin.

"We are so hot," Simon says smugly, reaching to grab the box of tissues to clean himself.

Benji moves to the side, tips his head and smirks in a lopsided sort of way. "Mmhmm, fish face and all."

Spicing Up Your Sex Life Tip: *Try watching sexy movies together to get in the mood! Or make your own!*

Good idea or bad idea: I am afraid, dear readers, that I am still undecided on this one. Some people find watching pornography works for them, some don't, and, really, either one is fine. We have different preferences and different ways of getting turned on, but it certainly can't hurt to try. (Read the descriptions! Carefully!) As far as making your own, proceed with caution. We did enjoy ourselves while making one, a little less so watching it. But it worked out okay in the end. Aim for soft lighting, know your best angles and edit judiciously. And, for the love of Paris Hilton, keep it safe and hidden. Unless you want to be famous for all the wrong reasons. (FYI: You don't.)

Chapter Twenty-Seven

January continues frigid and gray; Dementors suck joy and warmth from the air. Simon tells Benji this on the way to work and Benji grins, and despite his teeth chattering and toes going numb after stepping in a puddle of freezing slush, Simon's chest glows.

Simon's happy. The series of articles has lead to him having some of the best sex of his life, and his skin looks freaking fantastic. Life is grand, he thinks and swings Benji's hand and doesn't even care at how saccharine he's gotten lately.

As badly as he'd wanted a real relationship, he had never imagined it would feel like this.

"Hey, loverboy," Tia chirps, stopping by for coffee and gossip. "Double date on Saturday again?"

"You know it."

After she leaves, he pulls up the pictures still on his phone of their double date at The Butterfly Conservatory inside the Museum of Natural History: bursts of tropical flowers, butterflies of all colors and sizes flitting by on shimmering wings, Benji chock-full of butterfly facts. Simon had watched a monarch sip juice from an orange slice; cocooned inside the humid warmth of the conservatory while the wind howled arctic outside, he couldn't imagine a more perfect moment.

Simon pauses at a close up shot of Benji's sweet smile, a blue morpho flying away over his shoulder. Simon had called Benji the most beautiful creature in the entire exhibit, and Benji had blushed and stammered and laughed.

That settles it. He closes down his document, stashes his phone in a drawer so there won't be any interruptions and casually meanders down the hall, around the corner, through the break room and down a short stairway.

The first time he'd come down to the IT department, Benji had swept out his arms dramatically and said, villain like, "Welcome to the dungeon."

It's sort of apt. Windowless and fluorescent lighted, it smells like stale dust and old popcorn. There's a brown carpet and two long gray desks with computers lined side by side. Phones ring and keyboard keys clack, but it's otherwise quiet.

The door eases closed, and Simon makes his way down the aisle to Benji's spot between Mark and Cassie. He looks up with a start when Simon touches his shoulders.

"Hey," he says, pulling his head set off. "I didn't think we were getting lunch together today."

"We aren't. I just... uh... needed to talk to you about something." Simon stutters out. Maybe trysts are supposed to be better planned out. Or does that defeat the entire purpose?

Mark gives him a look, and Cassie giggles before catching herself and angling her chair away.

"Sure. Just let me finish this call?"

There really isn't anywhere to sit so Simon perches on a stack of cardboard crates filled with printing paper. Benji puts his headset back on, and Simon watches.

He's so patient. Both of their careers involve helping people; it's just that Simon gets to say something clever, drop some advice and then dash away like the Robin Hood of sex tips. Benji talks them through it, figuratively and, sometimes, literally holds their hands and never gets frustrated at things that would have long ago made Simon want to reach through the phone line and throttle people with their fiber optic cables.

It's the same way he is with Simon, or with Walt when he knocks over the trashcan, eats a moldy lime and gets sick. It's the way he is with Peggy despite her yowling at their closed bedroom door and her middle of the night ankle attacks. Simon's eyes go hazy as he imagines, for the first time in his life, a baby in his arms, his gentle, soft-hearted husband cooing at her.

"You ready?"

Simon jumps; the cartons wobble a little under him. "Yeah, yep, just—Daydreaming, sorry."

Benji kisses his cheek. "About that food truck with the meatball subs, right? Me too."

The room has cleared out; everyone's already gone to lunch. "Actually..." Simon hooks a finger into a pocket on his jeans. Benji is wearing a dark green T-shirt with a cartoon Godzilla printed on it, snug along every line and angle of his torso. The color makes his eyes look incredible.

"Maybe we could... stay here for a little longer."

"Oh." Benji looks around the now empty office and smirks. "Yeah, okay." He leans in, then stops suddenly. "Just in case though—" He leads Simon to the back corner, behind a huge shelf that's blocking a door.

"The graveyard," he says, in the same screechy villain voice.

A dark closet with computer parts littering the floor, teeming in piles and spilling from shelves. A museum of computers; huge hulking monitors and CPUs so massive, heavy and obsolete they're now about as technologically sound as cinder blocks. There are battered old boxes filled with wires and keyboards and circuit boards, as well as a desk with a severely bent leg and a bicycle with only one wheel.

Simon shuffles in sideways, trips over a box filled with random computer parts and ends up wedged in between the bicycle and the slanted, busted up desk.

"I don't even know where that came from or why," Benji says, squeezing in front of Simon, his ass resting on the desk edge as he nods at the bike. Then he breathes out, "Well, good afternoon."

"Hi there," Simon replies.

"So we're doing this?"

"Oh yeah." Simon leans in, pleased that their positions mean he's taller than Benji for a change. He cups his jaw, tips his chin up and kisses him. He bends over and bumps the bike's one wheel. The handlebars shift and dig into his hip, but he ignores it. It adds to the excitement. Simon pulls away, presses his lips to Benji's jaw and cheek and temple.

"Do you think anyone has fooled around in here before?" Simon asks, a little breathless already.

"I doubt it." Benji dips his head, then makes quick work of opening Simon's fly, palm pressing deliberately at the bulge of Simon's twitching cock.

"Oh. But we did find a dead raccoon in here once."

Simon stares down at him, a groan rumbling in his chest at Benji's fingers cupping him. He shoves his hand inside of Simon's underwear to grip around the shaft. "Can we not talk about dead rodents when your hand is on my dick?"

Benji starts to jerk, a little rough and dry but so, so good. He nuzzles his nose into Simon's neck. "Sorry." Simon loops his arms over Benji's shoulders and Benji's head rests on Simon's chest. "They aren't actually rodents though, they're in the—"

"Honey, not now," Simon says, then gasps when Benji's fist pulls tight.

"Right. Sorry."

Simon drapes his weight over Benji's shoulders, closes his eyes and just lets the pleasure build and build. They don't really have time to draw this out, and Benji's gotten so good at knowing just how to work him that it's not going to last long anyway.

Benji mouths up the column of his throat, gets a little enthusiastic in a spot just under his ear. Simon lifts his head to tell him to not leave a hickey, since they aren't fifteen and making out under the bleachers.

But instead he blinks at the ceiling of this dark closet that's tucked away in the back of a high-rise building in the middle of a huge metropolitan city and—"How did a raccoon get in here anyway?"

"I know! Crazy, right?" Benji bites at his jaw, hums happily and starts to jerk faster, harder, shoulder flexing under Simon's arm. The closet is filled with the sound of Simon's heavy breathing and the smack of Benji's lips, hungry and hot on Simon's skin.

"Close. Is there... tissues... shit shit shit..." He can feel it build, feel the heat draw up tight, feel his thighs shake and his hips pulse staccato.

Benji stretches back a bit, says, "I've got you. Come on." A cloth of some sort brushes the head of his cock, Benji kisses him and he whines into his mouth and spurts into the towel.

Simon presses their foreheads together and laughs a little.

"I hope that wasn't the towel they found the raccoon on," Benji says.

Simon stands up, tucks himself back into his pants. "Okay, I was going to blow you, but now you can forget it." He zips his pants and looks warily at the grimy soiled towel pinched between Benji's fingers.

"I'm joking! They found it in a box of printer ink." He hops off the desk, tosses the towel in a trashcan nearby. "It's okay, we don't really have time now. That was fun, though."

Simon spreads his hand flat on Benji's stomach. "I owe you one."

Benji grins. "Deal. Come on. let's get out of here. I do have to work with these people."

They straighten each other out; Simon fixes Benji's extra messy hair, and Benji sets Simon's shirt to rights. He checks Simon's neck for bruising, calls him clear for takeoff, and Simon gives him a jaunty salute.

When they emerge from the closet, it looks at first as though they made it in time to avoid running into Benji's coworkers. Simon promises to rock Benji's world later and says good-bye.

He runs right into Mark in the doorway.

"Oh hey!" he says a little too brightly.

Simon mock-punches his arm awkwardly and jogs away.

Back at his desk, he tries not grin like a guy who just got a pretty fantastic handjob in a closet. There are five missed calls from his mom. One voicemail. Simon squints in confusion. She knows he's at work, and the most she'll usually do is send a text.

The message is not his mom's voice at all, but a deep bass with a slow, honeyed southern accent.

"Si—Simon. This is uh. This is Darryl. I'm your mom's neighbor? Um. I have some bad news. Your mom is in the hospital. I'm not sure if she... uh. Just call me back at this number? Okay. This is Darryl."

Several tense minutes later Simon waits for his flight confirmation and hastily adds an ending to the document he'd already been working on. He sends it off, sick to his stomach and shaking. How could this happen? How could he let this happen?

Spicing Up Your Sex Life Tip: *Plan a sneaky midday tryst at his work or yours!*

Good idea or bad idea: This is a great way of connecting with your partner at a time when you're usually focused on other things. Just try to not forget that the rest of the world still goes on existing while you're busy getting off in a supply closet. This one I'm forced to call a bad idea. Sorry.

⌐☐ Chapter Twenty-Eight

Ask Eros: Hold the Hamburger Phone

Q: *I'm pregnant. And seventeen. I'm getting pressure from everyone about what to do, and the more they want me to figure out what I'm doing, the less I know. Maybe you can give me your unbiased opinion. Help?*

A: *Well, here's the thing about my opinion, and everyone else's for that matter: It's not up to us. You don't mention the other person involved in this so I'm going to assume immaculate conception? Kidding. I'm assuming he's being an immature snot who's left you high and dry. I talk a lot about empowered sex, and that includes safe sex, but we're still fallible human beings. Now you are empowered in a different way. Being pregnant is a big deal. Having a child is an even bigger one. Parenting is possibly the biggest deal of them all. You can opt out of all of the above, or you can have a child but choose not to parent. You can do all of them. But you have to choose, and you can because you are smart and capable and in your heart of hearts, you know what the right choice is. But rest assured, not choosing **is** a choice. My opinion? Don't do that.*

Simon never has been great at waiting. He gets way too impatient with tourists blocking the sidewalk or descending en masse on his favorite

Chipotle. He hates waiting for videos to buffer or a late train to arrive. He spent his high school years so desperate to get away from Florida that it sometimes seems he was never really there.

He wanted and got early career success and close friends. He just needed the right guy to finish the puzzle, the missing piece in the life he'd imagined for himself.

He got him, though he first had to stop trying to cram the wrong one into a spot that he would never fit, but he found him, and now—

Now he's fidgeting and sighing and craning his neck to see what the damn hold up is. *How fucking long does it take to put your luggage away? Christ.* He's sitting on the runway waiting for take off and wondering how all of the interlocking bits and pieces of his life shattered and crumbled so easily.

He's selfish, that's how. He's dragged Benji along with these articles and before that with his own hangups about Andrew. He left Florida without so much as a backward glance so he could go live some fantasy life. He wants to help people, but maybe he's only helping himself.

If he had been there, this never would have happened.

The buckle-seat-belt light dings on, finally, so Simon checks his phone one last time for an update.

Nothing more from Darryl. Nothing from his mom. Concern and love from Tia and James. And from Benji. He doesn't reply, instead checks his email as the flight attendant pulls the air mask over her face.

From: Daisy Martinez, Editor In Chief, *Ravish* Magazine
To: Simon Beck
Re: unpublished articles

Thanks Simon, this should cover it while you're gone. Don't sweat the series on spicing up sex life. Just send something if you can. I'll be praying for your mother.

From: Andrew Klaff
To: Simon Beck
(no subject)

The stunt in the bar was cute, got my attention. When you
get tired of playing house with the redhead, you know where
to find me.
-Andrew

He stares at the message, then the plane starts to taxi, and he has to
turn it off. He rests his head against the seat, closes his eyes and waits
for lift off.

Once they're in the air, he's even more impatient, right leg jogging
nonstop. He can't get comfortable, just shifts and sighs and drums
his fingers on the seatrest until the guy next to him asks, "First time
flying?"

"No," Simon replies curtly.

He looks over and moves his hand to his jumping knee and immediately feels bad for being rude.

His seatmate is an older man with gray hair and glasses. He doesn't
seem upset and asks, "Do you ever think about it? What a marvel of
human achievement flying is? We just take it for granted."

"I get it. It's not the destination, it's the journey." Simon presses his
shoulders back in the seat, tries to breathe a little slower. "But my mom
is in the hospital, so I just really need to be there already."

"I'm sorry to hear that."

"Thank you."

"Still," the man says, pulling open a tiny bag of pretzels. "Right now,
this is where you are. Pretzel?"

When they finally touch down, Simon practically vaults over his seat
to get off the plane. He doesn't have to stop for luggage, just hitches
his duffle bag onto his shoulder and makes a beeline for the car rental
kiosk. They hand him the keys to a Lincoln Town Car, a behemoth
that makes Simon feel as if he's at the helm of a ship. The sun glare
is unrelenting; the leather seats are scorching. The metal buckle is a
burning brand on his skin. So starkly Florida. Jimmy Buffett comes on
the radio as he pilots the beast onto the turnpike. Simon has to laugh,
a shocked hysterical noise, and turns up "Margaritaville."

"Joan Beck? I'm her son."

The hospital isn't far from the airport; all bright white flat expanses of parking lots, palm trees and white stucco buildings. He gets lost trying to find the entrance to the heart center, and, by the time he locates the automatic doors leading to the front desk, his shirt is sticking to his back and his hair is limp from the humidity.

It's blessedly cool inside. Simon pushes his hair back from his forehead, tugs at the collar of his polo and waits. And waits.

She's not in a private room, just in one bed of many in a white on white corridor. A blue curtain is pulled around the area. There's a small window above the bed. She looks tiny and frail with her eyes closed and her chestnut brown hair spread on the pillow behind her. Her bangs are swept to the side as if someone had been stroking them. An IV is in one arm, and a heart monitor is steadily *beep beep beeping*. Simon sits and stares at the little lines keeping time to his mother's heart, as if that's really her in there, steady and sure and safe, and not this pale broken thing in a hospital bed.

"Mr. Beck?"

The doctor, young and cute and the sort of tall blonde and tan he'd expect a doctor here to be, comes from behind the curtain.

"Simon," he says, standing, voice croaking, his throat dry and rough as though he'd swallowed sand.

"Simon." She smiles. "Your mother had a minor heart attack. Luckily she got to us in time. Her body has been through a lot, but she's going to be fine."

Simon releases a breath, as if he finally broke to the surface after free falling from the high diving board. "Thank you so much."

After the doctor leaves, he sits back down in the uncomfortable plastic chair and turns his phone back on. He replies to the messages from Tia: *She's ok.*

"You scared the shit out of me," he tells his mom. He can say that to her while she's unconscious and not risk a disapproving glare or a blithe *I'm fine, don't worry about me.* Because he does worry. Because it was just the two of them. The whole world was him and her, and she nearly killed herself being everything to him and he just... left.

Simon slouches over in the chair, rubs at his burning eyes with heels of his hands, guilt tearing and clawing at him. His phone vibrates in his pocket.

Benji: Tia told me. Thank God. Give me a call when you
             can.
Benji: I love you.

He puts his phone back in his pocket and doesn't reply.

⌐◡⌐ Chapter Twenty-Nine

When he hears the curtain scrape open and then closed again nearly an hour later, Simon is still in the same hunched over position. He expects it to be the doctor, but it's an older, dark-skinned man with curly, graying black hair clipped short. He's wearing Bermuda shorts and a button-up Hawaiian-style shirt.

"You must be Simon," he says, and sticks out the hand that's not holding a Styrofoam cup of coffee. "I'm Darryl."

Simon stands, shakes his hand and greets him. Darryl's eyes flicker from Simon to Simon's mom in the bed, and there is a lot more in that look than concerned friend.

"Thank you. I'm so glad you were there and brought her in."

Darryl looks into the cup of thin, watered down hospital brew. "She gave me quite a scare. Been having chest pains and back aches and wouldn't go the doctor even though I told her. At any rate, she was working in the garden and I was watering my lawn when she collapsed. So that's lucky, I guess."

"Wait, you live next door?" His mom's house is on a corner in the center of a subdivision, facing the cul-de-sac where Simon used to ride his bike, play dodgeball and wait for the bus. Next door is the green and white ranch house where he'd get yelled at for cutting across the lawn. "When did the Rosenbergs move?"

"I've been there... let's see, six years now?"

Simon frowns and shakes his head. How has it been more than six years since he's been home? How did he leave his own mother for so long?

Darryl sips his coffee, and Simon stews in his realization that he's a terrible son. He hasn't heard from Benji again and Simon still hasn't replied to his message, so he can add terrible boyfriend to the list.

"Simon?"

"Hey, Mom. Don't sit up."

She looks around, sluggish and confused, frowns at the IV in her arm and then seems to realize where she is.

"What are you doing here?" It's barely more than a wheeze. She puts her hand to her throat and clears it.

"Darryl called me, so I left work and took the first flight I could get."

Darryl looks sheepish, studies his coffee very closely and shuffles back a bit.

"Well. That wasn't necessary. I'm fine."

Simon sits on the bed, one leg propped beneath him, the rough hospital blanket under one hand. "Mom, you had a heart attack."

She licks her lips, clears her throat again. "Darryl, would you be a dear and see if you can track down some hot water with lemon?" She waits until he leaves, sits up a little and fixes him with the look Simon knows all to well. "It's not your job to worry about me."

"You have a heart attack, you're here all alone, and I'm not supposed to worry?"

"No."

"You are impossible." Simon curls up next to her, head on the pillow and barely managing to lie down in the space left on the edge of the mattress. "Don't ever do that again."

His mom strokes his hair and hums, and Simon closes his eyes. He almost lost her while he was so busy being caught up in his own life.

"Everyone I love keeps trying to leave me." First Tia gets married, then Walt gets sick. Now this. Not even a single birthday card or phone call from his own father his whole fucking life, and who's next?

"I'm still here," his mom says and kisses the top of his head. "I can hear you thinking too much."

"Sorry, I'll stop thinking forever," Simon mutters petulantly. She yanks at his ear. "Ow. Okay." He leans into her, warm, alive, and asks her the thing that's really been on his mind lately. "What if I'm trying too hard?"

"With Benji? Or with everything?"

"Both, I guess. Maybe it is too soon. Like I'm so afraid he'll leave that I'm forcing it."

"Oh, fuck that."

Simon whips his head up. "Mom!"

"Listen," she raises an eyebrow, presses her mouth flat sternly and says in her wheezy, weakened voice, "Your whole life you have believed in true love. Even when you didn't get to see it in your own parents. Even when other people tried to tell you that the way you loved was wrong or that happily ever after wasn't for you. Even when you did try to force it with the wrong person at the wrong time."

She coughs, motions for the pink plastic cup with a lid and straw. Simon reaches over and holds it for her while she takes long sips. She looks a little better now; she has some color in her cheeks and her eyes are brighter. Nothing like a good lecture to get the blood pumping.

"You never let the naysayers harden your heart and you never stopped believing. And Simon, I really think you found him." She pats his hand; the clear plastic IV tube brushes his arm. "I know you think you have to have all the answers, so if you were asking yourself for advice, what would you say?"

Simon pulls at a loose string on the blanket and sighs. "Fuck that, probably."

"There you go."

Simon grins. "All along my advice column has been your voice inside my head. Who knew?"

Darryl returns with a second little cup. "The doctor says you can have herbal tea." He has a fond look.

"Thank you, dear."

Simon narrows his eyes, looks back and forth, but decides to let it go for now.

"How do you feel, in your heart?" she asks as she sips her tea, curls of steam drifting around her face.

"Like..." Simon starts. She nods. "Like not being with him doesn't make any sense. Like he gets me and he makes me better. Like love."

When she smiles, she's looking at Darryl, but says to Simon, "Would you mind going to the house to make sure I didn't leave the oven on? Maybe water the plants and finish pulling up weeds while you're there?"

Simon pushes up from the bed and straightens out his clothes. "I know you're trying to get rid of me, but since you just suffered a traumatic event, I'm going to go ahead and let it slide."

He gives them both a nod, raises his eyebrows and pushes the curtain aside. He'll call Benji soon. Just. He's not quite ready yet.

The house looks the same for the most part: salmon colored and tile roofed, the flat driveway on the flat lawn with clipped green grass so fat and thick it crunches under his feet. A line of red ants marches to the garage door. He'll have to sprinkle that natural citrus scented repellant his mom insists on. He'd torch the bastards with a flamethrower if it were up to him.

Inside it's cool: the air conditioning humming happily, ceiling fans rotating steadily. The oven isn't on. No lights have been forgotten.

His old room is a guest room now, a purple lace bedspread on a double bed that was never his. There are a matching wicker nightstand and dresser and a generic pastel Monet print in a yellow frame. Simon sets his bag down, arranges his phone and wallet and keys on the nightstand. He looks at Benji's last message, *I love you*. And goes to water the flowers.

The hibiscus plant has gotten huge and is bursting with color. Simon squeezes the nozzle on the hose, and cold water trickles down his arm. His mom is right, of course. But can he be blamed for freaking out a bit at just how much he feels for Benji? How much and how fast and it's as though... as though it just all finally caught up with

171

him. He's been in this bubble, and he has maybe wanted things too much. He moves on to the geraniums. So much and yet so amazing. He hopes it's been the same for Benji. He hasn't really stopped to ask.

And maybe that's at the root of it. Has Benji just been happy to go along? Sweet, agreeable Benji? Blinded by the admittedly amazing sex.

No. No, of course not. Benji loves him. He sprays down the begonias, the petunias and the cactus plant just because he feels bad skipping it entirely. Probably the Florida sun is frying his brain. God knows it's been a day. He yanks up a few weeds, winds up the hose and goes inside to call Benji.

Who doesn't answer. So he skims the pool and sweeps the cement around it. Calls again. Still no answer. Sits on the couch and flips through all 789 channels. Benji's phone rings and rings and goes to voicemail. He should really be home by now.

Simon: Where are you?

Still nothing.

It's getting dark out: sky darkening to twilight blue, stars winking on, crickets chirping, cicadas hissing. A different kind of loud. He calls to check on his mom, and she sounds better still. She's excited to come home tomorrow.

He is settling down with a sandwich, enjoying the view of the wide open sky in the overstuffed chair at the sliding glass door when Benji finally calls.

"Hi!" he says, almost completely drowned out by background noise: cars whooshing by and people talking and some kind of steady, loud rumbling.

"Are you walking home?"

"No. Uh. Hold on." Some shuffling and a thump and the traffic noises mostly disappear. "Better?"

"Yeah." And not just the noise. It's so good to hear his voice. "Is it weird that I miss you?"

"No? Should it be? I miss you. I was worried when I couldn't get ahold of you." He still sounds strange. Muffled and far away.

"I was kind of—"

"Freaking out and feeling guilty and thinking too much?"

Simon sets his half-eaten turkey on rye on the plate. "Pretty much."

"This wasn't your fault."

"I know."

"And you don't have to fix it."

"I know."

"Okay, then."

Simon pulls the lever to recline the seat, stretches out and finally the anguish of the day lifts from his shoulders. "So how was your day?"

"Mmm. Started off great. Kind of took a dive though."

Simon thinks about the last time they were together, the tryst in the supply closet. He smiles to himself at that memory, then, "Oh no. I kind of left you hanging, didn't I?"

Benji laughs, warm and deep in his ear. "It isn't really a priority anymore. I'll be fine."

Simon, alone and lonely and missing him, wrung out emotionally and feeling raw and needy, hums a little. "Well, if you want I could... Help you out."

Benji's breath catches a little. "Yeah?"

"Are you somewhere private?"

He hesitates, then says, "Close enough." More shuffling, as if he's moving somewhere. "So, how would you, uh, help?"

Simon's face stretches in a grin, and he spreads his legs and drops his hand between. Just resting there for now. "I think I'd take you back to that closet, kneel between your thighs and open your pants."

"Good." A zipper snicks down, and Benji sighs. Simon can imagine him, stroking slow and loose at first. He likes to build up to it, not jerk off fast and hard just to get it over with.

"I'd take your cock out, put my mouth on you. Deep right away, make you squirm and moan and pull my hair."

"Your mouth is so good, yeah," he breathes, ending on a soft moan. Simon shoves his hand into his own pants, wrist constricted and bent at an awkward angle, pulls at his cock as best as he can like that.

"Right down my throat until you cry out, then I'd pull off and lick my way up." Simon moans.

"Are you—"

"Yeah. Yeah gonna come just thinking about you. I want you so much."

"Shit, I'm..." He can't hear it, but he can tell by the clipped words and the high strain of his voice.

"Yeah, come on. Come all over me, I wanna feel it, come on."

Benji gasps and groans, then just breathes heavily for a little bit. "And the day takes another turn."

Simon laughs, then whines, orgasm pulling tight at the base of his spine and building in his groin.

"You close?" Benji asks.

"Yeah. Just. Say something."

"Um. That was... hot?"

Simon grunts. "Something else."

"Right. Uh. What would you want me to do, if I were there right now?"

Simon shoves his pants down, phone trapped between his ear and shoulder. He cups the gaping, purpled head of his dick with one hand and strips the shaft quick, desperate. So so close. "Kiss me, just kiss me." He thinks about Benji's lips on his, thinks about losing himself there, and comes into his hand.

He recovers and cleans himself off. The noise from Benji's end of the phone picks up again. Where on earth is he? Walking Walt to New Jersey?

He tells Benji about the Town Car cruise ship he's renting. How he'd forgotten what a warm, sunny winter is like. Fills him in about his mom. Minor heart attack, she'll be fine. Home tomorrow. He thinks she's having an affair with Darryl from next door.

"Hey. Go to the door."

"What?" Simon says.
"The door. Go to the front door."
"Why?"
"So I can kiss you."

Spicing Up Your Sex Life Tip: *Try phone sex for a new kind of connection!*

Good idea or bad idea: We are lucky to live in an age of communication. Personally, I'll always prefer face to face. There is something about having that person in front of you, warm and real and living that just can't quite be replicated. I have to admit there is value, though, in being able to say certain things with only a voice and a tentative connection to tell someone what you're really thinking. Good idea. Just make sure you're alone and the line is clear so nothing is misheard and no one else jumps in on the fun. Unless you want them to, of course.

⬭⬭ Chapter Thirty

Ask Eros: Insert Raunchy Banana Joke

Q: *Do I have to use condoms for oral? They don't exactly taste great.*

A: *You know what really doesn't taste great? Herpes. Yes, you should be using condoms. The polyurethane types taste better than latex. Or try flavored condoms. I recommend the banana, if only to amuse yourself. I know it's not ideal, but, unless you know that the person on the receiving end has been tested and is clean, it's just not worth the risk.*

The bed is smaller than theirs at home, but without Walt sprawled between them and Peggy curled up on his feet, it seems huge. And even though Benji is there now, he still feels so far away.

Simon flips to his stomach, reaches across to skim his fingertips along his arm and jaw and brush his hair back. Benji doesn't stir at all. Simon's chest feels tight with how beautiful he is.

He gets up, finds eggs and bacon and whole milk—he will be talking to his mom about her eating habits. He doesn't care how annoyed she gets. He settles on toasted English muffins and black coffee, and eats breakfast in one of the lounge chairs by the pool.

Benji gets up and finds him when his coffee mug is empty and his plate with crumbs has been set down on the concrete. He mumbles something unintelligible, and joins him in the chair, head on Simon's chest and legs twined together, his arm flung across Simon's stomach. They stay quiet, warmed by the sun, a briny ocean breeze caressing their skin. A little piece of paradise with a tall cedar fence and a kidney-shaped pool.

"This is nice. We should live here."

"Hmm, come back in August and see what you think."

Benji drags his head up to Simon's shoulder, stretches and yawns. "It was eight degrees when I left. That's just wrong. That's Hoth levels of wrong."

"Hey, I get that *Star Wars* reference." Simon turns his face to the sun, closes his eyes against the fiery brilliance of it. "I'm really glad you're here."

Benji kisses his shoulder, props up on an elbow and squints. "Is there cereal?"

He calls his mom while Benji is in the shower, delighted that the guest bathroom has a dolphin theme. He tells her that Benji is here, and that they'd like to come see her. She insists he get the house ready for visitors, and that Darryl can get her home just fine. Would he be a dear and put out some food?

"It feels like it takes longer to get dry here. Am I imagining things?" Benji walks out still damp, hair wet and clad only in shorts.

"Humidity. Just wait until you see what it does to your hair." Simon frowns and pats his limp coif. "Hey, did you see that grocery store on the main road when you were driving in? Publix?"

"Yeah, I think so."

"Would you maybe pick up a party sub, whole wheat, and some fruit and veggie trays? I guess she's having people over."

"Sure thing."

Simon vacuums, dusts and tidies up. He puts her magazines (*Reader's Digest*, *National Geographic* and every recent issue of *Ravish*), stack of mystery novels and basket of knitting supplies away in her room. She changed the decor, Simon isn't sure when: all purples and yellows, a different dresser and new desk. There are letters from charities she's been working with that Simon doesn't know about, as well as framed pictures of people he doesn't recognize.

He still can't shake this feeling of disconnectedness from his mom and her life now, and from Benji and where they go from here. As if, by coming back here, he put his old skin back on—lonely and never belonging—and it doesn't quite fit anymore. It's not him, but he doesn't know how to shed it again.

Simon makes a pitcher of iced tea and puts a red-checked tablecloth on the dining room table. He unearths the most random assortment of paper plates and cups possible: Christmas, birthday, *Congrats Grad,* and a few from a baby shower she must have thrown. Who had a baby?

"That store is amazing! Seriously, I love Florida."

Benji comes back wide-eyed and smelling musky-earthy like the outdoors. He helps Simon set up the food, then cracks open two beers and tips them together. "To Florida."

Simon just laughs.

Darryl drives a Prius, so they're still hanging out in the dining room when the door opens. Simon had been expecting a loud gas-guzzling truck. He rushes to the door to help, but his mom waves him off.

"I'm not an invalid."

"Actually, invalid can just be referring to someone weakened by illness or injury," Benji pipes up.

His mom smiles and gently lowers herself to the couch. She looks a little weak still. Tired, but better. "Benji, in the flesh. Let me see you."

Benji sits, angles his legs towards hers. He looks so gangly all folded up on the couch next to her. She smushes his cheeks, turns his face this way and that. "Oh, he is handsome. Can't really see those adorable freckles on the computer."

"Alright, Ma, he's not a specimen."

"It's okay," Benji says through squashed lips, cheeks going red under her hands.

"So pale, though. Both of you. You should really get out in the sun a little. Go to the beach."

"This may come as a shock to you, but in some places it's cold in the winter."

She purses her lips at Simon, releases Benji and looks kind of exhausted after the excitement of coming home and shrewdly assessing Simon's boyfriend.

"I'll get you a blanket and something to drink," Darryl says. Simon has to admit, he's very attentive.

A steady stream of visitors starts soon, and the house slowly fills with flowers and balloons and cards. Casseroles and jello salads cram the fridge and freezer. Work friends. Neighbors. People she volunteers with, people she's helped, people Simon can't even remotely place, but who seem to adore his mom.

He catches Benji from across the room here and there, mostly focused on keeping the food stocked, opening the door and chatting. Benji always seeks him out with a smile and clear eyes, just for Simon, and the too-tight old skin itches and tugs uncomfortably.

"This is Laverne. She runs a local LGBTQ teen helpline that I've been working at." His mom's nibbling on carrots and patting the couch next to her for Simon to sit. "I was telling her that maybe you could put together some info on safe sex for the clients?"

"Absolutely, I'd love to. Let me know if I can do anything else. Sex education for gay kids is still sadly lacking in most places."

His mom nods and snorts. "Remember how I found you that book about sex? And then demonstrated putting a condom on a banana?"

"How could I possibly forget?" He was fourteen, with braces, short and scrawny. He had confirmed the day before that he was gay. It was mortifying. But if nothing else, it gave them an open dialogue, and he learned how to talk about sex without shame or fear.

"You're lucky to have her," Laverne points out.

"It's true, I am." Simon hugs her close with one arm. He's so lucky he still gets to have her.

"Have you boys been tested?" his mom asks, breaking the moment.

"Yes," Simon groans. "Jeez."

"And you know, I still have that book, just in case—"

"Okay, here's Benji. Why don't you traumatize him for a while, and I'll make more sweet tea?"

Benji looks afraid when he sits gingerly on the edge of the couch. Good. He should be. *Sorry,* Simon mouths, then makes his escape to the kitchen.

Where Darryl is.

"Good sub," Darryl says after a long awkward moment. Simon moves some grapes around and counts the number of cups left.

"New York has the most amazing food in the world and yet I still miss Publix party subs," Simon replies, finally popping a grape in his mouth after spending so much time fiddling with them. "Don't tell anyone. I'll lose my street cred."

Darryl doesn't laugh, but nods seriously.

"Um," Simon begins. "Listen, I'm really glad you're here for her. I haven't been around like I should have been, and I'm really grateful."

Darryl dips his head again. "She's a wonderful lady. I'm glad to do it."

Simon gives him a small smile, moves the half-empty iced tea pitcher closer to the cups, leaving a ring of condensation behind on the tablecloth. He's determined to make an effort to come home more, to ask her about her life and her friends more.

"She's really proud of you, you know. Talks about your fancy New York life all the time. She's happy." Darryl rests a strong hand on his shoulder, squeezes it and leaves the kitchen. Simon feels a little short of breath; his chest is tight and his throat is constricting. He pours a cup of tea and sneaks outside.

"Hey, you alright?"

Benji finds him at the clothesline stretched out at the back corner of the fence. His mom always claimed air drying was better for the fabrics, but Simon was convinced it was just to embarrass him by making him hang out his wet underwear to dry in the wide open. Not that anyone could see over the fence unless they were really motivated. But still. He hooks the line with his finger and tugs it down. Maybe she was right after all.

"Just needed some air. Starting to get a little claustrophobic in there."

"Yeah, I don't think I can chat about the weath—Shit." He smacks at his arm. Flails around and smacks at his neck and leg. Mosquitos.

Simon tries not to look too smug about it. "Welcome to Florida."

⚭ Chapter Thirty-One

It's dark by the time the last guests clear out and Darryl heads across the lawn to his own house. Simon's mom thanks everyone for their prayers and good thoughts. She should have been in bed hours ago. She makes a joke about sleeping when she's dead that is just entirely too close to the bone.

"Not funny," Simon grumps and Benji pretends his laughter is a coughing attack.

She lets him tuck her into bed and fuss over her a bit. He fluffs her pillow and tugs the blanket just right, kisses the top of her head. They chuckle at the role reversal.

At the sliding glass door, Benji eats from a little pink plate with a stork on it, piled with one of the many cheese-laden casseroles that have been stacked in the fridge.

"It is beautiful here at night, I have to admit."

Benji agrees and swallows. "I was thinking we should stay here until we eat all of this amazing food."

Simon steals a bite. "Enjoy it while you can, because I'm getting her a nutritionist right away, and I don't think any of those cheese and red meat monstrosities are going to survive the purge."

Benji takes another bite and looks away from the door. "She's lucky to have you."

Simon isn't too sure, but it's nice to hear anyway. "I try. I think I'm going to try a little harder."

Benji leans into him and it's like being on solid ground again.

"Hey, can we go swimming?"

"Didn't bring a suit. Did you?"

"No." Benji frowns. "I guess I wasn't really thinking about bathing suits with it being the planet of snow and ice at home."

"We could... go without." Simon's never done it, and maybe it's a terrible idea.

He takes the plunge first.

"How is it?" Benji fidgets at the edge, his towel still wrapped around his bare hips, toes curling over the edge.

"A little cold. Kind of weird." He kicks his feet, treading water in the deep end, enjoying the cool glide of it all over his naked body.

"You're sure nobody can see? And your mom is sleeping?"

"Yes," Simon assures him again, and says softer, "Probably."

"What about the mosquitos?"

"They aren't going to bother you in the water, Benji. Come on."

"Okay." He grips the towel, starts to slide it off, then pauses. "How's the shrinkage situation?"

"Benji, I already know how big your dick is. Just get in the damn water."

"All right." He drops the towel, and Simon lets out a low whistle. With just a yellow porch light and the slivered moon and the glow from the bottom of the pool, he can't tell if Benji is blushing.

He slips in with a soft splash. Droplets of water hit the dry cement and splash Simon where he waits in the middle. Benji swims over to Simon. He ducks under the water and emerges with his hair plastered down and eyelashes clumped together.

"Hey, this is fun."

"I've corrupted you in so many ways," Simon says, paddling closer so he can slide his arms over Benji's shoulders.

"Thank God," Benji replies, grabs Simon by the ass and hoists him up. Simon's legs wrap around his waist.

The water makes everything slow and muffled. His cock is pressed against Benji's abdomen, and Benji's is brushing along the underside of Simon's thighs, nudging up against his balls. There isn't enough friction, even though being together like this outdoors is thrilling.

They kiss, slow and soft and wet. Benji tastes a little like chlorine, and a little like ham and cheese casserole.

"Feeling better, now that she's home?"

"I guess."

They drift into the deeper end of the pool. He loves Benji's height advantage, especially when he backs them into the wall, and all Simon can do is cling to his wide, strong chest.

"It's weird. I feel out of place," Simon says as Benji drops cold-lipped little kisses to his cheeks, jaw and neck. "I had a good childhood, don't get me wrong. But I never felt like I fit here. Then I went to New York and thought *finally*. Finally I fit. I still didn't. I thought if I had the right job and lived in the right neighborhood and dated the right guy, I'd belong."

Benji pulls back, eyes sad and serious.

"But I was wrong again. Being back here it's like... I don't know who I am here."

Benji thinks, scrubs his hair back and shakes off droplets all around them. "I think maybe you shouldn't worry so much about figuring out who you are. Who says you have to only be this one person, right? *Do I contradict myself? Very well then I contradict myself. I am large, I contain multitudes.*"

"Did you just quote Whitman at me?"

Benji's answering grin is smug. "I think I did, yeah."

Simon drops his legs and glides in to press their bodies together. He kisses that grin off Benji's lips, their cocks pressing and slipping together now. There's a strange feeling of Benji hot and hardening against him while the cool water swirls around them.

"That morning, after Walt's chocolate disaster," Simon tells him in a whisper against the hinge of his jaw, "I woke up to you, all curled up with Walt and that was it. That was the first time I felt like I was right where I belonged."

"Simon…" Benji tries to pull him impossibly closer, fingers digging into his back.

"You're happy, right? You aren't just… going along with everything?"

Benji's eyebrows knit together so tightly a little divot creases between them. "Of course."

"Just making sure." Simon says, trying to be casual and flippant, but his thick voice gives him away.

"You're better at words than I am, and maybe I'm not great at telling you how I feel. But when I say I love you, it's because I mean it. And when I say I'm happy, it's because I am."

Suddenly, Simon doesn't want to talk anymore. He feels as free and calm as the gentle waves of the water.

Simon loses himself in kissing Benji and touching him. He moves his arms from Benji's shoulders to run down his chest, forgetting he's in the deep end and slipping down into the water.

Benji hauls him up and laughs. "Don't drown on me."

He coughs and clears the water from his face. Benji's eyes flash with an idea, and he hauls Simon up again, lifting him until he's sitting on the edge of the pool with water cascading down.

"Okay, that was really hot." Simon leans back on his hands, lets his knees drop to the side and his legs float easily in the water.

Benji licks his lips and glides between his knees.

He's only half-hard because of the chilly water, but that changes quickly, Benji reaches out of the pool to pump his cock a few times, then runs his lips along the underside of the crown.

Simon shivers.

"Are you cold?"

"No, it's just you."

Benji flutters his eyes closed and sucks the head into his mouth. He hums a little and presses his tongue into the slit. Simon watches him, drops his mouth open and huffs out a little *ha* when Benji sucks him down. The tight wet heat is all Simon can focus on, then the slick drag back up.

He bites down on moans and curses, trying to not alert the entire neighborhood, Pleasure floods his veins and makes his skin prickle with goosebumps. He looks up and spares a brief thought to the realization that his gorgeous boyfriend is blowing him in the pool where he grew up playing Marco Polo. What would younger Simon think? Hell, what would Simon from just a year ago think? And it's true, isn't it? How had he not realized? He's all of those people, and none of them, and what the hell does it even matter anyway?

He's here, Benji is here, and he's happy. That matters.

Benji increases his pace, takes him deeper and *Jesus fuck*, he's gotten good at this.

Simon buries his hand in Benji's wet hair to warn him, doesn't get much farther than that before everything pulls tight and snaps. Benji pulls up to the tip to swallow as Simon twitches against the rough cement underneath him.

He lolls his head back, lungs heaving, then slips back into the water once he can get his muscles and brain communicating again.

The pool water feels amazing against his overheated skin. "Up," he tells Benji.

Benji looks like sin spread out on the edge of the pool, alabaster skin luminescent in the dark.

"I'm happy to report that there has been no shrinkage," Simon announces, fist curling around Benji's cock. It juts, stiff from between his legs.

Benji smiles down at him, cups his cheek and says, "I love you."

Instead of answering, Simon ducks down and sucks Benji's cock into his mouth.

Spicing Up Your Sex Life Tip: Get in touch with your wild side, and do the deed outdoors!

Good idea or bad idea: Sex outdoors does present some logistical challenges like bugs, finding a secluded spot, risking sunburn, getting sand in unpleasant places or being poked with the wrong kind of stick. There is something thrilling, though, about giving in to some of your baser, more natural impulses while out in the wide open. Take some precautions. Think ahead, bring supplies and don't do anything illegal. (Despite what porn might have us believe, the cop isn't actually going to join in on the fun. It will just be mortifying.) Remember that condoms are more likely to slip off in water and keep the old adage in mind: Take only memories and leave only footprints. Clean up after yourselves, is what I'm saying. Good idea.

⌒⌒ Chapter Thirty-Two

Ask Eros: There's a Hair Down There!

Q: *I'm sixteen and ready to have sex for the first time. I'm on birth control, and we've had conversations about both of us wanting to do this together. But I am still so nervous. Like, what if he notices the weird stretch marks on my thighs? My body is not even close to being perfect. Will my soft stomach gross him out? Should I wax down there? Should I wax everywhere?*

A: *It's normal to be nervous your first time. Keep in mind that he's probably just as nervous as you are! Because you are very wisely having sex with someone you know and trust, what he's going to see when you're naked together is you, the person he loves. It's okay to start slow, maybe with just some soft candlelight, exploring each other under the covers. It doesn't have to be a wild night of naked debauchery if you aren't comfortable with that. The point is to feel good and connect and enjoy yourself in whatever way that means for you. And if a guy is grossed out by a woman's body having curves or hair, then he has not earned the honor of having sex with a woman. He already loves you, imperfections and all. He surely thinks you're beautiful and sexy and, when he sees you naked for the first time will be thinking something along the lines of: HOLY SHIT, I GET TO HAVE SEX!*

"That's where I used to watch the older boys skateboard." Simon nods toward the parking lot of a bait and tackle store, which has a dock in the back and a weathered table for gutting fish. He realizes that it's a little strange to have the rank smell of fish guts bring back childhood memories, but he had some good times in that parking lot.

"Ooh, skater boy phase. Interesting." They're holding hands, walking side by side behind his mom and Darryl on the narrow sand-dusted sidewalk.

"It was either that or the goth boys. If you wear a black trench coat when it's ninety-nine degrees outside, I have to question your mental stability."

"But they're so dark and mysterious," Benji teases, running his finger along an aloe plant growing on the corner of someone's beachfront yard. The place has a white picket fence with two bicycles propped against it and a manatee-shaped mailbox. The quaint yellow cottage boasts a wraparound porch complete with rocking chairs and lazily-rotating fan. Benji lingers for a moment, deems it *adorable* and jogs to catch up.

Simon takes his hand again. "I think I prefer sweet and bright to dark and mysterious."

"Right? I'm telling you, we should live here."

Simon rolls his eyes, and then they're at the public beach access, trudging through the blazing hot sand. It's quiet; a young mother with two toddlers, a group of women with wide brimmed hats. Their beach chairs are set in the shallows so the low tide can lap at their feet. A fisherman is off in the distance, and a sailboat bobs on the horizon.

Darryl sets up two folding chairs as Simon shakes out the towel draped around his shoulders. It catches the wind, twists and flaps around until Benji snags the other end and helps him lay it flat.

The water is too cold for his liking, so he sits on the towel with his legs bent and feet dug into the sand. He watches Benji stand in the waves up his knees as he tracks a boat for a while with both hands cupped over his eyes. He moves on and builds a lumpy, lopsided sand-castle that's almost immediately swallowed by a wave. He puts his hands on his hips and pouts until he spots a crab scuttling by and takes several pictures.

Benji takes pictures of the seagulls, even though Simon tries to explain that they're basically flying beach rats. He finds some spiral whelk shells and takes pictures of those. A picture of Darryl and his mom with their beach chairs pushed together. A picture of Simon.

"Send some to Tia," Simon requests. He hasn't had a chance to talk to her much; she'll be glad to see they're all doing just fine.

"Okay." Benji plops down on the towel, gets sand on about a third of it. Simon brushes it off while Benji messages Tia. Behind them, Simon's phone chirps.

Tia:	You're glowing.
Tia:	Did Benji get you pregnant?
Tia:	Did you run off to Florida to hide your shame?
Simon:	Hilarious.
Tia:	:D
Simon:	I'm just happy. Really happy.
Tia:	About time.
Simon:	Shush or I'll have Benji send a picture of every sea-shell on this beach.
Simon:	That's what he's doing right now btw.
Simon:	God I adore him.

When Benji finds a tide pool on the rocks nearby, he starts taking videos. Simon doesn't really think about much beyond the warmth of the sun on his skin, the comforting rush of the waves, the sand under his feet and the salty air in his lungs. Peaceful.

"Thank you for coming, sweetheart," his mom says, reaching down to ruffle his hair. "I'm sorry I gave you a scare. But I'm glad you're here."

"Me, too." Simon shades his eyes with his arm so he can look up at her. "I'm gonna try to be better about visiting more often." He glances over to where Benji is still recording his tide pool documentary, now with commentary. "I don't think it'll be hard to drag him back."

"Benji is a wonderful man. He's good for you."

"Yeah," Simon agrees, looks past her to Darryl, who offers Simon a stoic sort of smile in acknowledgment. "Yeah, he is."

They manage to book two seats on an early flight the next morning. His mom is up with them at the crack of dawn, making egg sandwiches and fresh orange juice. She swears she'll eat better, stress less and go to cardiac rehab. She hugs them both tightly and sends them out the door.

"My rental car looks like it could swallow your rental car whole," Simon remarks, heaving the trunk down with a slam that echoes through the sleepy subdivision.

"Yeah, I kind of felt like I was driving with my knees on the steering wheel." Benji scratches at some mosquito bites on his legs and neck and grimaces when he touches the sunburn there.

"I can't believe you jerked off in that thing."

"It was really awkward."

"You could have just told me you were here." Simon pulls open the door and fishes the key from his pocket.

"I didn't want to ruin the surprise! And then you said all that... stuff..."

"Stuff, huh?" Benji pulls a face, so Simon winks then slides into the stuffy, hot car. "See you at the airport, stud."

"Ugh, I hate Florida," Benji whines, about two hours later. It seems as if every business person in Palm Beach County is flying out this morning; they have an extra-long wait for baggage check and then a lengthier security screening for them both due to their last-minute ticket purchases.

Their gate is in the back corner of the airport, and, after their trudge through the entire busy terminal, the sky has turned dark. The rumbling thunder turns into a full-fledged tropical storm. Delayed flight. No word on when they'll be leaving.

So they wait. Benji scratches his bug bites and winces when his scorched skin touches the seat back. He's bright pink from his scalp to his shoulders, all the way down his back, on the tops of his arms, and across the bridge of his nose and his cheekbones.

"Aw sweetie, want me to see if I can find some aloe?"

Benji scratches and scrunches his nose and shifts around some more. "In the airport?"

"You aren't the first pasty white guy to come here and get sunburned," Simon points out.

The loudspeakers crack with an incoherent announcement, which Simon is somewhat positive is a weather update.

"Did you catch that?" Benji wiggles and sighs in his chair, stares in confusion at the ceiling.

"I think they said it's starting to pass. Hopefully we'll get out of here soon."

As long as they're still waiting, Simon figures he can catch up on some work stuff, let Daisy know he's coming back and everything is fine. He emails her and adds that he has an article rough draft written on his phone so they can get back on track with the series right away.

Benji has distracted himself from his misery with a game of *Plants vs. Zombies* on his phone.

"Andrew emailed me," Simon tells him, just now remembering.

"That guy does not give up." He pokes his tongue out and swipes furiously at his phone screen. "Just ignore him. He's trying to mess with your head."

"Ignoring him seems to make it worse," Simon points out.

"Strongly worded letter?" Benji offers.

"You know, I think I'll just call him."

He stands and hikes his bag onto his shoulder, then Benji's, too, since his shoulders are so sunburned. The corner by a huge window looking out at the planes is quiet, so Simon finds Andrew's blocked number and hits call.

It rings and rings, and the rain pours down. Benji stands across from him leaning against the rain-streaked window with his arms crossed, face drawn and stormy.

"Voice mail," Simon tells him.

This is Andrew Klaff. I regret that I'm unable to take your call. Please leave a message and I'll get back to you if I am able. Have a blessed day.

"Christ, I forgot how obnoxious his voicemail was." The line beeps, loud and abrasive. "Andrew, it's Simon. I got your email, and I thought that this was the best way to respond." He shifts his weight, watches the rain come down in sheets, howling wind and bursts of lightning.

"First of all, his name is Benji, and you know that. And I'll take some of the blame for this because I haven't been totally upfront with you either. But let me be completely clear now: You and I are not together in any way, shape, or form. We never were. I am no longer interested in being a dog at the end of your leash just hoping you'll give me a tug."

Benji grimaces and shakes his head.

"That sounded dirty. I didn't mean it that way. Please don't contact me again. I'm with someone that I genuinely care about, and I truly hope that someday you'll find that, too." But then, because he's needed to say it and has held back and taken the high road and been the better person so many times he adds, "By the way, you poisoned Walt with your pretentious chocolates."

He jabs the end call bar, and Benji says, "The end was a nice touch."

"It felt right."

The speakers crackle again. The storm is moving out, and they'll begin boarding soon,

"What do you say we come back in July?" Simon asks as they head to the line waiting to board. "They do this whole lame parade and street fair. It's sort of fun."

And for all his grumbling and current misery, Benji's face still lights up. "Sounds great."

"We have got to travel more. You are way too excited about this place."

He shrugs. "I like liking stuff."

"I know," Simon says, moving forward a little, both bags hitting the backs of his legs. "It's one of my favorite things about you."

"And my butt."

Simon laughs. "Well, of course."

Benji leans in close, as close as is doable in a crowded airport in Southern Florida. "You are my favorite everything."

Simon fights back a goofy grin and reaches into his bag to find the tickets. "See, now I know we have to get back to New York, because I didn't find that even remotely cheesy. I've lost all my cynicism."

They board the plane together, settle in side by side, and Simon doesn't feel impatient or annoyed or lost anymore. He feels as though he could fly without needing an airplane at all.

ᗣᗣ Chapter Thirty-Three

"Okay, just start."

"Um. It's... good?"

"Benji, seriously. You aren't even trying."

"I am so! I just—You're looking at me."

"I can't look at you? You realize you have your fingers in my ass at this very moment and *I* can't look at *you*?"

"I feel like I'm giving a speech or something!"

Simon pushes himself off Benji's chest, one leg hitched over his hips. Benji's fingers slip free. Simon sprawls on his back, turning his head to look out the window.

Outside, the sky is blue and clear and hints of winter finally coming to end. The birds are back in the trees that line their streets. Walt recently tried to befriend a goose who had a nest nearby at the park and nearly got them both maimed. Peggy is shedding, and the days are a little longer, a little warmer.

"I can just do it, if you're uncomfortable. I don't mind."

Benji pushes up on one elbow. "I know. You're really good at dirty talk. That's why I wanted to do it. I feel awkward is all."

"You kind of have to barrel on through the awkwardness. That's the secret." Simon pats Benji's bare thigh, bent at an angle so his knee is against Simon's hip. "Hey, I have an idea."

Simon sits up to a kneel, and, instead of the usual, uses Benji's thigh for leverage. He positions himself over Benji's hips but facing his feet, his back to Benji still lying prone on the bed. His legs stretch and flex, giving Simon a fantastic view of his lean, strong muscles.

"Oh, shit," Benji breathes.

"See, better already." Simon reaches for the bottle of lube, squirts some out to slick Benji up.

"That wasn't uh—" Simon's fist pumps him a few times, holds the base. "Wasn't dirty talk. Just an involuntary expletive."

"So, use that. Just say what you're thinking and don't hold back."

Simon raises higher and flushes a little at the view Benji is getting right now, but takes his own advice and just moves on through the awkwardness.

Benji is quiet and then says, "I think that there's a term for sudden expletive. Coprolalia."

"Mmm, yeah, talk vocabulary to me baby." Simon breathes in, presses the blunt tip of Benji's cock just right and sinks down slowly, thighs burning with the effort.

"Love how you feel inside me. So big," Simon moans out, getting the ball rolling. Benji grips onto his ass and he bottoms out, full, tipped forward with his hand on Benji's legs where the muscle is thickest. He lets his head drop and grinds his ass down in little circles.

He's seen Benji naked plenty of times, but never with this vantage point. He notes, for just a moment before starting to lift up again, that Benji's thighs are kind of hairy.

He drops back down, starts a slow rhythm, scratches his fingers through the thick, reddish fuzz and grins to himself.

Benji curses again, makes an aborted sort of squeaking noise, then, "You look amazing right now."

"Yeah?" Simon's voice already breathy. Riding is always more work than he remembers it being. But, as a reward and encouragement, he speeds up.

"Watching you. Uh. Watching you..." His fingers twitch on Simon's skin and he swallows audibly. Simon rises and falls, rises and falls, waiting for him to struggle through. "Watching you take it."

Simon lifts up, slams back down and Benji cries out. "Make me. Make me take it." He pitches forward again, giving Benji space to fuck up into him, holding onto Benji's knees as his legs bend and his hips move.

"You're so—" Hard smack of flesh on flesh. Simon is jolted, holds tighter to Benji's knees as he pistons up into him. Everything's getting hot and slippery now. "The first time I saw you, I thought you were so fucking hot. I couldn't stop thinking about you, needed to see you," Benji grits out, the words loosened like a stopper now so Simon meets him, thrust for thrust, doesn't touch himself yet even though beaded drops of sticky pre-come are leaking steadily from his aching cock.

"I fantasized about you," Benji admits on a whisper, like he's not sure how Simon will react.

"Did you think about this? About fucking me just like this?" Simon manages, Benji close, frantic now.

"Yes."

"Did you think about coming inside me? Marking my skin? Making me yours?"

"Yes. I thought about you bent over your desk. How you'd look under me with your wrists pinned down. I thought about your mouth on my cock and mine on yours and I—Oh fuck, oh God, yes." He plants his feet, snaps his hips up one last time and stays there as his cock throbs so hard Simon feels it in his belly.

He is in immediate danger of sliding right off Benji's lap, pushed up high and off to one side and barely managing to cling to his legs. Benji releases a gust of air, falls slack to the bed and his softening cock slips free.

Simon jerks himself, wishes he wasn't just looking at Benji's legs and feet but, oh well, he'll make do. Then two fingers slip inside where he's open and wet, an easy glide through the lube and still warm come and it's a filthy mess. Benji crooks them just right, and it feels amazing.

Then he's coming, streaks shooting across Benji's thighs and knees and the bedspread between.

He lists off to the side, head at the footboard and feet on his pillow.

"How was that?" Benji says to his toes.

"Very good." Simon wipes his hand on his stomach. "You should apply to Toastmasters, you'd be a shoo-in."

He sits up. He needs a shower now, and they should probably go grocery shopping. Then he needs to call his mom and confirm with Tia that they'll be at her dinner party, and the cat will not stop meowing at the door. Simon shakes out his wobbly limbs and asks, "Did you tell the super about the water heater?"

Benji's eyes are closed, mouth lax and arms and legs flung out to the side, starfish style. "Yep."

"Dibs on the shower."

"Mmkay."

"Hey." Simon pokes at his side and his eyes open to slits. "Did you mean it? You wanted me like that?"

He pulls Simon's hand over, spreads it flat on his abdomen and traces the fourth finger on his hand with a barely there touch. "I wanted you from the moment I saw you."

Spicing Up Your Sex Life Tip: *Talk dirty to your man to really get his motor revving!*

Good idea or bad idea: I personally don't have a problem with the quieter in bed types. In fact, I've found that those are the ones who often surprise you with their enthusiasm and dedication to a job well done. Sometimes it's best not to rock the boat when earth-shattering orgasms are involved. But. It can be nice to hear exactly what your partner is thinking; the filthy, debauched things that zap across their brains in the throes of passion. Just be aware that you may learn things you were happier not knowing. But you may also discover that your partner has things on his mind that you never expected. Good idea.

◯◯ Chapter Thirty-Four

Spring hits warm and vibrant; the city blooms with colors and life everywhere Simon looks. His series is a hit, and the advice column still gets so many messages he can't keep up with them. Tia saves the ones that aren't questions, but *thank-yous*. The ones he used to breeze past because he just writes a silly advice column; he's not anyone important.

He gets it now, how just reaching out and offering empathy and kindness and caring makes a difference. How he doesn't have to be anyone but himself to matter. How a gentle heart can go a long way.

They have one last installment to do before bringing the series to a close, and it's around then that Benji starts to get cagey.

One evening, Simon is going through messages in his home office, editing an article here and there while talking on the phone with Tia. He's trying to talk her into convincing Daisy to be more inclusive with a new series, *What Men Really Want,* that she's asked him to write for the print magazine.

"I'm just saying, how many articles do we need about straight men wanting women who wear tight clothes that show off their bodies, but looser clothes because they should leave something to the imagination, Or how they should wear makeup because it shows they care, only don't wear makeup because it looks like they're trying too hard?"

Tia laughs in agreement, as Simon takes the phone with him to the kitchen to grab an apple. Benji is at the kitchen table, laptop open, Peggy winding back and forth under his hand and purring loudly.

"I'll try," Tia says. She'll call back and let him know. When Simon reaches over Benji to the bowl of fruit in the middle of the table, Benji jumps and slams his laptop closed.

"Nothing!" he replies, to a question that Simon never asked.

"All right..."

He takes his apple and gets back to work, but he can't help straining to hear when Benji starts to talk to whomever he had been on Skype with.

"I know but," he's saying and then, "I just don't think that we can get more time off, we both already took a week in July."

Then Benji just listens for a while, offering a *yeah* and *that's true* and *okay*. Simon can't tell who he's talking to or what they're saying, so he focuses on finishing his tasks. He really shouldn't be working from home in the evenings so much anyway.

Benji is many things: sweet, genuine, open, honest. All of those are wonderful, of course, but also add up to him being a terrible, terrible liar.

"Who was that?" Simon asks, tossing his apple core in the trash.

"It was, um—" His eyes shift, his jaw works, then he looks at Peggy. "The vet."

"The vet called you over Skype?"

Shifty eyed again. "Yes?"

"Mmhmm."

He lets it go, mostly because Tia calls back and tells him Daisy wants a pitch ASAP. He trudges back to the office down the hall with a sigh.

That weekend, Simon is exhausted, mentally drained and just wants to sit on the couch and watch cheesy sitcoms. He can't even enjoy *Boy Meets World* because Benji is so wound with nervous energy.

"Got a hot date?" Simon asks as Benji hops from foot to foot by the window.

"What? No. No. What?"

"Honey, I'm kidding. What is your deal right now?"

Benji stares out the window, up at the sky, then down at his phone. Bites his lip and worries it between his teeth. "It wasn't supposed to rain. But it looks like rain."

"Why can't it rain? Did you plan a romantic picnic or something?"

Benji's face goes extra pale, and his eyes pop wide. "A picnic? Yeah, yep. Just a picnic and nothing else. Excuse me for sec."

He rushes off, making a phone call and closing the bedroom door behind him. Simon isn't stupid. He knows something is up. He just doesn't have the brainpower to deal with it right now. He trusts Benji, so whatever he's cooking up, Simon decides he'll just leave him to it.

"Ah, Shawn Hunter. I have to you to thank for my sexual awakening. The things that *Tiger Beat* magazine saw..." Walt adjusts his position on the couch, looking at Simon with a sigh and a groan. "What? Don't judge me."

The following Saturday is the trip to the Museum of Natural History that Benji insists on, even though Simon is really not in the mood for dinosaurs. He doesn't care how much Benji argues otherwise, sometimes a guy just isn't in the mood for dinosaurs.

Benji practically drags him at a run from the subway station to the train and then all the way to Central Park West and Seventy Ninth.

They can't even get in the door, it's so packed. They wait in line outside, Benji with his hand jammed into one pocket, looking more frustrated than Simon has ever seen him. It's kind of sexy.

"Did the entirety of Germany decide to fly in and visit the American Museum of Natural History at the same time today? What the hell?" Benji spits out.

The family in front of them turns around, gives them both dirty looks and mutters something in German that doesn't sound very nice at all.

"Let's come back another day. Weekday mornings are quieter and we can play hooky from work."

"But—"

"Let's go home. I'll make it worth your while." He tickles his fingers on the small of Benji's back, makes the face that Benji can't resist for some inexplicable reason.

"Okay," Benji agrees. though it's with much less enthusiasm than Simon would prefer. He tries not to take offense. He's being *so weird.*

They don't get a chance to go back to the museum. Benji mopes about it for several days. Simon has some concerns that the dinosaur fixation may be getting a little over the top.

The weekend after that one, they decide they deserve to let loose a bit. Both of them have been working too hard, so they meet Tia at Bloody Mary's. Benji insists on taking a cab both ways, though Simon doesn't think they'll be getting that drunk. Benji tells the cab driver to take them through Times Square of all godforsaken places. The traffic is so horrific that the driver curses the whole time, and they crawl through at a snail's pace, nearly plowing down a group of tourists. Benji checks the time on his phone every five seconds.

The cabbie sees a break in traffic, guns it and breaks free. Simon sighs, "Thank God." Benji moans, head in hands, "*Oh no.*"

"What's wrong?"

"Uh." Head whipping up, blinking at Simon in the dark. "My aunt. It's her birthday. I... forgot."

"We can send her flowers right now. There's even an app." He rubs his back. Poor thing really does need to relax a bit. "No biggie, right?"

"Right," Benji says, but doesn't look like he believes it at all.

When they get to the bar, Tia rushes them, pulling Simon into a tight squeeze and makes a high-pitched cooing sound in his ear. Benji does a motion just over his shoulder, and Tia freezes, releasing him with a fake laugh.

"It's been so long!" she says, patting at his shoulders.

"I saw you four hours ago."

She pulls the collar of his shirt down and tuts, "Well it feels longer. What was that? Coming, James!"

She runs off, even though James is not anywhere in sight. She must already be hitting the cosmos hard.

The Monday after that strange night is the quarterly planning meeting at the magazine, nothing too exciting. Simon doodles on the handout, yawns, draws a little picture of a penis, and shows it to Tia.

She punches him on the arm. *Ow* he writes, with a little sad face cartoon. She snatches his paper and turns the penis into a rocket ship. The *US Pocket Rocket II.* He snorts as Daisy sends them both a glare.

After the meeting, he catches Daisy to work out some details about the newly titled *What Your Lover Really Wants.*

"Did you want to be more like *Spicing Up Your Sex Life* or like the *Good Sex* series because—"

"This can probably wait," Tia interrupts, tugging at Simon's arm.

"Not if I want to get started." Simon yanks his arm free. "What is your problem?"

"I wanted to get coffee," she says, code for *I have juicy gossip.*

"Give me five minutes."

But five turns into ten which turns into twenty. Daisy wants to expand the idea, maybe make it ongoing. She brings some other writers into the discussion, and despite Tia's numerous sighs and looks of irritation, forty-five minutes pass.

They go down to the coffee stand in the lobby. The line is slow because almost everyone in the building is on the last few minutes of their lunch break. Simon orders a cappuccino and a toasted bagel, extra toasty. Tia looks as if she's going to blow steam from her ears.

"You should eat something," he tells her. Her nostrils flare, and she stares up at the ceiling for a very long time.

"You are so lucky I love you both."

Simon's order is called before he can ask what the hell she's talking about. They get back upstairs, round the corner to Simon's desk, and he can see something has been placed inside. Huge bouquets of roses are all over the desk, the floor and the computer.

"Oh my God."

"Surprise," Tia says, voice flat with sarcasm. "Benji wanted you here on his lunch break but..." She lifts both hands, palms up. "We missed him."

"Oh, you should have said. Is this for the anniversary of when we met? Is that what he's been up to?"

Tia growls, spins on her heel and says something about being through with the both of them. She does not have time for this shit. Simon shrugs it off and smells his beautiful flowers.

Simon:	You are so getting laid tonight.
Simon:	And Tia told me.
Benji:	WHAT
Simon:	For our one year meeting each other anniversary.
Benji:	I
Benji:	Yes.

"Do you want to go to a baseball game this weekend?" Benji asks. They're at home in bed, both of them sticky and spent and still catching their breath.

"Like with your dad?"

"No, just us."

"Uh. If you want. Since when you do you go to baseball games unless it's a bonding thing with your dad and brothers?" Simon scratches his hand through the coarse hair low on Benji's stomach.

"I don't. It was stupid. Never mind."

Simon tilts his head. "You sure?"

Benji pulls him down by the back of the neck for kiss. "Yeah, I'm sure."

He asks how Simon feels about hot air ballooning one night over dinner. Then, if the top of the Empire State Building is romantic or clichéd or possibly both.

"What are your feelings on flash mobs?" Benji asks one night when his toothbrush is hanging out of his mouth and Simon's face is covered in foaming face wash.

"Con," Simon tells him, ducks into the sink and rinses before Benji has to spit.

> **To:** Simon Beck
> **From:** Tia Robinson
> **Subject:** This week's advice column
> I know you usually pick these yourself, but I want you to run this one. Gird your loins, it's a doozy.
> XOXO Tia

Simon scrolls down, confused, then stunned and then so beyond thrilled that he can't seem to make his fingers work on the keyboard. He's shaking and reading the screen through blurry vision while his heart pounds in his chest. He manages to make it through, then takes off for the IT office so fast that he flings his chair into the desk behind him with a crash.

Ask Eros: Happy Endings

Q: *I've been trying to ask my boyfriend to marry me for about a month now, and it seems like the universe is conspiring against me. It just keeps going to crap despite very careful planning and scheming. But then I realized: maybe I'm trying too hard. After all, falling in love with him was simple. As easy as the sunrise. He told me that. He said he wanted be a poet once upon a time. I think he still is. So, instead of trying to ask him to spend his life with me while a One Direction cover band serenades him at the duck pond where we had hot dogs, or at the museum where I looked at him under a blue whale and imagined our forever, or at the beach in Florida where he looked so beautiful even the sun couldn't compare. Or at his desk, the place that I first saw that he was even more amazing in person. Instead of a billboard in Times Square or a hot air balloon ride or a flash mob or the Jumbotron at a baseball game, I decided to ask in the very first place I connected with him, an advice column in a women's magazine. Reading it, I felt like someone* *was finally listening. that someone was telling me that I deserved a happy ending too. Though I didn't know then that he'd become my best friend and my partner and my love, I felt a connection and I felt cared for. I want, more than anything, to have that every single moment for the rest of my life. Simon, you are the most amazing man I have ever met. You challenge me, you make me better. I love you with all my heart. Will you marry me?*

A: *Yes.*

⬭⬭ Chapter Thirty-Five

(8:00 am)

Simon: Hi, husband.

Benji: Hi, husband.

Simon: What are you wearing?

Benji: You know what I'm wearing. You're sitting next to me. You picked this outfit out.

Simon: I acted as a consultant.

Benji: You say consult, I say harangue.

Simon: Excuse me for liking you in that blue shirt.

Benji: Because it made you want to jump my bones the first time you saw me in it.

Benji: Or my bone...

Simon: Obviously.

Simon: Speaking of bones.

Simon: Can you pick up a new rawhide for Walt? And canned cat food?

Benji: Again, sitting right next to you.

Simon: This isn't very sexy.

Simon: I think we're doing this wrong.

(8:30 am)

Benji: Come here often?

Simon: To our kitchen? Yeah, pretty often.
Benji: I'd like to see you come often.
Simon: Still no.

(10:00 am)
Simon: Ok, gonna try sending a naughty pic.
Benji: !
Benji: That is a peach.
Simon: It reminded me of your ass.
Benji: If you say because of the fuzz, I swear I will go get a full body wax right now.
Simon: No!
Simon: Because it's round
Simon: and succulent
Simon: and I want to bite it.
Benji: Okay maybe we're starting to get the hang of this.

(12:30 pm)
Benji: What is your favorite body part of mine?
Simon: Is this a trick question?
Benji: I mean. Besides the obvious.
Simon: Your eyes.
Simon: Especially the way they look when you're sucking me off.

(12:40 pm)
Simon: Too much?
Benji: No. Just.
Benji: Maybe a little much when I'm waiting in line at the deli.
Benji: We should probably find a new deli.

(3:00 pm)
Simon: Benji!

Benji: What? I'm sexting. Do you want me to sext or not?
Benji: You don't like it :(
Simon: Of course I like it.
Simon: But maybe warn a guy before you send pictures of your junk.
Simon: The subway is crowded.
Simon: I think the elderly woman next to me saw.
Benji: Oh. Crap.
Simon: Well at least she looks happy about it.
Benji: I'm not so sure that makes it better.
Simon: And... she gave me a thumb's up.
Benji: Threesome?
Simon: Sexting is the worst idea I've ever had.

(4:00 pm)
Benji: How is your meeting going?
Simon: Terrible. You would think that no one could talk about dental dams for an entire hour, but you would be wrong.
Benji: Well... I'm scrubbing the grout in the bathroom.
Benji: On my hands and knees.
Benji: And it's really hot, so I'm just wearing those athletic shorts.
Benji: You know the ones.
Simon: God you make scrubbing grout sound sexy.
Benji: When is scrubbing grout *not* sexy?

The ride home had been near torture, crowded, hot and sticky, and that was without factoring in the sexual frustration. Benji, all sweaty in those shorts that hang off his hips just right. Benji waiting for him, teasing him. He'd had to keep pressing his rapidly warming bottle of water to his neck and temples in an effort to stave off the hot throb of want.

"Benji?" He closes the door, immediately losing his shirt, dumping his wallet and phone and keys on the table. He listens for Benji's response over the whoosh of the huge box fan in the living room and the cacophony of noise outside from the open windows.

He follows the sound of music playing, the enthusiastic last few verses of "Maybe I'm Amazed" with Paul McCartney's signature *ohs* and *oohs* and *yeahs* crooning over a fading electric guitar solo.

"In a Wings mood, eh?"

"Hey! You're back!" Benji grins at him through the fogged up mirror, towel cinched low around his waist. He dries his hair, scrubs on deodorant and crosses the bathroom to kiss Simon's cheek. "I tried to stay in my sexy shorts for you, but I got kind of gross."

"It's okay." Simon slips a finger under the towel. "I'm gonna shower too. Wait for me?"

As he washes the sweat and grime from his skin, Simon's irritation from the meeting and the commute drift away under the cool stream of water.

They've both been so busy: IT is updating the entire system and format for the online magazine; Simon works all day and then locks himself in the office and writes late into the evenings. He'd really been looking forward to doing this last installment of his *Spice* series together, but with work picking up so much for both of them, they've barely even had time to talk.

Though he does have to admit that the sexting was fun. Not that it worked entirely as it was supposed to; titillating each other all day long, was more frustrating than exciting. But it's nice having that connection throughout the day, something more than *pick up a gallon of milk* or *what the hell is the wifi password again?*

It's domestic without being boring.

He pulls on a light cotton shirt and soft linen shorts and pads barefoot to the living room. The rapidly circulating air raises bumps on his cooled skin. Benji is now dressed in jeans and a Loch Ness Monster T-shirt, perched on the counter and eating a banana. Simon smirks and saunters over.

"Is that a banana in your mouth, or are you just happy to see me?"

Benji waggles his eyebrows and takes a bite.

"Hey, since this is our last hurrah for the *Spicing Up Your Sex Life* article, we should make it good. Give everyone something really hot." Simon leans over the counter on his elbows to move closer, but Benji hops down.

"I guess," he says, throwing his banana peel away and standing with his back turned to Simon.

"And then," Simon continues, reaching for his phone and opening up a new note on the app, "I thought you and I could do something for the *What Your Lover Really Wants* series. I think we could really—"

"No."

"—add something with our experiences." Simon looks up from his phone. "Wait, did you say *no*?"

"Yes. No. I said no, yes." Benji sighs and walks out of the kitchen.

"What did Brandon say to you? Is he teasing you again?" Simon calls before following him to the living room.

"Nothing." Benji spins around. "Don't make this about me and my insecurities." His ears are turning red and his eyes narrow.

"Then what is it about?" Simon replies, wishing his voice didn't sound as clipped and annoyed as it does. "Please enlighten me."

"This is about you agreeing we would be done sharing our most intimate moments. This is about your need to be validated by strangers," Benji says, and his voice wavers a little but he pushes on. "This is about me just wanting something that's only for us."

Simon swallows down a variety of sarcastic and defensive replies, takes a minute to *hear* Benji instead of just trying to gloss over the problem or shove it back at him.

"Okay," Simon starts, moving a little closer. "Maybe I do like when people see me as some kind of sex genius. I mean, who wouldn't?" Benji smiles a little. "But you know those articles were never about proving our relationship, right? You know I'm in this for real?"

"Honestly, Simon." Benji gives a defeated little shrug. "Sometimes I don't."

"Well, I am. You are my anchor. My lighthouse in the stormy waves. The gentle guiding current to my ship adrift at sea. The—" Simon snaps his fingers a few times. "Help me out with more ocean metaphors."

"I think you've got it covered." Benji's posture shifts as he relaxes into Simon's space.

Simon squints one eye. "No but... Something about fish in the sea. Hmm, trout in the sea?"

"Trout are freshwater fish," Benji huffs.

Simon reaches for Benji, winds his arms low on his waist, looks down and says, "I love you so much."

He wants to make sure that he never takes Benji for granted, and not just today, with the texts and pictures and Benji's worries. But every day. Just because they're married now, just because they promised forever, doesn't mean he can coast on the idea of happily ever after. It's easy to forget how a promise made is still not a guarantee. People leave, people change. He never wants Benji to doubt just how much he means to him.

"Are you saying *I love you* to me or my dick?"

"*Benji*." Simon tugs him closer and looks up with narrowed eyes.

"Alright, okay. I know. I do." He leans down for a kiss and Simon is happy to oblige him.

"So," Simon pulls away and kisses across his jaw and down his throat. "What does my lover really want?"

Benji wriggles out of Simon's arms and he steps away. "I really want there to be no more articles. No more public discussions of our sex life."

"None?"

"Nope."

"Not even a little?" Simon wheedles.

"Not even a little." He heads to the hall closet. "I'm gonna walk the dog."

Simon slumps dramatically down onto the couch. "Ugh, fine."

"You know what?" Benji opens the closet and ducks inside. "Every once in a while is okay. Like if you want to talk about the rave reviews my junk got on the train, I won't stand in your way."

He emerges with the leash and a bright grin and more eyebrow waggling. Simon laughs. "Deal."

Benji calls for Walt and gets the leash hooked. "And you know what I really, really want? Boring married people sex. Like, in the dark. Under the covers. And then we just—" He unlocks the door and makes Walt sit and wait. "Roll over and go to sleep and don't talk about it with friends or coworkers or family or strangers at all."

"Okay, okay," Simon says.

Benji opens the door. "Or maybe no sex. Maybe we could just do a puzzle."

"Now you're talking crazy," Simon tells him, sitting up as Benji and Walt leave. "I have my limits!"

Simon sprawls on the couch for a while, hands folded on his stomach and smiling to himself. Peggy walks across his chest for some ear scratches, then hops onto the back of the couch when he gets up.

Simon:	Of course you bought a 3-D glow in the dark dinosaur puzzle.
Benji:	Oh good choice!
Simon:	Nerd.
Benji:	You're excited don't lie.
Simon:	Maybe. But only because we're doing this just for us.
Simon:	And no one will ever know.

He takes the puzzle to the kitchen table and dumps out the pieces, busying himself with arranging them in neat rows while he waits for Benji. The apartment is quiet and calm now and Simon hums to himself. He could get used to boring married life. As long as it's with Benji.

Simon:	Where are you? I'm ready.
Benji:	Right around the corner.

* * *

Spicing Up Your Sex Life Tip: *Send your partner sexy texts throughout the day to make sure they know just how much you desire them!*

Good idea or bad idea: Good idea. In fact, take as many opportunities to tell your partner how much you want them. How you can't stop thinking about them. And if you've been together for a while and assume that they already know, you especially should. This whole column has been about connecting, opening yourself up and finding ways to spice up the mundane. But don't forget why you were in that rut in the first place: Because sharing your life with someone means sharing everything: the good, the bad, the thrilling and the monotonous. Some days will mean paying bills and picking up prescriptions. Some days will mean handcuffs and blindfolds and riding crops. (Wait, did we not get to that one? Just use your imagination.) But the sum total of all of that is a relationship. And if you don't find it with whipped cream or morning sex or bondage, or in exhibitionism or voyeurism or sexting, then keep looking. Find your own spice. Find joy. Never settle for just good enough. For Ravish *magazine, I'm Simon Beck encouraging you to be safe, be sensible, and most importantly: Enjoy all your happy endings.*

THE END

Acknowledgments

I'd like to thank the Interlude Press team for their dedication, encouragement and unwavering support, with an extra shout out to Annie for her belief in this story and my ability to tell it.

To my parents, who not only read my romance novels, but enthusiastically and proudly recommend them to their friends and acquaintances. You always knew I could do this, and it turns out you were right. As usual. To my mother-in-law Anne, for helping me a take once-in-a-lifetime opportunity, and to all three of you for the gentle nudge and quiet assurance that I am capable of more than I think.

I'd like to thank Allyn for her excitement and enthusiasm and for being the kind of best friend who always has my back.

To my sisters for always being around, always. To Candy, thanks for the hand-me-downs. To Kait, sorry about the hand-me-downs. I'm so glad we have each other. And Justin, too. He's cool.

For everyone in my life that I neglected while I wrote this, thanks for your patience and understanding. (Most of the time.)

To the fandom that started this journey, thank you again. I will never forget the immense gift that community has been to me. Wherever we go from here, I'll always carry you in my heart.

And finally, to Joshua, thanks for all the happy endings. ❧

About the Author

Lilah Suzanne has been writing actively since the sixth grade, when a literary magazine published her essay about an uncle who lost his life to AIDS. A freelance writer, she has also authored a children's book and has a devoted following in the fan fiction community.

Her novella, *Pivot and Slip,* was published in 2014 by Interlude Press. ✯

Questions for Discussion

1. Simon writes a romance advice column, yet his own love life is in a shambles. How can someone who is bad at relationships be good at giving relationship advice to others?

2. Why is Simon interested in Andrew? Does he match up with Simon's "list" of character traits for the perfect partner, and if so, has he created a barrier between idealized love and real life?

3. Why doesn't Simon pursue Benji right away?

4. What about going home causes Simon to reevaluate his approach to relationships?

5. How does writing about his relationship with Benji interfere with Simon's ability to achieve true intimacy with him? Can Simon have a relationship that doesn't become part of his column?

6. Why doesn't Benji give up on Simon?

7. Benji ultimately proposes via Simon's column. What are your thoughts on public versus private marriage proposals? Does it matter? ❧

Broken Records

by lilah suzanne

LA stylist Nico Takahashi loves his job—or at least, he used to. Fed up and exhausted from the cutthroat, gossip-fueled business of Hollywood, Nico daydreams about packing it all in and leaving for good. So when Grady Dawson, sexy country music star and rumored playboy, asks Nico to style him, Nico is reluctant. But after styling a career-changing photo shoot, Nico follows Grady to Nashville where he finds it increasingly difficult to resist Grady's charms. Can Nico make his peace with show business and all its trappings, or will Grady's public persona get in their way of their private attraction to each other? And can Nico's time in the South change his perspective on life and love and what really matters?

Chapter One

This is rock bottom. It has to be. Nico clings to the last tiny thread of hope that this is rock bottom, because if he sinks any lower than being elbow deep in the plunging neckline of the red bandage dress—carefully considered and procured and the fourth outfit of the night for one Hailey Banks, former child star and current trashy tabloid star—then he's packing it in and leaving LA for an off-grid eco-shack in Montana or Wyoming or South Dakota. One of those square-shaped states. He's not picky.

Hunched and contorted in the backseat of a BMW X4 that's parked in an alleyway behind a club in West Hollywood at four a.m., Nico grunts and struggles with the silicone pads and tape, lifting Hailey's perky A-cup breasts and mashing them together to give the illusion they've magically become bounteous C-cups.

"Lean over," Nico hisses, struggling with the left breast that stubbornly refuses to rise over the line of the bodice evenly with the right breast to become a perilous attempt at cleavage.

He had once imagined helping Hollywood's elite look and feel their best—stepping out onto the red carpet at The Oscars or Golden Globes with the sort of joy that comes from knowing, deep in their souls, that this who they are, this is what they want to the world to see.

What Hailey Banks—once the adorable chubby-cheeked tot who starred in movies and her own TV show, once the angel-faced, squeaky-voiced It Girl of Hollywood and every talk show's go-to guest for a sure dose of adorable and sweet and sky-high ratings—wants the world to see is apparently her nipples.

"More," she says, bending lower to strap on her black and red suede platform six-inch stilettos, making Nico bend with her and nearly topple from the seat and onto the floorboards. She narrowly avoids Nico's crotch as she kicks one foot out. "Ugh, I hate these shoes."

"The shoes you made me fly to New York to find and all but get down on my hands and knees and beg for? The shoes by an elusive designer who seems to think they should only be worn by Brazilian supermodels and the ghost of Jackie Kennedy Onassis? Those shoes?"

Nico hauls himself back up onto the seat and finally hikes her stubborn left boob up evenly. The dress is tiny, and her pale skin is garish in the flickering light of the alleyway.

"Yeah, I dunno. They're pointy and shit," she rasps, lighting another cigarette and making no effort to direct the smoke toward the open window and not Nico's face.

He coughs and waves the smoke away. "There, that's as good as you're going to get."

Hailey takes a drag and says with smoke drifting from her mouth, "It's beyond time for me to get a boob job."

Styling Hailey may be a nonstop nightmare for Nico, but it's his job to look past the bratty, out-of-control behavior and figure out how to make the person beneath shine. And if she ignores him, well, it's not as if Hailey Banks has been listening to any sound advice since she was twelve and throwing diva fits over the wrong brand of bottled water.

"Look, they're your uncooperative breasts, so do whatever the hell you want, but I've told you before we have so many options with the shape you have now. Look at Kate Moss. Look at Twiggy. Audrey Hepburn!"

Nico fixes some stray hairs that have come loose from her top knot; a red carpet premiere and an after party and an after-after party have taken it from *carefully disheveled* to *just woke up on the floor of a public bathroom after a bender.*

He would know, because he's seen Hailey rock that exact look on the front cover of *CelebWow* magazine and every gossip site on the World Wide Web.

She waves him off, takes one final long drag from her cigarette and flicks it carelessly into a cup holder. Nico sighs and drops it into a half-empty (Italian-imported-sparkling-natural-mineral) water bottle instead. Hailey sends a text on her phone; the sunken contours of her face are illuminated. She looks forty-five instead of nineteen, her once cherubic features are hardened and sharp and world-weary.

"Wish me luck." She winks, and when she cracks the door open just a scant inch, there's a blinding barrage of flashing lights and voices shouting her name. She turns away from Nico, making her mini-dress even more mini and—

"Hailey, we fucking talked about the underwear." Nico groans.

Hailey pushes the door open the rest of the way, which initiates shouts and flashes and bodies shoving against the car so hard it rocks from side to side. "If I'm gonna give them a show, may as well go all in."

She steps out and closes the door, and the cacophony of light and sound goes with her, leaving Nico in a dark alleyway all by himself, climbing into the driver's seat so he can park the car somewhere safe and legal, and then figure out how to get back to his own car parked across town at Hailey's first event. That shack in Montana is starting to look better and better.

When he finally gets home, Nico collapses onto his bed, doesn't even bother to brush his teeth or take his shoes off, and still smells like cigarettes and booze and that god-awful perfume Hailey uses to cover up the stench of cigarettes and booze. He's so exhausted and drained he doesn't care, just drops off to sleep at five a.m., knowing he has to be back at it in just a few hours.

He wakes to a bird chirping in the tree outside his bedroom window. "Shh," he tells it, covers his head with his pillow and tries to go back to sleep. The bird seems to chirp even louder.

"Shut up, bird," he grumbles into the pillow.

Chirp. Chirp. Chirp chirp chirp chirp. Twee twee twee chirp chirp twee. CHIRP.

"Oh my god, shut the fuck up!" Nico yells, then pushes up on his elbows to throw his pillow at the window. The bird, unfazed, keeps chirping and tweeting away.

He glares at the bird, then at the clock on the nightstand next to his bed. It's nine thirty. He has a meeting with some record producer's daughter for one of those events for the sake of having an event and calling it "networking" that Hollywood is so fond of.

"Fuck, fuck, fucking fuck." He sends his business partner Gwen a message saying he's on his way, which is sort of true, then scours his cabinets for something edible as he hasn't had time to grocery shop in weeks. He manages to find an old protein bar on a top shelf and eats it while he waits for the water to warm up in the shower.

He dresses simply: a striped crew neck shirt, distressed jeans, a dog tag necklace, white leather belt, white leather shoes and aviator sunglasses to hide the hideous bags under his eyes.

He hooks the sunglasses in his shirt for now, ignores the dark circles, and fixes his hair: black and straight as a pin, cut in short soft layers to de-emphasize the way his ears stick out and highlight the sweep of his cheek bones and his naturally dark, thick eyelashes. He shaves, slides his index finger over the arch of his eyebrows, dabs on a touch of cologne and—

He may feel as if he was run over by a luxury super stretch Hummer limousine several times over, but his look says: Nico Takahashi, calm, collected and put-together stylist to the stars. For now that will have to be enough.

Sitting in barely moving construction traffic at—he glances at the clock—ten sixteen, Nico lays on the horn again. It doesn't do anything, he's aware, but he *feels* better. Looking put together and feeling vindicated when a sliver of the left lane opens up and he speeds past those suckers in the center lane are really the only things going for him today.

After he gets off the highway and leaves the traffic behind, he gets excited and takes a turn too fast while he sips his coffee. It dribbles down his chin and spills on his sleeve, and he now has to pretend that breezy rolled-up shirt cuffs is the look he was going for all along. He cuffs his jeans high at the ankle, too, while waiting for yet another light to change. Gotta be able to adapt on the fly.

He continues to catch every single goddamn red light, cursing at them and willing them to change with the sheer force of his irritation.

By the time he makes it down Sunset Boulevard to the boring, standard office building on a side street, he can't find street parking. He has to slowly, slowly, *so fucking slowly* follow a woman in an unfortunate baggy beige pants suit around a parking lot until she finally remembers where she parked her car.

He bolts from the car, slams the door, mutters a few curses under his breath for good measure, and then just outside the street exit he steps in a puddle of something that is definitely not water. By the time he's trudged up the stairs to their office, Nico has decided to tell Gwen to cancel their appointments so they can focus all of their energy on researching the wilds of Montana for suitable land.

Chapter Two

The meeting with the record producer's daughter goes fine, especially since Gwen had already taken her measurements and written down what she was looking for, so Nico wasn't the one trying to get at the specifics of what "something nice, but not nice" could mean.

Nico scours photo sets of recent runway shows, the usual fashion sites and blogs, puts some auctions on watch, saves images and takes notes, and calls a couple of contacts. He shovels down the spinach and quinoa salad Gwen shoves at him late in the afternoon, two more coffees and, after that, a bottle of (regular, boring, probably from the tap) water and two aspirin.

The day is winding down and Nico is finishing up, very much looking forward to crawling into bed and sleeping for at least ten hours, when Gwen comes in with a stack of magazines. Gwen's look is always a variation of goth-punk-pixie, one not many can pull off, but with her dramatic bone structure and round kewpie-doll eyes, hair dyed blonde and cropped in a short jagged style, she somehow turns tartan prints, corsets, black leather and carefully placed chains, hooks and zippers into something totally fresh and interesting: today, leather pants with fishnet side panels, a frilled white blouse with a draping bow, heeled leather boots and a thin silver chain hooked tight around her neck.

"Two things: One. Cosima, our spoiled Daddy's girl from this morning, called and requested that she only work with you because..."

Gwen hikes the magazines into the crook of her arm and reads something she scrawled in ink on her palm, holding it in front of her face. "I wrote this down so I'd get it right. She 'likes to surround herself with exotic people.'"

"For God's sake..." Nico looks up with fingertips pressed to both temples. "Did you tell her I grew up in Sacramento? And so did my parents?" Gwen bobbles her head and gives him a look that says it wouldn't matter if she did. "Can we at least charge her extra?"

"Already did." She moves across his office space; their suite is small, a reception area with racks of clothes and shoes and accessories, two glass-walled offices side-by-side with small windows facing the street. White walls. Gray carpet. Nothing special, despite their plans to make it so.

"This is why I keep you," Nico says, going back to his notes.

"I think it's the other way around, but whatever makes you happy." She drops the stack on his desk and sits in the chair on the opposite side of his desk. Nico drags the top one closer with the end of his pen. "Second order of business," Gwen announces. "We have a problem." She flips to a dog-eared page.

Hailey Banks punches photographer in ripped Herve Leger dress and peekaboo sheer thong!

"I'll call her manager. I'm not paying for that." It's awful, it was a stunning dress, really, but he dresses her, instructs her team on hair and makeup and sends her off. After that she's someone else's problem.

"Oh, it gets worse." Gwen pulls a different magazine.

Who wore it better?

"Oh no," Nico groans, his head pounding around his skull like the thump of a bass drum.

Troubled child star Hailey Banks steps onto the red carpet in stunning Gucci jumpsuit... after model Claudette Babineaux already strutted her stuff to the delight of the crowd.

"Fuck, fuck." Nico drops his head in his hands and scrubs his hands through his hair. "She's gonna lose it."

"On the bright side, they identified both designers and called the jumpsuit stunning. I wasn't sure about it, but you were right." She pats his head.

Nico looks up with his cheek on his fist, slumped in his chair. "Maybe she'll fire us."

Gwen smiles placatingly. "We can always hope."

Nico sighs and spins his chair to face to the little window behind him. He keeps meaning to get rid of those sad vinyl blinds.

"Uh-oh, he's staring wistfully out the window," Gwen mutters.

"Don't you ever get tired of it, Gwen? The whole bread and circuses. It's all so fake and pointless. Put on a show, build people up, tear them down. Rinse, repeat. "

"It's entertainment. It's art. It's fun, Nico."

Nico swivels back. "Yeah, it's fun until you're in the back alley of some skeevy club waiting for vultures to eat you alive."

Gwen tips her head and looks at him with her huge, round eyes soft and affectionate. "It's sweet that you care about Hailey."

Nico runs both hands through his hair and sighs, "I really wish I didn't. It's exhausting." He leans forward and reaches for her. "Run away with me Gwen; let's move to Montana and learn how to ice fish and hunt buffalo and grow radishes and beets."

"I think my wife would probably object to that."

Nico waves at hand at her. "Flora can come." He twists his lips and considers. "Does she know how to ice fish?"

"Okay, I think you need to take a break now." Gwen closes his laptop despite Nico's objections and pushing his notebook aside. "I brought you a little pick-me-up."

This magazine is a more respectable publication, with high fashion photo spreads and sit-down interviews instead of close-ups of celebrity beach bodies and the latest infidelity scandals.

"Not bad," he allows.

"Not bad? That is a fine specimen of man and you know it."

"And how does your wife feel about you ogling fine specimens of men?" Nico wonders, as he straightens the magazine.

The splashy headline reads, *Grady Dawson: Country Music's Sexy Bad Boy Strips Down and Opens Up,* the words just to the left of a photo of what Nico has to admit is a very attractive man. A naked, save for a strategically placed acoustic guitar, very attractive man.

"Ogling is completely allowed within the confines of our relationship; besides, just because I don't want him doesn't mean I can't appreciate the aesthetics. It's part of my job to appreciate aesthetics. In fact..." She flips the pages and grins wickedly. "On page eighty-six he's wet and wearing nothing but white briefs." Gwen flips to said page. "You're welcome."

Normally he'd roll his eyes and call it a desperate bid for attention and say he prefers his men in a nicely tailored suit, which is true, but it's been a shitty two days, he's running on very little sleep and Nico may very well be down to nothing but base instincts at this point, so what the hell.

He lets himself enjoy the images: damp sandy blond hair in a mass of thick, tight curls; plump lips and chiseled features; just the right amount of rugged scruff on his strong jaw; gorgeously sculpted torso and thick thighs; and, from what he can tell in the wet underwear shot, pretty impressive assets as well.

"Okay, fine, you win. I would lick him if I had the chance," Nico says, closing the magazine and looking up at Gwen.

She grins. "Well, maybe if you ask him nicely..."

"Gwen, please tell me he's not here."

"He's not here," Gwen says. Nico sighs in relief. "Yet."

"Not today," Nico groans. "Even if I wasn't beyond tired and in a shitty mood, I can't deal with one more entitled, self-absorbed trainwreck right now. I've got nothing left to give."

Nico stands and steers her out of his office by her shoulders. More than anything, he just wants the sanctuary of his own quiet, simple home and his own cozy, simple bed.

"I know, but his assistant called and said he really wanted to meet with you and that *Mr. Dawson's* time is limited, and I had to make a quick decision," she says, rapid fire and breathless. He steers her to the left, into the open door of her office.

"As opposed to my time?" Nico says. He has to continue this never-ending day because some pretty-boy music star thinks everyone should just bow to his demands? "No. I need this day to be over. Go home to your wife, Gwen."

She resists, bony little shoulders twisting from Nico's grasp. "Just meet with him. This could be the sort of fresh opportunity you need. Try something different, see what happens."

Nico grabs her bag from under her desk, plops it against her stomach, and holds her shoulders again, shuffling her towards the exit and—

Outside the door to their suite, one hand raised to knock, there he is. Grady Dawson himself. Even more gorgeous and ruggedly sexy in person. Just fantastic. The nightmare day continues.

Gwen greets him, claims to be a fan, which is news to Nico and explains so much, then skips away, back to her office.

"Thank you for meeting with me," Grady says with a noticeable southern twang, after getting settled at Nico's desk.

"Well, I was informed your time is very valuable," Nico says with a bite that makes Grady wince a little.

"Yeah, I'm really sorry about that. My assistant can be a little... pushy. But, I've been working on my next album here and in Nashville and after that is the CMA Awards and then I leave for a short promotional tour." His eyes are a lovely light shade of blue; his lush golden curls spill down his forehead and spiral over his ears and softly brush his neck.

"And you're here because..."

"Oh." Grady smiles. Perfect teeth, beautiful smile. Nico sighs heavily. "I saw you working an event recently and— Let's just say you caught my eye." His accent is thick and viscous like honey; his voice is deep and rough-hewn and stupidly sexy. "I can see you have the article where I talk about wanting to change my image?"

Nico raises his eyebrows and glances over at the magazine spread he'd been ogling earlier. "Yes. I... certainly read that article." And did not just drool at the pictures.

Grady smiles again. "Great. So you get it. I want something new. Something different. And when I looked into your work, I knew you were the person who could help me."

Nico falters, releasing a breath and trying to think through the fog that is his brain right now, but the last thing he wants is another needy client too full of themselves to listen to anything he has to say. He's just so *done*. "I don't think I can help you. Sorry."

"So you won't do it?" Grady frowns and leans over the desk. His eyes are low and imploring, his mouth is lush and pouting, and Nico really, really wishes he didn't find that so damned appealing.

"I don't think—" Nico starts.

"How about just for this photo shoot I have tomorrow. No commitment," Grady offers. He flutters his eyelashes and smiles hopefully. Nico can only imagine how often that look gets him exactly what he wants and more.

What Nico really wants is to go home. And the easiest way to do that is to tell Grady, "I'll think about, okay?"

Grady stands, with tight jeans and a tight black T-shirt on that incredible body, grins and holds out a hand for Nico to shake. "It's at noon. My assistant will send the details." His hand is soft and warm and strong.

"I didn't say yes," Nico tells him.

Grady's answering grin is sly, cocky. "You didn't say no, either."

To Be Continued

❧

ALSO BY
LILAH SUZANNE

Former Olympic hopeful Jack Douglas traded competitive swimming for professional yoga and never looked back. When handsome pro boxer Felix Montero mistakenly registers for his Yoga for Seniors class, Jack takes an active interest both in Felix's struggles to manage stress and in his heart, and discovers along the way that he may have healing of his own to do. Faced with the ghosts of his athletic aspirations, can Jack return to his old dream or carve out a new path, and will their budding romance survive the test of Felix's next bout in the ring?

ISBN 978-1-941530-03-0

One **story** can change **everything**.

Now available from

interlude press.

Chef's Table by Lynn Charles

Chef Evan Sandford steadily climbed the ladder to become one of New York City's culinary elite. But in his quest to build his reputation, he forgot what got him there: the lessons on food and life from a loving hometown neighbor. Patrick Sullivan is contented keeping the memory of his grandmother's Irish cooking alive through his work at a Brooklyn diner, but when Chef Sandford walks in for a meal, Patrick is swept up by his drive—forcing him to consider if a contented life is a fulfilled one.

The two men begin a journey forging a friendship through their culinary histories. But can they tap into that secret recipe of great love, great food and transcendent joy?

ISBN 978-1-941530-17-7

Love Starved by Kate Fierro

Micah Geller considers himself lucky: at 27, he has more money than he needs, a job he loves, a debut book coming out, and a brilliant career in information security before him. What he doesn't have is a partner to share it with—a fact that's never bothered him much.

But the romantic in him isn't entirely dead. When a moment of weakness finds him with a contact to a high class escort specializing in fulfilling fantasies, Micah asks for only one thing: *Show me what it's like to feel loved.*

ISBN 978-1-941530-32-0 | **Available April 2015**

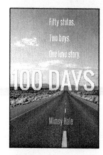

100 Days by Mimsy Hale

Jake and Aiden have been best friends—and nothing more—since the age of six. Now college graduates, they take a road trip around the USA, visiting every state in 100 days.

As they start their cross-country odyssey, Jake and Aiden think they have their journey and their futures mapped out. But the road has a funny way of changing course.

Fifty States. Two Boys. One Love Story.

ISBN 978-1-941530-23-8 | **Available April 2015**

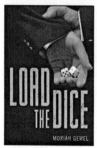

Load The Dice by Moriah Gemel

Eric left the BDSM scene years ago because he couldn't find the right partner, opting instead to meet men in quiet coffee shops and piano bars. But when his friend invites him to a posh hook-up party, he meets first time sub Jamie, whom he convinces to detail his sexual fantasies during a passionate night together. The pair soon embark on a relationship that introduces Jamie to the BDSM scene, and plays out his fantasies one by one. But as they approach the final fantasy, will Eric be able to walk away?

ISBN 978-1-941530-18-4

One **story** can change **everything**.

www.interlude**press**.com

interlude 🧩 press.

One Story Can Change Everything.

interludepress.com

Twitter: @interludepress *** Facebook: Interlude Press
Google+: +interludepress *** Pinterest: interludepress
Instagram: InterludePress

CPSIA information can be obtained at www.ICGtesting.com
Printed in the USA
LVOW07s0446180515

438860LV00001B/73/P